A DRY HATE REVIEWS

The story is familiar to those of us living in Arizona—sadly too familiar. You did a good job articulating our sad story—the future as yet uncertain.
—**Sandra Day O'Connor (retired)**, U.S. Supreme Court Justice

As a judge targeted with three bogus felony charges by the Sheriff and County Attorney depicted in *A DRY HATE*, I can confirm that this book accurately portrays the illegal immigration hostility that drove the Sheriff and County Attorney, aided by their sycophants, to abuse their powers and violate the civil rights of many people, both citizen and undocumented alike. Nancy Marshall also references the attacks the Sheriff and County Attorney mounted against county officials and judges because officials dared to question the Sheriff's spending on neighborhood raids and his displeasure over the building of the Central Court Tower. Unfortunately, many events described in *A DRY HATE* happened, and the Sheriff's Office (funded by taxpayers) settled significant lawsuits by unjustly prosecuted civilians. While the leading players portrayed in *A DRY HATE* eventually lost at the polls or were disbarred from law practice, the same caustic rhetoric about immigration continues today.
—**Gary E. Donahoe (retired)**, Arizona Superior Court Judge

A suspenseful storyline brings current events to life as author Nancy Marshall weaves fact into fiction, providing realistic, sometimes sympathetic characters and motives. In addition, she provides an excellent backdrop of First Amendment issues and a display of power and propaganda in action—an easy, worthwhile read for those who want to understand Arizona immigration politics. Marshall, former director of the Arizona Civil Liberties Union and defense attorney for a jailed activist, is thoroughly familiar with the Constitutional issues that surface throughout the novel.
—**Terry Goddard,** Former Arizona Attorney General

A DRY HATE is about a Sheriff arresting Latinos and activists in Maricopa County, Arizona. But it is much more. This complex and readable tale is set in the summer of 2010 when the Arizona Legislature passed SB1070 (the state anti-immigrant law). Author Nancy Marshall exposes some of the most intimate details of the abuse of power and the hard work done to combat that abuse. An attorney with in-depth knowledge of unconstitutional arrests and jailings, Marshall crafts characters from the Latino community and various other backgrounds who come to life and give us a real opportunity to appreciate the people affected by official abuse of power.
—**Daniel R. Ortega, Jr., Esquire**

Nancy Marshall's *A DRY HATE* blends her considerable knowledge of the law and Arizona into a fast-paced novel of ideas. Her book rewards readers with novelistic excitement and a deeper understanding of local politics, culture, and the heated debate over immigration in our state.
—**Sam Coppersmith,** Former U.S. Representative

Nancy Marshall writes with a passion for justice. In *A DRY HATE*, she provides a complete cast of characters—whether you like them or not—who make an intriguing story to keep readers engaged. The politically naïve college professor, the Sheriff's Deputy, his son in the professor's class, a young woman who graduated high school with honors but without documents, a dedicated—but secretly perverse—Assistant County Attorney, and a timid secretary who overhears everything are some of the actors who keep your interest. It's complex but not confusing, and it has a few heart-stopping twists before the climax. For book groups, there are discussion questions at the end. For teachers, there are tools to analyze propaganda. Curious about Arizona's immigration meltdown? A summary of SB 1070 gives you the bottom line. And for those who love a hike in the wilderness, Ivan, the professor, goes to the mountains and creeks of Arizona, where he learns more about the universe and himself. All of these make this such an exciting read.
—**Steve Nakamoto,** Writer's Digest Award-Winning Author

There is a delicate balance between reciting the facts and telling a readable tale. In her novel, *A DRY HATE*, author and lawyer Nancy Marshall tells a page-turner of a story, capturing vital details of incredibly true-to-life incidents. Readers will appreciate the complexity of Arizona's people and politics and begin to understand the abuse of power that threatens us all.
—**Randy Parraz,** Co-Founder and President of Citizens for a Better Arizona; Executive Director of the Arizona Education Association; author, *Dignity by Fire: Dismantling Arizona's Anti-Immigrant Machine*

The toughest Sheriff teams up with the most unethical prosecutor, a power-mad politician, and ALEC (look it up) to carry on a reign of terror against Hispanics reminiscent of Bull Connor, to the shame of Arizonans who wish this story was fiction. This ripped-from-the-headlines fictionalized account of the horror that is Sheriff Joe Arpaio uses a clever device of a summer school class on communications to dramatize how propaganda works and how one person can terrorize an entire community, violate the law, and destroy all vestige of human rights in the 21st Century. A College professor insists on exposing his class to an analysis of how different groups use communication to advance ideas or ideologies and to free or attack groups. He runs afoul of the Sheriff, and with the help of some creative students, a spirited woman attorney, and a secret weapon, he brings down the house, but not before getting a taste of it himself. Nancy Marshall's story will be a pivotal piece of history in fifty years. Today it's a living example of the uprising of the Hispanic civil rights movement, with Arizona as its epicenter. *A DRY HATE*, exposing the imbalance of power in society, makes for memorable fiction.
—**Dianne Post,** International Human Rights Attorney

Author Nancy Marshall bases the name of her book, *A DRY HATE*, on the phrase "dry heat," used by Arizonans referring to the scorching 120-degree summer heat. Inspired by a true story in Arizona, she brilliantly and intimately draws the reader into the lives and thoughts of numerous characters—while revealing the 5,000-ton elephant in the room, who was more than a bully—he was a megalomaniac filled

with tyrannical hatred toward others whose reflection in a mirror differed from his own. As this book astutely reveals, the number one criminal in Arizona for many years was the man entrusted with enforcing the law. *A DRY HATE* is a "wake-up call" for all Americans.
—**Elizabeth Graham,** author of *AMERICAN DREAM* and *DEMOCRAZY Version 2020: A Warning to all U.S. Citizens*

In *A DRY HATE*, retired Attorney Nancy Marshall captured the fear many felt when the former Sheriff and County Attorney arrested and prosecuted the innocent and those guilty of minor offenses. I can attest to the frustrations of Judges and Prosecutors because the County Attorney refused to let his Assistant County Attorneys negotiate with Defense Attorneys, thus limiting the flexibility of his own office.
—**Thomas W. Haines (retired),** Victim-Witness Advocate, Office of the Maricopa County Attorney

A DRY HATE
Power *Versus* The People

A Novel

Inspired By Historical Events

Nancy Hicks Marshall

NUGGET PRESS

Phoenix, Arizona, USA

Paperback ISBN: 978-0-9828259-2-1
eBook ISBN: 978-0-9828259-3-8
Library of Congress Control Number: 2023907191

Assisting Publishing House: Spotlight Publishing House™ in Goodyear, AZ
https://spotlightpublishinghouse.com
Editor: Lynn Thompson, Living on Purpose Communications
Cover Images: Adobe Stock
Portrait: Vance Marshall
Book Cover: Angie Ayala
Interior Design: Marigold2k

Other books by the Author

Out of print:
SEX AND THE LAW
DEAR GRANDMA

Available on Amazon:
ROSIE'S GOLD
THE BOOK OF PRO-S

A RATTLER'S TALE won First Place for Children's Fiction, 2023
National Federation of Press Women's At-Large Communications Contest

For information, contact, and to order books:
www.nuggetpress.com
nanmar4009@gmail.com

Dedicated to
those who uphold Free Speech, Press, and Assembly
and who persevere despite injustice
and for
Jason, Joel, Kristy, Monica, and Raquel

FOREWORD

When I read historical fiction, I look for three components. First, I want a plot with a compelling storyline and characters who bring the story to life. Second, I expect historical and geographical accuracy and imaginative events to enhance my understanding of the period of history in which the story occurs. Third, I look for an account with sensitivity to injustice and a passion for justice. In *A DRY HATE: Power Versus The People,* Nancy Marshall achieves all three.

I met Nancy Marshall when the Arizona Civil Liberties Union Board of Directors hired her as our Executive Director in 1975. I worked closely with her throughout her five-year tenure and have continued to work on justice issues with her since then.

In her book, *A DRY HATE,* Marshall achieves the first two components that I look for by providing a mix of plots and sub-plots in which the tension builds with several twists and turns and some surprising conclusions. Also, as a person who lived through this period of Arizona history in the place where the events occurred, I appreciate her accurate description of locations, including the Westward Ho, the U.S. Post Office, and downtown Phoenix around the ASU Cronkite School of Journalism.

Several events in the book actually occurred as described. Deputy Sheriffs did arrest and jail newspaper editors, an ACLU lawyer, several activists, and a County Supervisor. Other events could have occurred based on the political climate of the time. The May 6th morning sweep targeting undocumented workers might not have transpired as described in the book. Still the Sheriff's office ran many sweeps in predominantly Hispanic neighborhoods, so the one in the novel is realistic.

Most of the major characters in *A DRY HATE* represent real-life people. For example, Maricopa County did have and continues to have a Sheriff, a County Attorney, and County Supervisors. However, Marshall's storytelling breathes life into the fictional version of these characters. Further, although it may be hard to believe today, some elected officials really did make the exact statements quoted in *A DRY HATE*. This combination of accuracy and imagination creates distinctly believable characters.

Finally, when I read about history and politics, I look for a third quality—a focus on justice and outrage at injustices that occurred or likely occurred.

As a long-time member of the ACLU (American Civil Liberties Union)—a hundred-plus-year organization that defends individual rights against government abuses—and also as a former President of the ACLU of Arizona and forty-plus year board member, I value books that highlight injustice and describe events through a justice lens. In the period covered by *A DRY HATE*—2000s through 2010, and continuing today—we as a nation have been faced with outrageous abuses of power. Elected officials have used propaganda and the power of their office to marginalize, discriminate against, and outright jail people because of the color of their skin or because they spoke out against government policies with which they disagreed. During the time frame covered in *A DRY HATE*, certain elected officials in Arizona repeatedly deprived individuals of their rights under the First, Fourth, Fifth, and Fourteenth Amendments to the U.S. Constitution.

We have educated others about these abusive policies by organizing marches, rallies, and other peaceful means like writing books and letters to the editor and holding workshops and discussion groups.

In writing *A DRY HATE*, Marshall ensures that we will not forget our recent painful history while telling a compelling, believable story that illuminates those specific abuses of power. *A DRY HATE: Power Versus The People* is a story that needs to be told, read, and understood so that we, as Americans, can recognize, identify, and thus prevent its recurrence.

—Rivko Knox, Former President of the Civil Liberties Union of Arizona, former Board Member of the League of Women Voters of Metropolitan Phoenix; former Lobbyist for the League of Women Voters of AZ with a focus on voting rights; and Democratic Precinct Committee person, 1967-77; 2003 to the present.

INTRODUCTION

A persistent desire for justice—from fair play in the home and school to equity in our government—inspired me to write *A DRY HATE*.

As a child, I experienced injustice when my older brother lied to my father, saying, "Nancy did it." I don't recall what "it" was, but I *didn't* do it, yet my father spanked me. It was not fair.

I've also observed unfairness to others and known it was wrong. Sometimes I've tried to right that wrong. When I was in high school, the students in the Honor Society—of which I was a member—almost voted to exclude one of my classmates. The criteria for being selected *into* this club were good grades and good citizenship. The girl they were about to exclude was both. I envied this girl. She sang in the girls' octet. She was cute, blonde, and popular with the boys—things I was not. She was also intelligent and a good citizen. As we went around the circle, each Society student member spoke about whether they would admit this girl. One by one, they wanted to exclude her. Even the faculty advisor was going along. Finally, it was my turn to speak.

Horrified, anger flaring, I spoke in a clear voice. "If you don't include her, you'll have to kick me out—because she is smarter than I am."

Stunned silence filled the room. Then, almost in unison, each student voted her in. In this instance, it took just one voice—mine—calling for fairness to halt the abuse of power.

As an elections volunteer in 1968, I witnessed power abuse in electoral politics for the first time in New York City Democratic primary. The Italian Americans working the poll hid the multilingual ballot information so the Chinese Americans could not read the ballot. More recently, during the 2022 mid-term elections in Arizona, I watched Donald Trump's daughter give a morning speech (in a slinky red dress) to her base while her Secret Service detail—employed by our government to protect the ex-President's family—used their government vehicles to block the entrance to the polling place in a Democrat-favored district. It took the insistent voice of an observer to make the Secret Service men move their cars.

Abuse by both parties is possible. However, bipartisan integrity is also possible—probably the rule in most elections. As paid poll workers in my precinct, a fellow worker and I noticed a violation of the election rules. Another paid worker spoke loudly to everyone in the room, "Those Mexican illegals are coming across and voting. It's fraud!" But there was no brown face in the crowd in our polling place. Worse, it is against the law to electioneer within 75 feet of the polling place.

My co-worker—a Republican, and I, a Democrat—looked at each other, locked arms, and walked over to the loudmouth. I listened as my Republican colleague told her to shut up, that it was against the rules, and if loudmouth continued, we would call our supervisor and have her removed. From both sides, we wanted fair elections.

I have had several encounters with the police. Most of them were even-handed and fair, even praiseworthy. However, one abuse of power still haunts me. In 1967, hundreds of thousands of Americans marched to the Pentagon to protest the Vietnam War. The next morning, the organizers called me and asked if I would drive to the Pentagon, where many had camped overnight, and shuttle them to the bus station in Washington, DC. Returning to DC, I crossed the Avenue C bridge and turned right. The roads were virtually empty. But a lone vehicle, a police car, pulled me over. They cited me for a "wide right turn" (unprovable and doubtful) and an improper driver's license. Both charges were misdemeanors and carried only a fine. But the police arrested me and took me to jail. I spent that day "inside," wondering if my one phone call would come through with enough money to bail me out. That stop should have been a ticket and a court date, but the police recognized the "hippies" in my car and decided to punish the protestors—or at least their driver.

Fast forward to the period of history covered in *A DRY HATE*. In 2008, I bailed a young man out of jail. The police had arrested him for applauding at a public meeting. As I watched the video of the arrest, I began to understand how one elected official, with many at his command and in disgusting detail, could abuse his power. Finally, in 2012, I felt compelled to write about it. While much of the novel draws from actual historical events, the characters in *A DRY HATE* are fictional, as are the thoughts, words, and actions attributed to each character.

Then, why re-publish in 2023?

First, we learned more about the events surrounding the summer of 2010 and incorporated them into the novel.

Second, we worked with an excellent editorial team. In the process, we corrected grammar and removed outdated content. And thanks to our dedicated collaboration, we've made the Second Edition of *A DRY HATE* stronger than the original.

Third, the themes so relevant in 2010 continue to be relevant today. History could have changed, but it has not. Abuse of power turns up with disappointing frequency—in the family, the hometown, the county, the state, our nation, and beyond. Citizens remain pitted against each other on issues of immigration, race, and power. Uncertainty and fear encourage politicians to abuse their power. Sadly, the essential elements in *A DRY HATE*—from racial profiling to families hurt by unresolved policies—continue to plague us.

If you want a good read, I hope you'll find it here. Also, if you seek a detailed understanding of the reality of abuse of power during the historical events that inspired this story, read the Afterword.

NHM

A DRY HATE

PROLOGUE: WHAT "IT" WAS

"What sort of a day was it? A day like all days, filled with those events that alter and illuminate our times. And you were there."
—Walter Cronkite[1]

Nobody agreed when it began. Or what caused it. But from all sides, they agreed—even if they wouldn't admit it aloud—what "it" was.

Geologists blamed it on the earth's mighty seismic upheavals combined with the Colorado River's cutting force, which formed the Grand Canyon. As a result, the rocks on the North and South rims, made from the same mountains and mesas, are virtually identical. Yet they stand miles apart.

Archaeologists claimed that the climate caused it over one thousand years ago. Lakes dried up. Dinosaurs got stuck, leaving their massive footprints in the mud of time. Disappearing jungles left our Saguaro cactus, the prickly-armed sentry that stands as a silent witness to the birth of a desert, as their legacy.

Anthropologists blamed it on the earliest humans. They trace man's presence in the Southwest to about 400 CE. Humans sought control over the environment and domination over each other. The First People fought among themselves long before the arrival of Europeans.

Historians say it was caused by more recent human events. Since the 1500s, the Pueblo peoples along the Rio Grande violently, although unsuccessfully, resisted incursions by the Spaniards into New Mexico. In 1821, Mexico declared independence from Spain. In 1846, the United States defeated Mexico in a war and claimed a huge swath of what for centuries had been considered, by the Mexicans, their land.

Those analyzing race say slavery caused it. During the U.S. Civil War, men fought in the Arizona Territory over whether Arizona could be, or should not be, a slave-owning state.

Sociologists, economists, and demographers claim that the invention of air conditioning caused it. Only in the 1950s did Americans of European ancestry flood [sic!] into this desert valley, when HVAC could bring living room temperatures from one-hundred-and-fifteen degrees Fahrenheit to a pleasant seventy-eight. Only then did "whites" begin to take over as the ethnic majority in a state with twenty-two Federally recognized Native American tribes and a legacy of Hispanic presence. Tribal and ethnic divides heated up precisely when Arizona gained the capacity to cool down.

Modern meteorologists suggest that the recent dry period, starting in the 1990s, caused it. Some call it a "twelve-hundred-year drought," one that will (theoretically) occur only every twelve hundred years.

But did drought cause it? We can confidently say that the notorious three-digit summers have birthed the well-mined nugget, "it's a dry heat." But the temperature did not cause "it."

Political pundits point out that Arizona has more than its share of activists on the extreme fringes of our traditional two-party system. Who knows? Maybe it's caused by politics.

In this volatile state, it's not surprising that a punster contrived an anti-slogan—a bull's-eye campaign button that would also become a bumper sticker. This sound bite became the *cri de coeur* that complained of a cowboy society un-holstering its sacred guns to repeatedly, collectively shoot itself in the foot.

It's an expression that brushed aside reason and culture and may even have been embraced by some. And, though we won't admit it, everyone knows:

"It's a dry hate."

CHAPTER 1

JAIL!

July 5th, 2010, Phoenix

Santana, a steroidal and muscular skinhead, shoved Ivan against the jail cell wall. "Ya got cigarettes, punk?"

Ivan threw up his hands in defense. Sweat poured down his back, sticking him to the cinder block.

Instantly Rambo, a huge, bald, and tatted detainee, touched Santana's shoulder gently. "Not him," he said, his *basso profundo* a quiet command. "We'll find you a smoke later." He effortlessly turned Santana toward the far corner of the holding pen next to the stinky latrine that served twenty-five men awaiting their initial appearance hearing.

"Thanks, Rambo," muttered Ivan as Sheriff Bardo's seasoned returnees shuffled away.

What an irony! Two months ago, he was a respected university professor. Today, Sheriff Bardo jailed him on felony charges.

In early June, Professor Ivan Wilder had met Ms. Emily Hartwell, hotshot defense attorney, at the door of his classroom. Last night they slept together under the shooting stars. This afternoon two Deputies stuck them in separate stinking jail cells. *How the hell?*

CHAPTER 2

THE PERFECT COURSE

May 2010, Phoenix

Six-foot-two, in his mid-forties, Professor Ivan Wilder parked his lanky frame into one of the mesh metal chairs near a table with an attached ashtray. He unloaded a stack of papers, opened a pack of Marlboros, withdrew a cigarette, lit up, and grumbled about the upcoming summer. They kept handing him the losers. *Do I have to teach a remedial Gov.101 course again?*

He had just zipped a final draft of his course by e-mail to the department chair of Public Service and Policy (PSP) at Arizona State University's undergraduate campus in downtown Phoenix. It was May 15th, the deadline for submitting his syllabus for the summer course in "Remedial PSP," as it was locally known.

Ivan often found himself alone in the shade of the north alcove outside the copper steel and glass tower. Diaphanous green paloverde trees and black-tipped agaves in mulberry glazed pots served as urban foliage for the concrete and steel *décor*.

As a professor in the Public Policy department, he prided himself on tracking political shenanigans and citizen reactions. Recent dramas ranged from Sheriff Bardo feeding the county jail inmates green baloney in pink undies to rowdy anarchists throwing rock-filled bottles at the equine police in a protest. The list went on: racketeering lawsuits against judges and county supervisors, a midnight sweep by Bardo's SWAT team against undocumented workers, and a ridiculous game of urban "Capture the Flag" on Valentine's Day at midnight.

And no, no, that was not all.

In April, hundreds of students had demonstrated at the capitol after the Governor signed Senate Bill 1070—the anti-illegal immigrant law. In late July, when the law would go into effect, over ten thousand marchers were expected to converge on downtown Phoenix to protest the law. So, the time was ripe for Ivan to teach a seminar on propaganda, not the "Gov. 101" class for the bunch of rag-tag misfits he was bound to greet on the first of June.

He sat back and took a deep drag. Warm smoke filled every respiratory crevice. He accepted the momentary relaxation. Exhaled. Watched the curl rise and dissipate. Sighed.

Marti would have scolded him had she still been alive. They'd been married almost fifteen years when she discovered a lump near her armpit, and they embarked upon the struggle against breast cancer—a short struggle, as things go: from diagnosis to death was just under twelve months. She'd been gone now just over four years. Her cancer had come not from smoking but from the fluke that surprises many people who eat right, sleep well, and exercise. She had done everything by the book, only to be felled by random cell metastasis. Huge waves of guilt buffeted him, but even her suffering and death had not persuaded him to kick his habit. Ironically, Marlboros had become his best friend. He'd feel calm and quiet, with the gradual intake softening the blow of his loss—for just a few seconds—repeated with each inhalation, down to the filter.

The local headlines blasted: "County Supervisors sue Sheriff and County Attorney!" Yet another round. The taxpayers were stuck.

Ivan's cell phone rang to the tune of "Yesterday." He plucked it from its belt holder. "Professor Ivan Wilder here."

"Ivan, this is Allen McNeil."

Unusual. No need for the dean of Public Policy to call him just now. He'd e-mailed his curriculum on time. "Doctor McNeil?"

"Ivan, I've been talking to Mitch Sullivan, dean of the Cronkite School of Journalism. Know him?"

"Heard of him."

"He and I have been discussing summer plans. We came up with something for you. Give him a call. Here's his number."

"Is there something I should know?"

"Something you should like." McNeil hung up.

Ivan dialed.

"Dean Sullivan here."

"Dean Sullivan, this is Ivan Wilder, over in Public Policy. Doctor McNeil said I should call."

"Thanks, Ivan, for the quick follow-up. Doctor McNeil and I think there's a course you might be interested in teaching this summer instead of the remedial one originally assigned to you. We've already sent it to be printed in the course catalog, with the teacher TBA—to be announced. Hope you want to do it."

That's odd. Even though the Walter Cronkite School of Journalism at ASU downtown stood a mere block from the Public Policy building, the two faculties rarely overlapped. Public Policy kids wanted to enter the thicket of politics. Journalism students just wanted to expose them—almost a natural antagonism.

"How can I help?"

"Ivan, the National Foundation for Excellence in Journalism has funded a special program for several journalism schools nationwide. One of them is Cronkite. As you may already know, Cronkite is the HQ of the National News 21 Initiative to help influence how upcoming students learn journalism."

"Go on."

"Each school chooses a cross-disciplinary topic under the general theme, Changing America. This summer, 2010, Cronkite has chosen the topic, Injustice in America."

"Where are you headed with this, Dean Sullivan?"

"Call me Mitch. By the end of the summer, you may be my NBMF—New Best Male Friend."

"Oh?"

"We'd like to have an interdisciplinary course this summer called Journalism and Public Policy 102: Politics and Propaganda. The Politics part would be for the Public Policy students you normally attract. But the class would also be mandatory for the students in the journalism program—highly-motivated students looking for the use of propaganda. So Allen and I thought it would be a natural fit for you."

"Are you serious?" *Natural fit? That would be a dream course!* Ivan dug up a noncommittal "Sure. I can do it." He paused. "Aren't there practicalities?"

"Minor details. But Ivan, you've been collecting something of a reputation as one of the most interesting and controversial professors we've had for a long time in ASU. You've also spent time teaching about power and propaganda. Isn't this a perfect fit?"

"Honestly, yes. But this isn't what I thought Dean McNeil had in mind for the summer."

"Not to worry. We have discussed the idea in depth. We're combining the normal Politics 101 with the more journalistically focused 102. With the budget crunch and economic downturn from 2008, McNeil won't have to pay. The Excellence in Journalism Foundation will fund the course for the full summer two-month block."

Interesting.

"There are a few details."

"Hit me."

"First, we will use the auditorium at the Cronkite building instead of the Public Policy building. Okay?"

"Not a problem. How many students will be enrolled?"

"Probably about one hundred. We expect the auditorium to be at capacity."

"And here I thought I'd be coddling twenty repeats. That'll be a lot of papers to grade."

"We've taken care of that. You'll have two grad students as teaching assistants."

"Anything else?"

"We thought you should have office space in our building with a phone, computer, and access to our equipment. It's not a big space, but it's handy. Okay?"

"Fair deal, sir." *Absolutely sweeeeet deal.* It didn't even occur to Ivan that this plan could have an unintended dark side. "I think I can adjust. Do you have any materials you want me to include?"

"No, your rep precedes you. And since this is a journalism group, you'll want to reference the local newspapers, radio, TV, the Internet, and especially the Cronkite student channel. You can use a lot of current events material. Now that Governor Middleton has signed Senate Bill 1070, it will go into effect on Thursday, July 29th, your last day of class. That might provide some grist for your mill—and heat up summer news."

"The news has been entertaining."

"But Ivan, I'll warn you. Some folks in power appear to be either paranoid, egomaniacs, megalomaniacs, or just out for blood. So don't be surprised to have spies in your class looking for a misstep."

"Hasn't this always been true?"

"Yes, but somehow the tone is different. I've been around for a long time. Some of the arrests in the past few years and some of the citizen-inspired ballot initiatives—I don't know. I just feel a need to tell you to watch your back. I can't protect you if you do anything foolish."

"I keep the class wide open. I keep an audio record of everything. I'll be okay."

"Well, then, we're on. Come over after lunch today, and I'll show you around. You have just two weeks. The class starts Tuesday, the first of June. We'll get you set up ASAP."

Unwittingly, the Public Policy and Journalism deans had dealt Ivan a sharp learning curve. For Professor Wilder, "it" began on June 1st, 2010, with Government and Journalism 102: Propaganda and Power.

CHAPTER 3

SIGNING UP FOR "IT"

May 2010, Tempe

In a small adobe house in Guadalupe, run-down on the outside but colorful on the inside, Lydia Flores signed up online for her first university class at downtown ASU. A casual observer might not expect to find the Internet inside or imagine her father's careful painting of the rooms and her mother's thoughtful attention to adorning the walls and windows.

The day of Lydia's birth in 1991 should have overjoyed her parents. But they lived in Sonora, Mexico. Between a chronically corrupt government and the effects of the North American Free Trade Agreement (NAFTA), they faced increasing struggle, poverty, and uncertainty. Determined to provide the best for their daughter, *Señor* and *Señora* Flores crossed the border into Arizona one winter night in 1993 with the help of a *coyote* (a paid-off guide). In *El Norte,* they would find education and opportunity for their firstborn child.

In the spring of 2010, Lydia was a senior at Tempe High School. Dark-eyed, her black hair pulled neatly into a bun, she looked unmistakably Latina. She had participated, with hundreds of classmates, in an April demonstration at the Arizona state capitol. They had joined together—Blacks, Hispanics, Anglos, Native Americans—citizens and non-citizens alike. They had marched against Senate Bill 1070, a new law signed by Governor Alice Middleton that declared it a felony to be in the state without proper documentation. Moreover, the legislation stated that any law enforcement officer could stop someone "suspected" of being in Arizona illegally.

In a week, Lydia would graduate from high school. She already faced hurdles. A few years earlier, most Arizona voters had passed Proposition 200, requiring all who could not prove legal Arizona residency to pay out-of-state tuition registration fees. She filled the bill. Despite seventeen years in Arizona, her flawless English, and honors in high school, she could not obtain a state driver's license. Fortunately, the university based its tuition policy on proof of residency, not legal citizenship. ASU maintained a vise-like grip on the privacy of its student records. Lydia's high school transcript would allow her to pay in-state tuition.

The climate was turning ugly. Sheriff Bardo had begun sweeps in Hispanic neighborhoods, stopping any car for a minor infraction. His enforcement teams patrolled Guadalupe, a town too small and poor to fund its own police force. Bardo had threatened to get all the "illegals" out of Arizona. Recently, the Federal government had passed a law, 287G, which gave local law enforcement the power to stop and question everyone who "looked" illegal. Lydia knew people who had been stopped and sometimes arrested, in her town of Guadalupe, on their way to Catholic Mass. Sheriff's Deputies would demand, "Where are your papers?" Residents were frightened.

"Mama, I'm worried. It's a different vibe out there now. After that demonstration this April, *Mamacita, yo no sé.*" Lydia helped her mother roll chicken burritos for lunch, folding in the ends carefully and adding a little extra *guacamole* for her younger brother Jesus. By an accident of geography and timing, her brother was an American citizen.

"Nonsense." Her mother's skilled fingers placed chicken and green chilies on the open tortilla, adding a few chopped onions. She scooped up some *frijoles refritos* and added a layer of *pico de gallo* before closing up her burrito. "We be here fifteen years, and there no has been problem. Thees is what we come for to America. You get college education. Your papa he save just for thees, for you, *mi niña.* We can do. You sign up for that summer class. Off to good start, *m'hija favorita.*"

"*Pero, Mamá, tengo miedo.* I'm scared. *Tía Beatrice* says I have good instincts for things. After the April demonstration, some people yelled, 'Go back to Mexico.' What if someone causes trouble?"

"Phoenix ees not that kind of ceety. You weel be fine, *mi* American *muchacha.* You are a young lady *muy bonita, muy inteligente.* Thees weel be good, your college education!"

Lydia shivered. To her, "it" was her heritage. It began the day she was born in Mexico.

Pissed at having just flunked Public Policy 101, Phil Strong sought out the repeat course for the summer. If he hadn't missed his mom so much after she died back in February, he might have been able to focus. Then it was just him and dad at home. And Burger King almost every night. He didn't like the teacher of the class, Professor Wilder. The guy made you work, and he encouraged all sorts of ideas. But it was a required course.

Sheriff Deputy Paul Strong had been angry, too, about his son flunking the course. Both parents had expected Phil to go to ASU to get a criminal justice degree and shortcut the career ladder into the Sheriff's Office. But Dad, always busy at work, didn't understand how hard it was for Phil to lose Mom. Winning one of the top deputy slots, and with this new immigration law and all the neighborhood sweeps for illegals and criminals, Dad was busier than ever.

Stressed and grieving, he railed at Phil for the "F" in Public Policy 101. "You don't have to stay at ASU—just pass this summer course, and we'll drop you back to community college. Then you'll be on your way to work for Sheriff Bardo. So don't flunk it this time. And lemme know what you notice about that Professor—I hear he's a liberal extremist."

"I don't like that Professor Wilder. Okay, I'll pass the course and tell you what I see."

Phil didn't realize it then, but a newly inserted summer course called Power and Propaganda would be a life-changer. For Phil, "it" began on June 1st, 2010, when he entered the auditorium of the Cronkite School of Journalism.

Winter 2005, the Maricopa County Board of Supervisors

Supervisor Asa Johnson listened, deeply disturbed, as Sheriff Bardo announced to the panel of supervisors that he had cut inmates' meals at the Fourth Avenue Jail from three to two meals a day. After the meeting, Johnson took Bardo aside. "Sheriff, up to a third of your inmates have medical and mental health issues. Cutting their food patterns can harm their health. Many have diabetes. Please reconsider. These inmates need to get regular food and have access to their medications, or their health conditions will deteriorate."

"I'm the Sheriff, and I'll run the jail the way I want to." Bardo glared and turned away.

For Supervisor Asa Johnson, "it" began with diabetes.

CHAPTER 4

BIRTH OF A BULLY

1992, Maricopa County

Born in Italy in 1936, little Giulio Edgar Bardo was not a pretty baby. Maybe he somehow knew that the Nazis were overrunning Europe, World War II was about to break out, and within a few years, the United States would engage in this worldwide struggle on both the Atlantic and the Pacific fronts. In any case, baby Bardo arrived looking decidedly grumpy—not a beautiful baby.

But Mama and Papa Bardo gave him a dignified name to honor his grandparents: Giulio, from the Italian paternal side, and Edgar, from the maternal ancestors in Spain. They left Italy and arrived, fresh off the boat at the end of WWII, as had so many desperate families seeking a better life, hoping to find it in America. They changed Giulio to Julius. They called their little boy "Eddie." It sounded American.

Eddie was the short kid in his class. Entering the sixth grade, however, he began to grow—out, then up. Suddenly the short pudgy-looking kid was now a size and force to confront. As he scrutinized the playground, he noticed that the regular targets of bullying were often ethnic minorities. World War II soldier-fathers returned with a host of names for the enemy. "Nazis," "fascists," "krauts," "frogs," "micks," "wops," "japs," "kikes," "chinks," and "spics." The playground was replete with insults.

Then came the Cold War against the Soviet Union. From this new evil empire arose more political insults— "commies," "reds," "commie-pinkos." Anyone opposed to Senator McCarthy became suspect. A favorite line was, "Go back to Russia"—even when you were born here. And a few sexual slurs—you could learn a lot on the playground— "pussy," "fag," "dyke." So, Eddie realized name-calling could become a bully's weapon intended to hurt the other guy and gain control. Eddie was interested.

The first time a kid called him a "wop," he pummeled the guy to the ground. Two other boys had to pull him off before he did any real damage. "Never call me that again, you pinko fag!" he yelled, not knowing what a pinko was except that it sounded like it might connect to fags.

What struck him after this incident at recess was that no one threatened him—no one at all. It was then that he figured out that he liked having control. So, at age twelve, on the cusp of puberty, Eddie decided nobody would ever again push him around.

Working his way through high school, Eddie noticed that a lot of his Italian buddies joined gangs—they sometimes called it the Mafia—and wound up dead or in prison. Others joined the cops. They wore uniforms, they looked tough, and they lived longer. Eddie sought out some justice and police-type classes at a trade school and began to find work in enforcement.

As the 1950s and '60s rolled by, Eddie learned about a man who became, for many people in high office, a formidable opponent. That man was J. Edgar Hoover, Director of the Federal Bureau of Investigation (FBI). Hoover investigated criminals and brought them to justice. He tracked down high-profile Mafioso. He put big names in prison for life. Hoover amassed power—lots of it. He kept files on everyone—from crooks and "commie-pinkos" to the President. That was how he stayed in power for so long—he had the goods on them all.

Eddie decided to call himself "J. Edgar." He'd be one tough law enforcement guy. He'd pick his power issues as he went. And keep files on everyone. After years in enforcement in Arizona, his big break finally came when the people elected Eddie, now popularly known as J. Edgar, as Sheriff of Maricopa County. For J. Edgar Bardo, "it" was the rise to power, and "it" began on Election Day, 1992.

CHAPTER 5

SUMMER SCHOOL DAY ONE

Tuesday, June 1ˢᵗ, 2010
The Walter Cronkite School of Journalism
Arizona State University

Ivan crossed the Taylor Mall through scattered wrought-iron tables and chairs and headed north. The Cronkite School ran a digital ticker tape marquee above the entrance announcing: "Welcome to Summer School."

Two young security officers who kept watch at the information desk stood in the lobby. One looked Native, with a black braid down his back. The other looked younger, with freckles. Ivan nodded and smiled with a "Good morning."

Off-white paint covered three auditorium walls, the fourth a muted slate blue. Ivan's desk squatted off to the left side of the wall nearest the doors, flanked by a wall-to-wall set of two large whiteboards—one for standard marker use, the other a state-of-the-art SmartScreen installed last year, ready for a PowerPoint presentation. The Stars and Stripes hung off to the side at stage right.

The surnames on the class roster suggested heritage from all the major continents—Europe, Asia (and the Middle East), Africa, North America, and South America. An asterisk marked about forty names of all types to indicate they were from the Journalism School. Realizing that he was making assumptions, Ivan nonetheless smiled to himself. *Should be an interesting mix.*

The auditorium quickly filled as students took their seats. Ivan explained the course and began. "This summer, we're combining a class in basic government structure with a journalism course. Following the direction of the Excellence in Journalism Foundation, we will emphasize elected officials—their power and propaganda. In a nutshell, when we talk about power, we're generally talking about elected officials and whether they uphold the law impartially and fairly toward everyone according to the laws, their oath of office, and the Constitution."

The first slide showed a three-pronged tree of the branches of the Federal government. Then, Ivan asked, "If the President is Commander-in-Chief, why does Congress declare war?"

A kid who had flunked in the spring answered, "Separation of powers, duh. So one branch doesn't become a dictatorship. High school history."

"Kudos on the separation of powers, Mr. History. Congress has the power to declare war. But Congress did not declare war in Iraq or Afghanistan, yet the U.S. is at war. Could you explain why?"

Stymied, Phil Strong hunkered down in his chair, arms across his chest.

Ivan asked students to introduce themselves for the first few days to become better acquainted.

A young woman who planned to become a journalist raised her hand. "Susan Goldstein. Because the President, as Commander-in-Chief, can order troops? And Congress can vote, or not vote, to spend money to support the troops?"

"Correct."

"Tony Mendez." The Mendez family had lived in Arizona for several generations. Working first in the mines, then in citrus, they ultimately developed real estate in Tempe. Tony had conflicting interests: he sympathized with the underdog but felt they didn't always take personal responsibility. After all, his family had succeeded in just a few generations. "How is it that the CIA and the FBI are under the executive branch in your diagram, but sometimes they seem independent from the President?"

Ivan asked, "Anyone else venture a guess?"

Susan spoke again. "J. Edgar Hoover, who ran the FBI for a long time, kept files on everyone. Like Martin Luther King supposedly being a Communist. And President Kennedy having an affair with Marilyn Monroe."

Ivan nodded. "But is it an abuse of power for an appointed official to keep files on his boss or fellow workers?"

"Jonah Whalen. Wouldn't it depend on what he does with them? It sounds more like Mr. Hoover wanted to keep info that was like—well, you know—like—"

"Blackmail?"

"Yes, sir."

Ivan said, "The FBI director did keep information about the President and members of Congress as well. So even if they wanted to reduce spending for the FBI, Hoover could essentially rat them out. For example, men in Congress were married and had mistresses or gay liaisons. Do any of you know what that was like, politically, in the 1950s?"

Mr. History sat back up. "Phil Strong. Yeah, I get it. Like, the Sheriff or Governor could out some legislator as a homo. That'd kill his career. At least, I hope so!"

"Actually," Ivan parried, "we have had two recent Arizona legislators, one in the House, and one in the Senate, who were openly gay men. One a Democrat, one a Republican. They were well respected. Is public acceptance towards homosexuals different today than it was in the 1950s?"

Jonah said, "I think it's different. And that's good." Jonah was currently studying public policy, but he wasn't sure. He might switch to a nursing degree. As a volunteer last summer at St. Joseph's Hospital, Jonah witnessed the controversy over healthcare delivery to the poor, especially those without documents. He met many heavy hitters, including defense attorney Emily Hartwell. She'd bailed him out after an arrest at a public meeting and went the distance for him as defense counsel, *pro bono*.

Ivan broached the dark side of J. Edgar. "Does everyone understand blackmail?"

Susan said, "Professor, I've just Googled, and how's this? 'Blackmail is threatening a person to expose criminal activity or a discreditable act—'"

Ivan added, "Blackmail doesn't have to involve money. For example, back to J. Edgar. Quote: 'If you don't vote for the full budget for the FBI, Mr. Senator, certain damaging information might come out that would affect your chances of re-election—or your marriage.' End quote."

"Ahhh."

After a mid-morning break, they covered the legislature, then the court system. "Does anyone know how they select judges in Arizona?"

Phil started, "My dad works for the Sheriff. He says a lot of them are crooks. Some of them have been charged with some crimes or something."

A young woman in a gray headscarf raised her hand. "I am Nazrin Pahlavi. In Iran, where my parents came from, the judges are all Islamic clerics. They dictate how we practice our religion and powerfully influence the government."

Susan said, "My father's a lawyer. He says a panel selects them by merit."

Ivan added, "Arizona is ahead of the curve in selecting qualified judges—at least in our two largest counties, Maricopa and Pima. First, they must be Arizona Bar Association members and actively practice law. By contrast, most elective offices, like City Council or Sheriff, require only minimum age and citizenship. What else?"

"In Maricopa County," Susan added, "a Judicial Nominating Commission with sixteen members reviews applications. The Governor appoints some lawyers and non-lawyer members. The Commission usually provides a slate of finalists." She paused. "Then the Governor makes appointments to fill a vacancy."

Tony asked, "That doesn't prove they can be good judges, does it?"

Ivan answered, "Not necessarily, but at least they have some experience practicing law. One last question. How many of you are eighteen or over?"

Every hand rose.

"Keep your hands up. Now, keep your hand up if you registered to vote here in Arizona or your home state."

Over half the hands dropped.

"Ladies and gentlemen, people worldwide have died for the right to vote. It's part of your responsibility as—" Ivan stopped in mid-sentence. Suddenly, he remembered students in this room might not have documents. "—as adults—to participate in our democratic institutions. It's not an assignment. Just think about it."

It would have been really dumb to make voting registration an assignment. Ivan dismissed the class and headed out for lunch.

CHAPTER 6

THE MOLE

June 1ˢᵗ, 2010, Phoenix

Maricopa County Attorney Robert Shatigan studied his mustache in the men's room mirror. Slicked a comb through his trim dark hair, jutted out his chin, and studied his profile from one side, then the other. Satisfied, he walked to his office.

A long hot summer lay ahead. After Governor Alice Middleton signed SB 1070, the anti-illegal immigrant bill, on April 29ᵗʰ, it was due to go into effect on July 29ᵗʰ. Sheriff Bardo would be corralling even more illegals. Activists would show up for demonstrations, just begging to get arrested for petitioning their government, as if they had special rights. Shatigan was eager to prosecute the resulting increase in criminal cases.

Running for the office of County Attorney in 2004 on an anti-immigrant platform, Shatigan had bonded with Sheriff Bardo and vowed to investigate and prosecute "illegals." He developed a similar slogan: "I will prosecute people here illegally to the fullest extent of the law." So, teaming up with Bardo became "it" for County Attorney Robert Shatigan. What if some of the men Bardo caught in his sweeps in Hispanic-dominated neighborhoods were U. S. citizens without any priors and had to be released? Many were illegal.

Today Shatigan gathered a few hard-liners in his office, including Bardo's right-hand man, Sid Bullard. "We need to collaborate on a list of troublemakers coming up. Do you have any new names besides the usual suspects?"

Bullard grunted, "One of our people at ASU tells me there's going to be a two-month summer class at Cronkite on something like Abuse of Power. Professor's been around a while. Bardo has a file on him going back to 2007. We need someone in that class. Do any of you have a kid around college age?"

A senior prosecutor, Harold Tanner, spoke up. "My son Harry. He's about to wrap it up at downtown ASU. He can take a summer class before his senior year. I think he's already enrolled. He'll be your mole."

CHAPTER 7

REVENGE ON THE PRESS

Autumn 2007, Phoenix

Deputies Paul Strong and Len Snyder were the most highly utilized officers in the Maricopa County Sheriff's Office. They were experienced, loyal, and, depending on one's viewpoint, capable—or ruthless. Bardo's second-in-command, Sid Bullard, frequently assigned them to cherry-picked duties. The early November action would be just that—arresting the editors of the *Desert Dirtbuster*, a local news rag that continually railed against the MCSO.

For Deputy Strong, weighing in at about 260 pounds, a decade of loyalty had paid off. He was now one of two chief Deputies under Bullard. At six-foot-two, he ordered the little people around.

Snyder, a man of slighter build at five-foot-ten, 170 pounds, brought agility to Bardo's shop. He'd be on the tail of a bad guy quicker than the click of a jailhouse door. Snyder assumed the role of CEO of each operation, making sure every pawn was in place when planning the final checkmate.

They split into two teams. The execution must be airtight. They would arrive at two different sites simultaneously and transport the two criminals to two different holding pens, isolated as far from each other as county regulations would allow. Strong would arrest Bradley in Paradise Valley; Snyder would apprehend Woodward in Tempe.

Bradley and Woodward were the two editors of the local weekly muckraking paper, the *Desert Dirtbuster*. Except for a smatter of raunchy personals, they ran copious ads for eateries, movies, and home entertainment centers. The advertising financed investigative pieces that exposed government officials; their latest gambit went beyond the pale. Bradley and Woodward had poked an editorial finger in the chest of Sheriff J. Edgar Bardo.

The battle had been raging for several years. Bardo would act; the *Dirtbuster* would react. Bradley and Woodward recorded almost every MCSO move for public consumption and condemned them all as an abuse of power and a violation of Constitutional rights. Finally, Bardo had had enough. He commandeered Shatigan to help him design a look-alike Grand Jury subpoena for all the records available from the *Desert Dirtbuster*. The subpoena demanded files, e-mails, lists of contributors, private sources, and information on subscribers and folks who wrote ads or letters to the editor—everything that made the *Dirtbuster* an award-winning newspaper. *And* the same stuff that made freedom of the press a valuable tool against power mongers.

The fact that an independent judge had not drawn up or signed the subpoena was incidental. The mission was to get the press. A process server duly delivered the fake *subpoena duces tecum* to the editors demanding that they produce all their records by a specific date in the offices of the MCSO.

Bradley and Woodward were furious. An attempt to crush freedom of the press? In violation of several major Supreme Court decisions upholding their rights? No! The privacy of their sources was sacrosanct! They fought back. They published the information about the subpoena on the front page of the *Dirtbuster,* including the address of the person seeking the subpoena—*el jefe* J. Edgar Bardo. They knew that to include the address was a class 1 misdemeanor. That modest misbehavior led to tonight's action by the MCSO.

Bardo had set the rules in person. He had joined Bullard in the planning session with Strong and Snyder. "These two editors think they can make fun of us. They think they can take liberties with our authority because they are the press. Men, your job is to prove them wrong. We know what they did. They published the information about the grand jury subpoena. That is a crime!"

Snyder asked, "How do you want this to go down?"

"Take Woodward from Tempe to the Jail on Durango and 35th Avenue. Haul Bradley to the Fourth Avenue Jail in downtown Phoenix."

The law enforcement officials knew that Bradley and Woodward were crafty. They had trampled on the Sheriff in print. They had exposed the overreaching nature of the subpoena. But as a further insult, they'd also dubbed him "Sheriff Bombardo." Not funny. Bradley and Woodward needed consequences. Hence "Operation *Dirtbuster"* would occur after dark.

Strong was eager to obey, wanting to prove to Sheriff Bardo that he was worth his weight in arrests. "Which one do you want me to take?"

Snyder took command. "You take Bradley downtown; I'll take Woodward to Durango. Either way, they're not gonna know what hit 'em."

The evening's uniform included black pants, T-shirts, and leather vests. They looked like thugs—their goal was to produce shock and awe.

With five other black-suited members of Bardo's "Special Enforcement Unit," Strong approached Bradley's front door at 9:58. He knew that Bradley had been out to dinner with his girlfriend and had returned home because he had tailed the couple from a posh local restaurant. They had dined with Woodward, his wife, and some professor from ASU downtown. Their plant inside the restaurant would provide details on the conversation. It occurred to Strong that maybe Bradley and his gal were in "the act." He became faintly aroused, then shut down. With the missus gone, "the act" wasn't likely to happen for him, not again in this lifetime. He snapped back to the situation at hand.

Flanked by another five MCSO minions, Snyder approached Woodward's home at 10:00 sharp. The house was dark, except for solar-powered lights that lined the brick walkway to the front door. Woodward and his family might have all turned in for the night. As if in unison, in two towns and two minutes apart, Strong and Snyder pounded loudly on the two doors. They rang doorbells. They kept pounding. Finally, in Paradise Valley, Bradley squinted through his peephole. In Tempe, Woodward peeked through his. They both saw men who looked like criminals.

Bradley and Woodward, unaware of each other's danger, each fearing for himself and his loved ones called 9-1-1. And each one of them, in consecutive shock and dismay, learned from the Paradise Valley and Tempe police departments that these thug look-alikes were, in fact, Deputies of the powerful Sheriff's Office with court-ordered warrants for their arrests. While Bradley's negligee-clad girlfriend stood helpless in the foyer, and Woodward's wife and children hid in a bathroom, Strong and Snyder entered their homes.

Strong grabbed Bradley by the arm and had two officers cuff him. "You're under arrest, sir."

In Tempe, two Deputies hauled Woodward in handcuffs out his front door. Woodward started to protest. "You can't do this. You don't know what you are doing—"

"Tell it to the judge, *sir,*" said Snyder. "Here's the warrant he signed this afternoon."

Allowed only one phone call each, Woodward and Bradley remained in custody overnight until their lawyer arrived at each jail to post bail the following day.

What had they done? For months they had applied increased scrutiny to Bardo's activities against inmates, illegals, and activists, including the death of at least one inmate under mysterious circumstances. In retaliation, Bardo had launched an official "investigation" that included subpoenas for stacks of documents within the *Desert Dirtbuster.* What Bradley and Woodward learned only months after that harrowing night in jail was that the alleged grand jury subpoena was a bogus document. Bardo and his ever-reliable sidekick, County Attorney Robert Shatigan, had created it on their own. To Bradley and Woodward, protecting sources was the heart and blood of independent journalism. Divulge names today— and tomorrow, you'll have none. Their arrests made headlines in the daily news.

John McCormick, attorney for *the Dirtbuster* editors, called ASU. "Professor Ivan Wilder?"

"Yes."

"John McCormick here. I'm the attorney for Bradley and Woodward of the *Dirtbuster*. Have you seen the news? They were arrested and jailed after dinner with you at the restaurant last night."

"Yes. It doesn't make any sense!"

"They asked me to call you. I understand you were having dinner with them and their ladies last night."

Ivan responded cautiously. "They've been solid friends to me since—"

"What did you discuss? I need to know to defend them properly, and they don't want you getting into trouble."

"I didn't want to talk about me. It's been a hard time for me since my wife—"

"I know. They told me. My condolences."

"So, I asked them what they were up to, and they talked about a grand jury subpoena from the Sheriff's Office they hadn't obeyed. They said there was no probable cause that they had committed any crime. The demand was vague and over-broad. They said Bardo was abusing his power, going on a fishing expedition, trying to intimidate them, and squashing freedom of the press. They were going to protect their customers and sources. The usual stuff. Any reason?"

"Yes. The prosecutors usually impose arrest and jail for domestic violence and assault felonies. The *Dirtbuster* charges are minimal. These arrests were unprecedented and over the top. They were both pretty badly shaken up."

"So why are you calling me?"

"We have reason to believe someone was spying on them in the restaurant. That means they probably heard the conversation you had with them. Think about whether there's anything dicey you might have said. Ivan, I'm sure you're now on the MCSO hit list. Any friend of the *Desert Dirtbuster* is an enemy of theirs."

"You're kidding."

"No, you know that Bardo takes after J. Edgar Hoover. He keeps a file on just about everyone. Even you. Even me."

"Well, I don't know how that could affect me. All I do is teach public policy and write an occasional letter to the editor."

Bradley and Woodward refused to miss a beat and were back in their offices by midday at the *Dirtbuster,* again writing exposés on Bardo and Shatigan. They knew they would have to pay a small fine on the "publication of information" charge. But they would not be bullied when it came to freedom of the press.

CHAPTER 8

NO SURPRISES

June 1st, 2010, Phoenix

As Phil unzipped in the men's room, a short, muscular guy sidled over next to him, doing the same.

"Phil? I'm Harry Tanner. Noticed in class how you gave the prof a run for his money. Say, we should get together and talk. We might find some way to make this class more fun."

Someone making friends with me? Phil re-zipped. "Uh, sure, Harry. Anytime. Have something in mind?"

"Sure. Got a little cash?" Harry smirked. "Let's go to lunch tomorrow after class at Hooters. We can ogle the waitresses."

"Okay. Tomorrow."

Lydia rode the Light Rail from Phoenix to Guadalupe in southwestern Tempe. She got off at Apache Boulevard and the 101 Freeway and walked the quarter mile back to her small adobe home clustered among several rental units. The landlord had agreed they could paint the interior walls something other than the ubiquitous Navajo White. Her father had painted the living room and kitchen walls to match his favorite chilies: bell yellow, Anaheim green, *habañero* orange, and chipotle red. The dark green of poblanos framed the windows and archways between the rooms. She found her mother preparing a corn soup with sweet red peppers in the kitchen. "Ah, smells good to be home again." She smiled, giving her mother a warm *abrazo*.

"How was eet, *mi angelita?*"

"Pretty good, *Mamá*. It's a big class. The professor is good. But there's one kid whose dad works for the Sheriff's Office. I hope there won't be trouble."

"Can you stay away from him?"

"*Sí, Mamá*. I am quiet. He won't know I'm there."

Ivan's cell phone vibrated as he left class. A call from Mitch Sullivan: "Come up and chat." Snatching egg rolls and a soda from the Chinese fast-food spot on Central, Ivan elevatored up to the Dean's office.

"So, Ivan, how was the first day?"

"Good so far. Having a course website allows me to offer information without the burden of a twenty-pound book. Plus, the students will be collecting source material through the news."

"Heard you are telling them to register to vote."

"Already? No, I did not tell them to register. I just suggested that they participate in our democracy. But I've hardly left the auditorium. Is it wiretapped?" Ivan smiled, making a joke.

"No, although we've been asked to do that." The Dean did not see it as funny. "But you said you tape everything anyway. Good idea. No surprises."

"Not planning on any. Some of my repeats have already made themselves known."

"Ivan, take a look at your student roster. They are all properly registered to take this class. Almost half of your students have an asterisk after their names because they are journalism students for the Cronkite program. Over a dozen have Hispanic surnames. I bet you have several undocumented students in your class."

"Am I supposed to make each student take a litmus test?"

"My sources say some students in your class have connections with the Sheriff's Office, the County Attorney, or anti-immigrant legislators who may try to collect names and cause some trouble."

"How can they know? Do they go up to students and say, 'Hey, I'm from the County Attorney's office. Are you illegal?'"

"Of course not," said Sullivan. "And frankly, I'm wracking my brain to see what issues they can manufacture."

"But I play by the book. I appreciate the warning, but I think you're wasting your time."

"Maybe, but the registrar's office has already notified me that someone—they weren't saying who—wanted access to their records and your class lists of students. Of course, that's impossible—the records are confidential—but I thought you should know."

The conversation with Sullivan rattled Ivan—*students coming to class specifically to spy on him or other students?* To shake off his unease, Ivan went to the ASU bookstore and arranged for them to carry a dozen sets of his printed materials. Next, despite the afternoon heat, he walked across Central Avenue and diagonally northwest to the Westward Ho to check in on his old friend from high school, Hector Muñoz, the security guard.

The Westward Ho, built as a luxury hotel in 1928, had fallen on less glamorous times and had been renovated as senior citizens' subsidized housing. Dark and cool, the interior offered a welcome contrast to the blazing sun outside. The lobby displayed several stained-glass artworks: Gambel's quail darting off saguaro and prickly pear cacti, Native Americans inside a tent with smoke shaped like a phoenix (the mythic bird) rising from the ashes, and a cluster of adobe homes on a dry mesa. In the corner of the lobby stood a large freestanding loom. Strings of rawhide ran from the top of the loom to the woven part of the half-finished Navajo pattern rug. But instead of a wool-woven base, stained glass patterns rose from the bottom frame. Geometric blocks of turquoise, copper, and claret surrounded a bronze-colored hawk in the center.

"Hector, how's it going?" Ivan asked the stocky security guard at the front desk.

"Ivan, long time no see." Hector extended his beefy paw to shake the hand of his old friend.

Ivan and Hector had been teammates on the football team at Central High several decades ago. Hector had been a fullback. As the years passed, Hector married and created a family while Ivan went on to graduate school, married Marti, and followed the professor path. Despite their disparate directions, a warm friendship grew as Ivan and Marti attended Hector's *Cinco de Mayo* and children's birthday parties. When Marti died, Hector and his wife Lupe were among the first to send flowers and condolences.

Glad to see Hector, Ivan said, "I'm teaching a double-session course at Cronkite this summer."

"So I've heard. My pal at the security desk there told me. Said he was worried. Thought the other security guy was looking for something to pin on you for either Bardo or Shatigan. From the local scuttlebutt, it sounds like it has to do with illegal immigration."

"News travels fast! I'm just teaching an interdisciplinary course in Power and Propaganda."

"Ivan, I know you can't keep your nose out of what's happening in the community. I'm just repeating the locker room gossip among us security guards."

"We will eventually cover Senate Bill 1070, so maybe you're right. But I'll invite all sides to talk to the class. Shouldn't be a problem."

A white-haired lady bending over her walker approached the desk. "Mr. Hector, sir, I am sorry to interrupt."

Hector immediately turned and smiled. "Mrs. Kerchanski, it's never an interruption for you. How can I help?"

A lightly-lipsticked smile transformed the elderly face into a glow of contentment. "There's a cabby outside who has my groceries and doesn't want to leave his car. Here's some money. Could you get them for me? There are only two bags. They aren't too heavy."

Hector took two dollars to tip the cabby and folded the rest back into her palm. "You wait here, Mrs. Kerchanski. I'll be right back."

He turned to Ivan. "Well, dude, I gotta get back to work. Let me know if I can be of any help. Stop by again."

"Thanks."

Ivan crossed the street to mail some bills. The old U.S. post office, still in operation, had been constructed under Franklin Delano Roosevelt during the Great Depression—a "make-work" project that supported the infrastructure of Arizona and gave unemployed men a job and hope. Murals adorned the east and west ends of the lobby. Two artists who otherwise may not have been able to express their talents had painted Arizona history for future generations to enjoy. At the west end, "Pioneer Communications" showed a Native American and a Spanish conquistador making hand gestures, the desert terrain receding in the background. At the east end, a triptych displayed "Cattle Roundup," "Cowboy on Horseback," and "Cattle Grazing."

Next, he walked north to Roosevelt Street and ducked into Carly's for an early dinner of beer and a sandwich. He spent a few extra minutes studying the tattoo curved from the front of the barmaid's chest around her neck onto her shoulder blade. The patterns were confusing, and she was a moving target, so he switched his gaze to the bar counter's array of hand-drawn humans and animals under the clear-resin surface. Finally, dinner finished, Ivan returned to campus and headed to the library on the second floor.

To the north, ceiling-to-floor windows offered a panoramic view of uptown. Several bookshelves stood to the west. The east wall highlighted a series of framed photographs spanning the career of journalist Walter Cronkite. In 1984, the Board of Regents changed the official name to the Walter Cronkite School of Journalism and Telecommunication.

The first photo showed Cronkite on the Morning Show. In the second, Cronkite discussed the news with the puppet Charlemagne. In the third, Cronkite presented "You Are There," illuminating events from history on television. The next photo showed Cronkite reporting on the death of President Kennedy. Finally, several images represented the Vietnam war—when President Lyndon Johnson said, "If I've lost Cronkite, I've lost middle America."[2]

Suddenly it struck Ivan. These kids didn't need a mumbo-jumbo on the branches of government. They needed to learn about freedom of the press.

CHAPTER 9

A SOUR TASTE

Autumn 2007, Phoenix

Within a few days, the arrest of Bradley and Woodward rocked the news world. It became the target of speculation and gossip in all circles—even the Maricopa County Board of Supervisors. Marcia Henderson wanted the Board to pass a resolution condemning the overreach by the Maricopa County Sheriff's Office. Chairman Ken Murdoch quashed her motion. Murdoch did not want to stir the pot with the Sheriff, who was gaining popularity. Sheriff Bardo carried a big stick—the power to investigate and bring charges against anyone. Murdoch was nothing if not careful.

Asa Johnson, one of four Republicans, had recently voted—again—to approve an increase in the budget for the MCSO. Sheriff Bardo enforced the law, and Johnson believed in law and order. Johnson wanted to be a fan of the Sheriff. As long as he could recall, he held to three basic tenets of faith: belief in a strong family, belief in law and order, and belief in public service. Johnson was lucky to have a good wife and several wonderful kids doing well in school. He had chosen to run for office because of his commitment to public service. And ever since the majority elected Sheriff Bardo, Johnson had supported his strong positions against crime, especially against the flood of illegals coming across the border and taking jobs from hard-working Arizonans.

But rumors about MCSO began to trouble him. Bardo had not backed down on implementing the two-meal-a-day regimen at the Fourth Avenue Jail. He also set up a "Tent City" Jail where they paraded the undocumented detainees in front of TV cameras. *And now these arrests of Bradley and Woodward.*

Marcia Henderson was the only Democrat among the BOS, and Johnson found her mantra on behalf of illegal immigrants tedious. First, she kept demanding that Bardo provide documentation of the spending patterns in his office. Now she wanted to sanction the Sheriff for the *Dirtbuster* arrests.

But Asa Johnson was troubled. It wasn't as if he liked the editors of the *Desert Dirtbuster*—not at all. Hadn't they already taken pot shots and him personally for allegedly shady real estate dealings, all untrue? And he had to chuckle at the idea of Bradley and Woodward being hauled away at night to jail. They were such bloodhounds for personal and political muck that a little turning of the tables satisfied his defensive instincts. After all, hadn't they printed the Sheriff's personal information right off the affidavit, a legal no-no?

But Johnson's better self knew better. The publication of the affidavit was a mere misdemeanor of a public record if anyone had wanted it. No one should be hauled out of bed at night and thrown in jail for a misdemeanor. Their arrest was an abuse of power, an actual violation of legal norms, and it left him with a pit in his stomach.

Johnson had supported Bardo consistently in his claim to be ridding the county of the illegals—people working with fake IDs in factories, picking up day jobs, and cleaning government office buildings under cover of night. So, when Bardo appeared at the BOS meetings and touted his record of arrests and sweeps, Johnson supported him even though the requirement that MCSO account for its spending patterns fell through the cracks. He should have realized that another budget item overseen by the BOS would soon come into direct conflict with the demands of the MCSO. Construction of a new Court Tower was a widely recognized need to house the Superior Court and all related offices. Johnson could not know but soon learned that his support of the Court Tower project—requiring over $300 million of County funds—interfered with Sheriff Bardo's ambitions for unauthorized equipment and expanded sweeps against the illegals.

For Asa Johnson, the issue of diabetes receded as budgetary battles intensified. Bardo had begun to hide his spending patterns from the Board of Supervisors. Regular meetings turned ugly as Bardo attracted an enthusiastic fan base who cared not a whit for the actual laws on the books but raved about the "toughest Sheriff in America." Rumors of money mismanagement mounted. Bardo's misuse of government funds soon became an "it" against which all other issues paled by comparison.

CHAPTER 10

WEARING THE FLAG

June 2nd, 2010, Cronkite Auditorium

As the T-shirts, tank tops, and painted toenails settled in, the SmartScreen displayed:

> "Congress shall make no law ... abridging the freedom of speech, or of the press; or the right of the people peaceably to assemble, and to petition the Government for a redress of grievances."

"Class," said Ivan, "where is this quote from?"

A quiet young woman in a middle row raised her hand. "Alicia Rivas. It is from the First Amendment to the United States Constitution. I learned this in my citizenship class. I became a citizen just last year. We did not have these freedoms in Venezuela. Although President Chavez says he is for reform, he tries to control everyone's education. He has shut down newspapers. He imprisoned my cousin for participating in a protest against Venezuela's totalitarian Education Law. His Attorney General got laws passed so he could arrest anyone who disagrees with the Government."

"Thank you, Ms. Rivas. And congratulations on becoming a citizen. Class, shall we give her a hand?"

Almost everyone gave a friendly round of applause except Phil and a kid in the back row. Nazrin added, "My parents fled Iran under the religious dictatorship of Ayatollah Khomeini. He closed newspapers. He persecuted educated people and religious minorities. What we have here in the United States is precious. We have a free press and freedom of religion, and we have no abuse of power by government officials. At least, I hope not."

Harry Tanner didn't join in the applause. As he saw it, he was in Professor Wilder's class to get information for Bardo and his dad. It would be easy to turn in assignments and get the grade, but class participation wasn't required, and it would work against his purpose if anyone noticed him.

"Let's review what we know about freedom of speech and press," said Ivan after the pause, "which has come to include freedom of expression. Any thoughts?"

Jonah jumped in. "Jonah Whalen. Wasn't there some objection to people wearing the American flag on their T-shirts during the Vietnam War? Didn't the Supreme Court finally say that was okay?"

Ivan answered, "Yes. So, should the government prohibit wearing an American flag T-shirt?"

Phil retorted, "No, wearing the flag is cool!"

Tony said, "I've seen bikers wearing the flag on the back of their leather jackets."

Susan added, "My mom took me to an exhibit at the Phoenix Art Museum when I was little. Every artwork showed the American flag from colonial times to today. Some were quilts; others were from the side of a barn or on chinaware. But one artist draped the flag in a toilet to express his anger about the Vietnam War."

Phil flushed with anger. "But that's anti-American!"

Susan continued. "The bikers thought so too. They felt the artist disrespected the flag, so they entered the exhibit hall and stole the flag out of the toilet." She noticed the look of disgust on some faces. "It was not a functioning toilet." A few students chuckled. "The museum put another flag right back in it."

Ivan asked, "What does the flag symbolize? Why does it matter? After all, it's essentially only a piece of cloth."

Tony said, "Doesn't it stand for our nation? So that how you treat the flag represents how you feel about America? If you treat it with disrespect, you'd seem to be unpatriotic?"

Ivan nodded. "Tony nailed it. But it prompts another question: how could wearing the flag on a T-shirt today be considered cool but be considered un-American in 1970?"

Phil looked confused. "So, I'd be labeled un-American in 1970 for doing what I think is patriotic?"

Susan suggested, "People's opinions change. Therefore, the meaning of the symbol changes over time."

Jonah nodded. "I think change is good. The Founding Fathers couldn't have known how to decide everything in the eighteenth century. So I can see how attitudes might change. But how does this always come back to the First Amendment? And how do we wind up with Supreme Court opinions on stuff like T-shirts?"

Susan answered, "My dad says most First Amendment cases get to the Supreme Court because some government officials arrest people and charge them with a crime. Those people hire a lawyer who challenges the law. If it seems to fall into the free speech, press, or expression categories of the First Amendment, the Supreme Court will take the case. Its decision will affect everyone in America."

Jonah added, "That's what happened to me! In 2008 I was arrested for clapping in a public meeting. That was freedom peaceably to assemble, another part of the First Amendment. Four of us were charged with disorderly conduct and jailed. We got lawyers to defend us. The judge found us innocent. Now we've filed a claim in Federal District Court that the Sheriff violated our civil rights."

Ivan asked, "Jonah, how does this all fit into the protection of the First Amendment?"

Jonah said, "My attorney, Emily Hartwell—you should have her come talk to the class—said clapping was a protected form of speech under the First Amendment. Speech can include talking, singing, clapping, some physical expressions, logos on T-shirts, and wearing the flag. So the First Amendment protects a lot of stuff."

Tony asked, "Did your case go to the Supreme Court?"

"No, just the Federal District Court. The judge has sent it to the County mediation people to try to settle without going to a big trial."

In the back row, Harry Tanner took notes. His dad had prosecuted that case.

Ivan moved on. "We've covered free speech and expression pretty well. So, let's get back to the freedom of the press."

Jonah said, "There was an awful situation here in 2007. The Sheriff's Office arrested two guys from a local newspaper for printing information about a grand jury subpoena. Woke them up in the middle of the night and threw them in jail! And even worse, it turned out, there hadn't been any grand jury. The subpoena was bogus!"

Phil argued, "But they did something wrong—"

Ivan answered, "You have a legitimate concern—publishing confidential information and deliberately breaking the law. The question is, was there any serious harm? Was the *Dirtbuster* case handled properly, or was there an abuse of power by the Sheriff and County Attorney?"

Susan asked, "Doesn't it have to do with the investigation?"

"What's such a big deal about an investigation?" asked Tony.

"It depends," said Ivan. "You may interview people informally. That's one kind of investigation. But journalists need to protect their sources. If the journalist has some damning evidence, the target of the investigation—like the Sheriff—could retaliate against the source."

"In Venezuela," said Alicia, "President Chavez is now imprisoning journalists and students, sometimes holding them without a trial."

Ivan clarified. "Exactly. A formal investigation by a government official differs from your investigation as a journalism or public policy student. The government investigator has much more power. For example, in 2007, the Sheriff's Office allegedly obtained a grand jury subpoena requiring the *Desert Dirtbuster* to turn over all phone records, e-mails, contributor lists, and other sources."

Susan gasped. "That would destroy the newspaper!"

Phil said, "But how else do you find out if someone is committing a crime? You gotta get the info."

"Not if they're just on a fishing expedition!" argued Jonah. "They should have some evidence before they get a subpoena."

Tony asked, "What's a subpoena?"

Reading from Google, Susan said, "'An official court document ordering a person to appear in court or at a judicial proceeding, or commanding a witness to bring documents.'"

Ivan added, "With the *Dirtbuster* case, it turned out that the County Attorney's office had made up a fake document to look like a subpoena." He continued. "In a significant case from the United States Supreme Court—*New York Times v. Sullivan,* in 1964—the Court said the government had no business trying to censor newspapers just because the story might embarrass a government official. The Court said: 'Criticism of official conduct does not lose its Constitutional protection merely because it is effective and diminishes official reputations.' The second case involved three newspapers printing the Pentagon Papers in 1971. Again, the Federal Government tried to suppress the publication of information about the role of the Pentagon in waging the Vietnam War. As the local courts ordered one newspaper to stop publication, a different paper printed the next installment. In that case—*The New York Times v. U.S., 1967*—the Supreme Court found that the three newspapers had published no secret information that would adversely affect U.S. Government interests. Therefore, the newspapers had a Constitutional right to print what they did—under the First Amendment clause on Freedom of the Press."

CHAPTER 11

"MR. ACLU!"

November 2007, Phoenix

On a crisp, cool Saturday in November, at the request of Al Freeman, Legal Director of the Arizona Civil Liberties Union, Ivan visited a demonstration organized by community activist Sam Aguilar. Ivan knew Freeman from a conference on the U.S. Constitution and when Freeman had spoken about the Bill of Rights in Ivan's class the previous school year.

"Ivan? Demonstrators outside Bennington Furniture on Saturdays are picketing to support workers' rights to assemble and seek work from passing vehicles. Could you come by and check them out?"

"Why me?"

"Because you write op-ed columns that get printed in the local papers, and you come across as an educated professorial type, more moderate than the activists. Meet me there at ten Saturday morning?"

Fresh on the heels of the *Dirtbuster* arrest, Ivan wanted to understand better what was happening locally. Sure, they were just men seeking honest work. But they were also primarily illegal immigrants. Maybe they were taking jobs away from American citizens. The interface between demonstrators, businesses, and law enforcement raised public policy issues.

This sunny Saturday was theoretically a day off for Deputy Sheriff Paul Strong. But, sipping a large mug at the local donut shop, he was on his way to a job that paid double time. He nibbled a jelly doughnut, chasing it with coffee. The lead story in the newspaper left by some early-bird patron ran the story: "Day Workers Clash with Local Businesses. Hispanic men, some without documents, crowd the parking lot seeking day labor. They have spread from Allenwood Hardware to the parking lot of Bennington Furniture. The local business owners say these men interfere with their everyday business and intimidate regular customers."

Strong wiped the powdered sugar from his lips and left a good tip like the missus would want. Then he headed across the street to Bennington Furniture.

Sam Aguilar, an elder activist among Latinos, had called a series of demonstrations at the furniture store across the street from Allenwood— men seeking day labor, all wanting work. The MCSO always called the day workers "them" or "illegals."

As Strong parked near Bennington Furniture and strode over, he saw Snyder and several other off-duty, double-time-pay Deputies lining up along the outer circle of trucks parked around Bennington's entrance.

Aguilar's group had been meeting on Saturdays for several weeks. Today, the "pro-illegal activists" milled around on the sidewalk down the street east of the entrance, obeying the law. Self-proclaimed "patriotic anti-illegal" demonstrators had clustered nearby for the past two weeks. He saw none of the patriots this morning. Strong counted Aguilar's crowd to be about thirty. He was glad he and Snyder had called other off-duty Deputies to work on this project to protect legitimate customers from the activists.

Dressed in a T-shirt and jeans, Snyder milled around with a legal pad and pen as if he might be a reporter or a Bennington customer making a list of things to buy. Snyder was imperceptibly but irretrievably disgruntled—the frustration was building. In recent years, hundreds of complaints had come into the MCSO on all kinds of sex crimes—rape, assault, molestation, and harassment— his main work for Bardo. But since the political wind shifted away from prosecuting dangerous felons to sweeping up illegals, Bardo had re-assigned him to the "Mexican detail." Bardo had even dropped the pursuit of hundreds of sex offense complaints. Snyder wanted to investigate perps and bring them to justice. Instead, he got assigned to a small, peaceful demonstration at Bennington Furniture that did nothing to pump his adrenaline.

Sam Aguilar had called Al Freeman at ACLU several days earlier and asked him to observe the next demonstration. "Every Saturday, super-patriots and neo-Nazis harass us because we're Hispanic. MCSO does nothing to stop them." Aguilar had pushed Freeman's First Amendment hot button. To Aguilar, Freeman had said, "They can be there too, but they don't have the right to endanger your guys. It's the job of MCSO to keep you safe. Be cool. I'll stop by."

Freeman was driving home on Saturday after running some errands when he stopped by the demonstration. He parked on the west side of Bennington's building, where the store did not have a "Customers Only" sign like in the parking lot. Then, careful to stay on the public sidewalk, he headed toward Aguilar's demonstrators. Citizen Al Freeman felt grumpy. A recent surgical procedure for a bulging disc and some over-zealous physical therapy had bound his back muscles into a knot. Feeling a pinch as he took each measured step, he just wanted to go home. His rescue dog still suffered abandonment issues every time he left the apartment. The visit to Aguilar would be just a quick stop on the way back to Fido and an ice pack.

Considered by many to be a giant in the fight against prison injustice and racial profiling, Freeman was a man of short stature, rotund at five-foot-five. He resembled a litigious Humpty Dumpty, except that he didn't sit on a wall—he stood unequivocally on the side of those oppressed by the government.

Large furniture trucks jammed the parking lot. A dozen uniformed men formed a ring between the trucks and the public sidewalk. The girdle of trucks and MCSO badges telegraphed the message "no trespassing." Freeman strode, outside the private boundaries of the furniture store, over to Aguilar. He recognized the white mustache and a full head of snowy hair framing the activist's walnut-brown face.

Meanwhile, just having arrived, Ivan parked east of Bennington near Allenwood. He walked across the street to meet Sam Aguilar as Freeman joined them.

"Hi, *Señor* Aguilar, I'm Al Freeman from ACLU. Remember? Hello, Ivan. I assume you two have met."

"No," said Ivan. "I've just arrived."

"*Bienvenido, amigo,*" Aguilar said to Ivan. "Nice to meet you," he added, shaking hands with each of them. "How are things going, *Señor* Civil Liberties?"

Freeman wished he had pain killers for his back. It was not going fine, but he faked it. "Fine. Glad I could make it."

Ivan added, "I'm glad to meet you. What's going on today?"

Aguilar motioned to a few demonstrators. "Miguel has been seeking work at Bennington for over a year. There have been no problems until recently." He turned to Miguel. "*¿No problemas en el pasado, amigo, verdad?*"

Miguel nodded.

"*¿Pero ahora, sí?*"

Miguel nodded again. "*Ahora, sí, hay muchas problemas.*"

Ivan failed to see any problems. "What kind of problems?"

"First," said Aguilar, "some property owners don't want us on their parking lot seeking work. That's why we're on the public sidewalk, away from Bennington, this morning."

Freeman's back kept twitching. He grimaced. "I don't see a hostile crowd today, though. Aren't you all doing okay?"

"Yes," said Aguilar. "No one showed up today. Maybe they got bored or had something they'd rather do."

Ivan asked a last question, "Any worries?"

"No, but thanks for showing up, both of you. Last Saturday, it could have gone any which way."

"Well," said Freeman, "I have a lonely dog at home, so if there are no problems, I'll take off. You have my cell phone number. Call me anytime."

"Guess I'll go, too, if you don't need me," said Ivan. He crossed the street, got in his car, and left.

Snyder wrote Ivan's license plate number as the car moved onto the main road. He watched Freeman walk away from the Mexican, along the sidewalk, and west, past Bennington Furniture.

Freeman retraced his path along the narrow public sidewalk, around the corner heading west toward his car. Strong kept Freeman in view as he passed Bennington's boundaries. Suddenly, he decided, *I don't like his cocky attitude.* He called, "Hey, you, come here."

Freeman glanced at Strong and kept walking. *I've done nothing wrong. If I obey, I'll have to step onto the parking lot, which he could label trespass.*

Strong amped-up his baritone. "Hey, you heard me. I told you to come here."

The nagging back pain dulled Freeman's hyper-vigilant antennae, inclining him, uncharacteristically, to cooperate. He approached Strong, leaving the legal safety of the public sidewalk to obey an officer of the law.

Snyder, Strong, and the wall of cargo trucks formed a solid barrier between Freeman and the band of protesters.

Strong spoke first. "What are you doing here?"

"I was observing."

To Freeman, the uniformed Strong was clearly part of the MCSO, but T-shirt was an unknown. "Who are you?"

With a mini-flourish, Snyder stuck an arm down his shirt and whipped out his badge. "MCSO. And I'll ask the questions from now on." He nodded to Strong as if they had rehearsed their performance. "Cuff him."

"What have I done?"

"Trespass three. On private property without permission."

"But—"

"You're breaking the law."

Freeman considered his options. He was on Bennington property at the insistence of the police. They should let him go. He said, "I'm an attorney. Besides, I have a dog at home, who has been sick—"

Snyder interrupted. "Stop talking. You're under arrest."

Freeman balked. "I think you should reconsider. Let me give you my card." Then, slipping a few fingers into his shirt pocket, he pulled out two and offered one to each deputy.

Strong flicked his card to the ground. Snyder read his card and tapped a finger against the logo. "Mr. ACLU. Well, now. A big fish. Howdy. Officer Strong, let's take him in."

Another call had greeted Ivan on the Monday after Freeman's arrest. "John McCormick again. Remember me from the arrest of Bradley and Woodward last month?"

"Yes. Good morning. To what do I owe the honor of this call?"

McCormick answered his question with a question. "Why do you keep showing up at these troublemaker situations?"

"What do you mean?"

"Where were you Saturday morning?"

"Nowhere in particular. Jeez, Mr. McCormick, what do you mean by that?"

"Call me John. Just after you left the demonstration at Bennington Furniture, the Sheriff's Deputies arrested Al Freeman. He had been just walking on the sidewalk. They ordered him into the parking lot and then declared he was trespassing. Ivan, I'm getting the sense that their *modus operandi* is to arrest people they hate when no one else is around as a witness. *Dirtbusters* at night, ACLU surrounded by trucks."

"You told me to watch out last month, John."

"Records are cumulative, Ivan. Bardo is up for re-election in 2008, and you've made it into his files twice in the fall of 2007. Of course, Freeman will fight this charge, but Bardo is surely building a record on you. So be on the lookout."

CHAPTER 12

HOOTERS

Wednesday, June 2nd, 2010, Phoenix

Harry was chatting with the freckled security guard when Phil arrived. The two students swung through the glass doors and headed east to the Arizona Center. They crossed the flagstone tile and passed a phalanx of four-to-eight-foot palm trees circling the entrance to Hooters.

Inside, ceiling fans whirred. A dozen TV screens flashed multiple sports broadcasts, from golf and tennis to auto car races. Memorabilia and hula hoops cluttered the walls. Orange dominated—seat covers, menus, the waitresses' shorts, and the orange Hooter letters across the bosom of each gal's white tank top.

Harry nudged Phil. "Look at those boobs. What a great name for this place—Hooters."

Phil nodded. Dressed identically, each waitress wore push-up bras, so their breasts showed cleavage. Harry ogled another waitress walking by. They took a high table and sat on stools. A waitress brought menus.

Focusing on her T-shirt lettering, Harry asked, "Can we have a drinks menu too?"

A petite five-foot-three with straight brown hair, the waitress asked with a bland smile, "May I see your I.D.?"

Irritated, Harry produced his driver's license. He was indeed twenty-one, so she brought the list.

"What'll you have, Phil?" Harry asked, inviting him to look at the beer selection.

"Uh, I'll have a Pepsi." Harry's behavior unnerved Phil. He couldn't quite put his finger on it. Harry acted like a good pal, yet he also seemed to need to appear older, richer, and sexier by choosing Hooters instead of going to McDonald's or a student hangout. And even though he went along with Harry, he was uncomfortable staring at the boobs—it didn't seem polite.

They both ordered mushroom burgers and fries; Harry had ordered a Bud Lite. They spent a few minutes chowing down.

Harry said, "Say, Phil, don't you think it's odd, the girl in class with the thick Spanish accent? That Alicia Rivas. Do you believe she's really a citizen?"

"Dunno. She said she was. Why?"

"You know, I sit in the back, so I can look around without being noticed. A lot of people look like they don't belong."

"Whaddya mean?" Phil asked. "Doesn't everyone have to register for class?"

"Yeah, but you either pay in-state fees, which are pretty low, or out-of-state. I've heard some kids came from out of state for Journalism. But a lot of others—well, you know, the group who sit together in two rows—look like Mexicans, like they could be illegals. My dad said that even if they're illegal, they can pay in-state tuition by proving they have a residence. Doesn't seem fair, them coming here illegally and getting the in-state bargain rate when real citizens from other states pay more."

"Oh?"

"Why should they even take up seats when citizens should have first dibs in the class? Not that this guy is a terrific teacher or anything. But you know what I mean?"

"Yeah. That's not right."

"I've been thinking. If we can find out who has papers and who doesn't, we could have them arrested and taken to ICE—you know, Immigration and Customs Enforcement."

"Cool! But how?"

"I don't know yet. That's for you and me to figure out."

"Sounds great. A sweep right in class! My dad has done plenty of sweeps at job sites."

The waitress approached with their tabs.

As they each put out money, Harry asked, "Say, Darla," staring at her name tag on the right breast, "can I have your phone number? Maybe we could do something later."

Darla took the money with another noncommittal smile. "Gosh, sorry. Company policy. I'm not allowed." She took their money and returned with the change.

Harry said, "That's okay, Darla, keep the change."

Phil nodded in agreement.

After they left, Phil felt strange. The idea of a sweep was exciting. And having a friend on the same side of his political scene felt good. He hoped he could figure out how to get some names of illegal students in class. But something still unsettled him about Harry. *The way he looked at the waitresses' T-shirts—geez. Mom would have killed me if I did that.*

───────────

At the University campus, following a quick lunch, Ivan sought a shady nook on Taylor Street for a smoke. Watching the curl rise, he pondered the morning's progress. It was eerie how the *Dirtbuster* case in 2007 had been so much on point today in 2010. And if the judge dismissed Jonah's case, there must have been a First Amendment issue regarding the applause. He reminded himself to enquire about Jonah's attorney, Emily something-or-other. He took one final drag, wishing he could talk it over with Marti.

CHAPTER 13

LIFE AT THE MCSO

June 2ⁿᵈ, 2010, Phoenix

Another day, a day like all days, but at least with Memorial Day, it's only a four-day workweek. Eleanor Jones unlocked the Maricopa County Sheriff's Office at precisely 6:57 in the morning. She held the key for the first door in her pale fingers, the rest slipping to a clump on the ring and jostling against her pinky. She turned the key to the right until she felt a catch. Then two notches counter-clockwise, followed by a full turn plus three to the right. The door unlocked. She entered and closed the metal door. She took a few short steps to the opposite wall and disengaged the alarm. Punching in the code correctly, she saw a green light and heard the blip. Silently, she said a Hail Mary. Once, when she was only two months into the job, she failed to enter the code on time. Insidiously, the alarm was silent. But in what seemed like less than the time it had taken for her to try the lock again, six members of a black-outfitted SWAT team had surrounded her. That two-second error triggered an internal investigation and several hearings. MCSO installed a new code panel and cleared her of wrongdoing. She kept her job as the front-office receptionist.

Eleanor needed this job. Jobs were not easy to come by, and she now lived alone with three children—two in high school and one in eighth grade. Shortly after the birth of their third, she had left her prominent, politically powerful, and physically abusive husband, the CEO of a major corporation, who had brought several hundred jobs to Mesa. Eleanor found safety at Sojourner Center, a domestic violence shelter for women and their children fleeing abuse, women who were struggling to make a new way in the world. She filed for divorce and obtained an Order of Protection. Then she got rid of her husband's surname. She had landed the receptionist position at the Sheriff's Office. It startled her to realize, feeling such relief at the sight of this morning's green button, how similar the MCSO felt to her former life—calm on the surface but with a perpetually tense undercurrent.

The MCSO customized the waiting room for top security. Visitors awaiting entry had to announce themselves into a grated speakerphone before being buzzed inside. Upon entering, visitors would notice that all four walls obstructed any view into the office or even back toward the elevator bank. On either side, they would see two plain brown walls with a mirrored glass panel covering the third wall, screening Eleanor from view. The fourth wall, at the visitor's back, was covered with plaques or photos commemorating Sheriff Bardo's achievements or association with various elected officials, from Arizona to the nation's Capital. If someone examined a few shots closely, they might recognize J. T. Reynolds, a self-proclaimed member of the American Nazi Party, immediately next to the Sheriff.

Eleanor walked down the hall to the staff kitchen. She brewed two pots of coffee to satisfy the needs of tightly-wound Deputies. She spread out the donuts from Bashas' Supermarket. Two Deputies chatted at a small table, ignoring her. Stashing her yogurt and fruit cup in the refrigerator, she poured a large mug and returned to her tiny reception room adjacent to the lobby. Eleanor placed her coffee mug on the platform near her computer. She waited in her small dark enclosure for the men to arrive.

Down the hall, in the one office with an expansive view of South Mountain to the south and the Papago Peaks to the east, J. Edgar Bardo asked Sid Bullard to lock the door behind him. The drawn blinds protected the office from the blazing sun. "I just ordered security to sweep the office for bugging devices, Sid. Do it several times a year. Can't be too careful."

"No, sir."

"Like the new chairs?"

"Yes, sir." Bullard appreciated the fact that, after he'd had to cram himself into standard issue, Bardo had finally installed two oversized steel-framed, leather-bound chairs.

"Sid, it's going to be a hot summer. We've accomplished a lot. Gotten rid of hundreds of illegals. Thousands of others are running scared, leaving the county, going back where they came from."

"What do you want me to watch for this summer, sir?" Despite the ostensible air of trust and collegiality, Bullard knew his place. He knew, also, that Bardo kept a file on him. Knew that Bardo knew he liked a drink or two in the evenings and an occasional trip to the casino on a nearby Indian reservation.

Bardo laid out his expectations. "As I see it, the activists will do their little business around SB 1070. Unfortunately, that Federal Judge is gonna knock a bunch of holes in the law. I have that feeling. But we've done a lot. And her little decision won't stop me. County politics aside, you deserve a huge amount of credit. We've rounded up hundreds of Mexicans, most of 'em illegal, and the rest are terrified. Our polls have never been higher. And that raid in May on the Milagro woman's house was brilliantly executed. You brought another activist to her knees, and your attention to absolute secrecy is impressive. I don't know anything about what went down, yet I know we have all the goods we want from that operation. No need to say more."

"No, sir. Thank you, sir. I'm pretty proud of that one, if I may say so."

Bardo continued. "Keep your ear to the ground and keep operations on track. And Sid, there's this professor at ASU downtown. Wildcat, or Wilder, is his name. I've built a fat file on him. Strong's kid is in the class. He stops by MCSO to see his dad sometimes after class. I'm sure he'll soon be feeding us tidbits. Tanner from the County Attorney's shop—his boy Harry is there too. We may get something on the professor in his little ivory tower by the time summer school is out. I'm sure he's got illegals in there. He's not rooting them out. They're racking up benefits illegally. Cheating citizens and taxpayers."

After Bullard left, Bardo called Snyder. "Len, come in and sit down for a minute."

Snyder felt dwarfed in the oversized chair, still warm from Bullard's imprint—both were aware of their status. Bardo was the boss. And although Snyder would never reach the top, he'd always have the Sheriff's ear because he collected information Bardo needed. "What can I do for you, sir?"

"Len, I like the intelligence you get from reading the press. I like how you branched out into the Internet and blogging. Also, TV talk shows. Keep your eye on that little Wilder guy at ASU downtown—you've given me some valuable intel on him. He's teaching a course called Propaganda and Power. I expect something to surface there. And, Len, if you ever get wind of potential sites for a newsworthy sweep on illegals, let me be the first to know. No, on the other hand, I don't need to know everything. I don't even want to know. It's getting more and more important that I do not know. Tell Bullard. He's in charge of all ops. I'll know, but I won't know, if you see what I mean."

"Yes, sir. No, sir. Got it, sir."

CHAPTER 14

PEACEFUL ASSEMBLY?

June 2010, Cronkite Auditorium

The next day in class, Ivan lit up the SmartScreen:

> *Amendment I, U.S. Constitution*
> "Congress shall make no law ... abridging ...
> the right of the people peaceably to assemble,
> and to petition the Government for a redress of
> grievances."

> *Amendment XIV, U.S. Constitution*
> "No State shall ... deny to any person within its
> jurisdiction the equal protection of the laws."

Ivan began, "Today, we focus on peaceable assembly. Note that this section of the Fourteenth Amendment doesn't restrict equal protection only to citizens. It refers to 'any person.'"

I wonder how this applies to me, wondered Lydia.

Jonah said, "The Fourteenth Amendment really matters! The Sheriff has tried to arrest people who might not be citizens."

Phil argued, "But they're illegal!"

"How can you tell?" demanded Alicia, looking straight across the room at Phil.

Ivan took a breath. "Both of you gentlemen have a point. And Alicia, that's an excellent question. Imagine there is a group of people demonstrating on a public sidewalk. They're peaceful. Can the police arrest any of them?"

Phil said, "The illegals, yeah."

Jonah argued, "If they're peaceful, no."

Alicia repeated, "How can you tell who is 'legal' and who is not?"

Nazrin added, "In Iran, my mother and several women were arrested for demonstrating peacefully, only because they were women. The Ayatollah was cracking down on educated women with professional jobs. My mom was a teacher. I'm glad I was born here. At least women and citizens are safe to demonstrate." She adjusted her headscarf ever so slightly, her dark eyes flashing. "Aren't we?"

Ivan continued. "In a case called *Edwards v. South Carolina*, in 1963, over 200 black students had peacefully marched to the state capitol to protest racial discrimination. The police arrested them all because they 'might' cause a riot, even though everyone agreed in Court that they were, in fact, peaceful. The Supreme Court said the state law was unconstitutional because it penalized peaceable assembly. Therefore, the students were innocent. What constitutes 'peaceful'?"

Phil answered, "If they're disorderly, they should be arrested, shouldn't they?"

"How can you tell?" asked Tony. "Who gets to decide?"

"Didn't everyone agree that the student demonstration was actually peaceful?" asked Alicia.

Phil asked, "Then how come the Supreme Court got involved?"

Jonah quipped, "Because the police arrested them all, duh!"

Ivan said, "True. In this case, after they were arrested and jailed, the students found an attorney who sued the police. The police released the students after their short stay in jail. Then the students waited almost a year until the Supreme Court ruled that the law allowing their arrest was unconstitutional. The Court found the students to be peaceful and innocent of any charges. Still, they had been arrested, jailed, and prosecuted before the Court made a final ruling that would protect against other such arrests in the future. On the other hand, the Supreme Court has ruled against unruly demonstrators who threatened violence. Furthermore, the Court has ruled on where people can peaceably assemble." He elaborated— on government property, public sidewalks, and areas where people had a right to distribute information but not disrupt traffic. "The Supreme Court has upheld the right of peaceable assembly for black students, labor unions, veterans, Nazis, Jehovah's Witnesses, and the Ku Klux Klan."

Jonah asked, "What about undocumented workers?"

Nazrin added, "Your law says equal protection for 'any person within the jurisdiction.' Doesn't that include the persons who are not yet citizens, legal or otherwise?"

Ivan said, "So far, it does."

Tony asked, "Can't Arizona make state laws to take care of problems we have?"

Phil looked over at Tony. *Yeah, we have too many illegal immigrants. He's smart.*

Ivan responded, "Good question. Is it a State matter? Or Federal? One last question. In the enthusiasm to arrest 'illegals,' or workers without documents, is it constitutional to arrest other people because they look 'illegal'?"

Jonah insisted, "No! And that's what Sheriff Bardo has been doing—arresting people on account of the color of their skin. He just arrests Mexican-looking people. He's racist!"

Susan added, "It's not just about Mexicans. A friend of my parents from India was pulled over at night for no reason and questioned. He was a doctor on his way home from the hospital. He wasn't speeding or anything."

Nazrin raised her hand. "I am a citizen." She cast a glance around the room. "Does anyone here think I don't look like a citizen?"

Harry wrote down her first name. He needed to get ahold of the class list.

Phil defended his dad's office. "But most people arrested have been either illegals or have committed some other crime."

Susan challenged him. "Why is 'most of the people' good enough? What about the ones who are innocent?"

Sitting in the front row on the end seat, Karen Young said nothing. As one of the TAs, it was not her place to participate in the class discussion. *But,* she thought, *Uncle Sylvester told me to watch for pro-illegal stuff in this class.*

CHAPTER 15

DOGGIE MASKS

December 6th, 2008, Phoenix

Paul Strong tapped on the receptionist's tinted window. "Hey, ma'am, more coffee. Now!"

Eleanor slid open the window and acknowledged his demand with a nod. It was a chilly Monday morning with coffee always brewing. Eleanor slipped into the hallway and hurried to the staff kitchen. She washed the coffee pot, placed a fresh filter in the top, spooned grounds into the filter, poured the water into the machine, and replaced the pot in its nest. She turned the button to "on." She washed the dishes in the sink.

Bullard and Snyder joined Strong in the cafeteria. They clumped together, speaking in undertones, ignoring Eleanor. They were talking about something about to happen. Bullard said protesters had gathered in the lobby of the County Board of Supervisors (BOS) offices—the Supervisors who funded Bardo's operations. Eleanor dried the mugs and put them next to the pot, where the little green light indicated that coffee was ready. She carefully rinsed the plates and silverware and put them in the rack to dry.

"Protective Services just called," said Bullard. "About thirty people, all wearing dog or cat masks. They need us to go over and surround them. Sheriff Bardo told me to enforce law and order in the BOS lobby."

"What's with the masks?" asked Strong.

"Seems these guys have been to the BOS public meetings a lot," said Bullard. "When one of our staff brings in a dog or cat to fundraise for the animal rescue program, the animals get more time on the agenda than these people. This little group thinks they are going to make a point."

Snyder broke in. "They may make a point, but they better make it fast because we're going to the BOS lobby right now to kick ass. We'll have them out of there before they can say, 'Woof, woof.'" He smirked at his joke. "Maybe we'll put a few of the punks in jail. Nothing else is happening today—it's only Monday. We might as well give the jail crew something to do."

Eleanor finished up at the sink.

As Mother Nature dumped an unexpected foot of snow on the Prescott National Forest one hundred miles to the north, thirty people in sunny Phoenix crowded into the BOS lobby, hoping to see a County Supervisor or at least to make an appointment. They wore face masks—doggie masks, kitty masks, lambs and piggies, and one "Big Bird" that covered someone's body. Protesters and activists, who had not been able to obtain a date for an appointment, wore masks as if to say, "Animals can get on the agenda. Why can't we?"

After punching the silent alarm button under her front-office desk for security backup, the secretary hurried back to the staff lounge. Soon, Maricopa County Protective Service officers arrived by a secret back elevator, marched into the public waiting room, and stationed themselves around the room against the walls. Right after them, as if in lockstep, more officers from MCSO entered. Twenty-five officers in full regalia surrounded the activists, who milled around like sheep in the center of the lobby. Strong stared. He'd never seen such an array of masks, not even on TV or in the movies.

Snyder told the protestors, "You need to leave. You have no public business here." *So what if they are all in a government building, in the public waiting room, during business hours? I'm here to enforce law and order.*

Effectively intimidated, twenty-six activists moved gingerly but promptly toward the bank of elevators, pushed the down button, and left. Four women stayed. They removed their masks, inhaled deeply, and sat in the chairs provided for members of the public coming to see their elected officials. They were petitioning their government. They believed Bardo was moving funds allocated for jail use to be spent instead on costly sweeps of Hispanics. They thought the supervisors should demand an accounting of this miscreant Sheriff. So, they decided to make a seated stand. They would try to make an appointment with one of their elected officials. It was the BOS waiting room, it was public visiting hours, and they believed they did have legitimate business.

Snyder motioned Strong to take over. With gun and taser on his hip, a walkie-talkie clipped to his pressed shirt pocket, Strong leaned over the shoulder of one of the two white women. *One of them should at least understand English. Those two others—well, they look like Mexicans.* "You'll have to leave, ma'am," said Strong, maintaining a polite facade. "You have no public business here."

No one budged.

"Ma'am. Tell the others. You need to leave. Now. You have no public business here." *After all, the secretary had pushed the button, and MCPS had called MCSO for help. The BOS crowd sure as hell needed someone in charge.*

Nothing.

One more time. "If you do not leave now, we will have to place you under arrest."

Still nothing. Silence.

Strong called to three other officers. "I am placing each of you under arrest," he said to the women. Strong and the Deputies grabbed their arms, making the four women rise to their feet. Then, the Deputies placed the women's arms behind their backs and locked the hard plastic bracelets on their wrists. Next, the captain from Protective Services pushed the elevator button, and the officers forced the women inside.

They headed down to the basement and through the underground passageway to the Fourth Avenue Jail. There, the women were booked and charged with trespass. Strong then turned them over to a female guard while he and Snyder waited at the far end of the hallway as the guard conducted a cavity search on each woman. First, she required each detainee to open her mouth for the "ah" stick. Next, she peeked up their nostrils and into their ears. Then she checked behind their ears, moving hair away if necessary. She ordered them to remove their slacks and underpants and squat, bottom-naked. Finally, she watched each backside to see whether a baggie of pot or cocaine would pop out, pressured by the squat, from the vaginal or anal orifices. "Cough!" she ordered to ensure clearance of the cavities as she physically spread the cheeks. After each woman completed the protocol, she told them to dress and line up. She then escorted them to their separate cells.

Strong glanced at the women and looked away. He'd seen his share of cavity searches. *Nobody's ass is pretty.* He recalled how his father would spank him, bare-assed, with a belt, if he didn't live up to Dad's impossible standards. He remembered feeling trapped, scared, and humiliated.

Snyder turned to Strong. "Remember the pregnant inmate we kept shackled on the way to the hospital?

"Yeah."

Snyder sniggered. "Pretty funny. As if she wasn't clumsy enough, already in labor."

Several months ago, a pregnant jail mate, awaiting trial on charges of possession of marijuana for sale, had gone into labor and started to dilate. They took her to the county hospital to deliver. The guards shackled the right hand and left leg to the table, even during labor and delivery.

Suddenly Strong's stomach soured. *I hate these activist women who are so disrespectful of authority.* But Snyder's reference to the pregnant prisoner repulsed him. *That goes too far—when a woman is in labor, giving birth.*

Supervisor Asa Johnson heard about the "mask" arrests by noon. He had not been in his office, but something was not right about the arrest. They had been in the public lobby. They had taken off their masks. They did have a right—a Constitutional right—to see a County Supervisor. He would have agreed to see them, unpleasant as they seemed. And concern was brewing about the Sheriff's spending patterns and his refusal to produce the Board-required monthly reports about his spending. As much as Johnson hated to admit it, these "mask" ladies might have a point.

The four women arrested at the BOS office that Monday in 2008 called Emily Hartwell from jail. She bailed them out in the late afternoon when the in-house bail judge presided over the holding room. The judge removed the odious clause, "can't frequent the Board of Supervisors' building or offices," from the terms of release. "The women had been nonviolent," the Judge told Emily and the defendants in the jailhouse courtroom. He wrote on the release order, "This is a First Amendment issue. They are free to assemble in a public place to petition their government."

"Then we'll go back," said one of the women as Emily accompanied them out of the building. "We have a right to be there— to make our voices heard. Emily, come with us. Watch what these thugs are doing. The Board of Supervisors holds its public meeting Wednesday. We'll speak in the public comments section after they conduct their regular business."

CHAPTER 16

THE DANGER OF APPLAUSE

Wednesday, December 8th, 2008, Phoenix

Flush with confidence from Monday's arrest and jailing of those animal activist women, Strong and Snyder flanked Bullard on Wednesday in the antechamber of the BOS public auditorium. Twenty Deputies, who could have been patrolling crime-filled neighborhoods, responding to domestic violence calls, or even transporting inmates from the jail to their hearings in the courthouse, stood at attention, awaiting orders.

"Men," Bullard began, "Protective Services just briefed us. Most of the same thirty people who were there Monday at the BOS office will be here today, during the public comments section after the Supervisor's business, to disrupt the meeting. They'll probably be wearing the same animal masks they wore Monday. Sheriff Bardo has spoken with me directly. Some of the women arrested Monday may show up today. Plus, members of that left-wing group with the red T-shirts. He has files on all of them. He has ordered that if we see the women or any red shirts, they are our priority. Get it? *Our priority.* Officially, your job will be to prevent disturbances in the meeting and uphold law and order. So, if anything is out of line, you will step in and make arrests. Snyder and Strong are in charge. Snyder will handle stage left. Strong will take stage right and the center aisle. And you—" he pointed a nail-bitten finger around the room and returned to mid-point, "—you will split yourselves and follow their command."

Snyder took over. "Men, we'll circle the auditorium, one man about every fifteen feet. Each of you has a pager. You can buzz me if you see a situation. Strong, anything to add?"

Strong shook his head. "Let's get out there and kick butt, officers."

The men took their places in the auditorium at 9:40 am. The official business part of the BOS meeting had been droning on since 8:00. They expected the disruption to occur sometime during the public comments segment, which would begin at 10:01. Soon, the room was lined with tan shirts and brown pants, all neatly pressed and bedecked with badges, hip-pistols, tasers, and pagers. The audience was largely unaware of the officers as they took their places behind and to the sides of the auditorium.

At about 9:55, four more visitors walked down the center aisle and sat quietly about halfway to the front, to the right. Strong recognized the two women who he had arrested and jailed Monday. *Who do they think they are coming here today?* Two young men sat next to the women, one a white guy with hippie-long hair, the other a black guy. All four wore red T-shirts.

The Chairman called for public comments. Two minutes each for any person who'd put their name on a request form. Snyder started feeling antsy. The Chairman would call your name, and you could go to the lectern and mouth off about anything. A dark-skinned woman began speaking in Spanish with some other Mexican woman translating for her. She claimed she was a citizen but feared Sheriff Bardo because of his sweeps. A large group of people in the crowd applauded her comments. As if on cue, about fifteen stood up!

Snyder didn't like the feel of it. *Too many people are standing and applauding.* He paged Strong, who was closer to the T-shirts.

Strong noticed it too. *Chairman Murdoch is pounding his gavel for them to sit down and shut up.*

One of the other supervisors said to the Chairman, "This is getting crazy!"

The Chairman called out, "Please sit down."

Strong's adrenaline spiked. He gestured to a few Deputies to follow him down the center aisle. At the same time, the fifteen settled quietly into their seats, including the four T-shirts.

Then, the Chairman called one of them—Thompson—to go to the lectern to speak.

Wait! Strong felt confused. *Hell! Thompson's walking toward the lectern, away from the other three!* Strong paged Snyder to grab her from stage left.

The Chairman pounded his gavel again when he saw Thompson in Snyder's custody. He called the next name. "Ms. Sanderson? A Ms. Sanderson?"

It's chaos! Making a split-second decision, Strong told the T-shirts, "Get up! You have to leave." Then he contradicted himself by directing the Protective Services captain and the Deputies to block their exit to the center aisle. "You cannot speak," he shouted. "You're under arrest."

At the same time, Thompson and Sanderson yelled to Chairman Murdoch, "The officer won't let us speak!"

Strong panicked. *Sanderson is disobeying my command to get up and leave! She's sitting again with the remaining two. What? She's pretending to get her purse. Bardo wants law and order enforced! It's now or never.* "Deputies, cuff the T-shirts." Right in front of the entire audience—*in case anyone thinks it might not happen to them*—the Deputies cuffed their hands behind their backs and marched the T-shirts down the center aisle, and out of the auditorium. A hush fell on the crowd. The rest was easy. Snyder brought Thompson directly from the lectern. Then it was down the elevator to the basement and over to the jail, where they booked all four on charges of disorderly conduct.

Although there was more time for public comments, Asa Johnson motioned to Chairman Murdoch to cut the meeting short. After the public had left the auditorium, he spoke to Murdoch. "What the heck was that? The MCSO was way out of line!"

Murdoch grimaced. "I was frantic. I called on people to speak, and the MSCO guys kept arresting them. Even after I had gaveled for quiet and everyone had sat down."

Asa looked around the room. "I used to think this was our auditorium, Ken, the Maricopa County Board of Supervisors. We oversee the county's budget, including MCSO. But today, it felt like Bardo's operation. Almost like we were in jail."

Strong and Snyder headed back to MCSO for a quiet recap in the staff room with a fresh brew from the lady at the receptionist's desk. An action-packed two hours had passed since their last mug, and they were ready for more. They went over details while she washed dishes.

Snyder spoke first. "I couldn't believe it. After the judge let them out of jail on Monday, two of the women returned."

Strong took a slow sip. "That Chairman is such a screw-up. Doesn't he know he is part of the problem? As if these women had a right to speak. They'd just been arrested two days before, for Pete's sake. He just kept banging the gavel and calling their names."

Snyder leaned back in his chair. "Don't worry, Paul, it doesn't matter. We got the four troublemakers out of there. One of our guys called me soon afterward. The silence in the audience after we left was awesome. We did our job. We established law and order."

CHAPTER 17

HOW TO MARGINALIZE

June 2010, Cronkite Auditorium

A 3x5-inch file card of red, white, or blue lay on each chair. Ivan told the students to pick them up. "Today is our first day to discuss propaganda." He watched the students as they silently read from the overhead SmartScreen:

> "Bandwagon," "Disinformation," "Marginalizing," and "Scapegoating."

"This morning, hold up your colored card when you raise your hand. Let's define propaganda. What is it?"

Hands rose. "Ms. Red card?"

"Isn't propaganda a false statement?"

Ivan said, "It does not have to be true. Mr. Blue card?"

Tony, with the blue card, asked, "Doesn't it mislead people? Like calling certain individuals or groups bad names? Right now, in America, we're labeling all Muslims as 'terrorists.' But the majority of them aren't. Most of them are refugees from the terrorists."

Soon the class agreed on Ivan's summary. "Propaganda is deliberately false or misleading information that supports a political cause or the interests of those in power. Propaganda is a technique used to change how people understand an issue or situation, to change their actions in ways that the interest group wants."

Ivan called on the students to give some examples. "Yes, Mr. Red card, in the middle?"

"The way the Nazis blamed the Jews for things that were out of anyone's control, like the economic depression."

Ivan asked, "How about in the United States? Mr. Blue card, in the back."

"We've had a history of discrimination against the Blacks and the Native Americans."

Susan waved her white card eagerly. Ivan looked directly at her, then called on one of the Somali girls who held up a red card. Several more students offered examples.

Soon, Ivan stopped. "Let's hold on for a moment. How many of you have noticed a pattern that differs from the previous days?" Many cards shot up. He then called Tony. "What did you see, Mr. Blue card?"

"It seemed that you only called on Blues or Reds. You refused to call on the Whites, even when they raised their hands."

"Exactly. And where are the Whites sitting? Whites, would you all raise your cards, please?"

Grudgingly, the students in the four front rows became aware they had been left out of the discussion and physically segregated.

"Now, Reds and Blues, show your cards."

The rest did so, and they saw that they were thoroughly scattered among each other, separate from the Whites.

"Mr. Blue, how did you feel when I called you, and you answered the question correctly?"

"At first, I felt okay, but then I thought you favored me unfairly."

"Let me check with the White cards. How did you feel when I refused to call on you?" He nodded at Susan.

"I was hurt. I did all my work in this class. I felt completely ignored. I'm, I'm—"

"Angry?" Ivan asked softly.

She whispered, "Yes, angry."

"Serves her right. She's a know-it-all anyway," blurted Phil, who held a red card.

"Aha! Mr. Red," said Ivan, "how did you feel while all this was going on? Didn't you notice that I was marginalizing some of your classmates?"

"So what?" Phil countered. "Everyone knows American history, but nobody says how we—the white males—are the victims!"

Ivan asked Phil, "Didn't it bother you that I discriminated against some students, without any justification, right in front of you?"

"I—I. Well, you didn't kick anyone out or anything. So, what's the big deal?"

Ivan pointed out how a specific propaganda tactic is to draw lines of separation between one group and another, to marginalize, then label and call them names. "You see how quickly those in the out-group can feel hurt, angry, and even afraid. Who among you has personally felt part of a minority that suffered at the hands of another group?"

Once released from the colored card game, students poured forth their feelings. From every part of the room, including many who had never participated before, they shared personal experiences.

Ivan shifted the focus to Isolation. "Has anyone been called a 'dummy' or a 'smarty-pants'? How about 'know-it-all'?" He glanced at Phil and met his awkward gaze.

He ended the class early. "I apologize to everyone whether or not you were uncomfortable being favored or left out. We have demonstrated how easy and often the separation and isolation of groups and individuals can occur. And how quickly we can slip into acceptance of this behavior. Watch out for how some of our elected officials will refer to minorities and other groups as 'them,' or just 'illegals,' as if they are not real people."

Harry tapped Phil's shoulder as they passed security on the way out. "Have you learned anything about where to get the names of illegals in that class yet?"

Phil hesitated. "So far, no. But my dad said something about the people in security maybe being able to do something."

Harry pushed the idea. "Most of the security guys train together. We could get a break if one of them knows anyone in Sheriff Bardo's Office. By the way, what did you think of today's Red, White, and Blue game? He put you on the hot seat."

"Geez, I hadn't noticed anything to start with," said Phil. "But we white men are victims. Sheriff Bardo says so."

Heading toward the Light Rail, Tony approached a classmate he'd seen ride the same route since the beginning of class. Although she looked very *mestizo,* her English was impeccable when she chatted with the other girls. Yet she hadn't spoken at all in class. "Say, you're in Professor Wilder's class too, aren't you?"

Startled, Lydia turned. "Yes, hi."

"I'm Tony Mendez. I noticed you take the Light Rail to Tempe. I do too. Want to sit together?"

"Okay."

"What's your name?"

"Lydia. Lydia Flores."

Tony and Lydia boarded the train and found a seat together.

Tony said, "I noticed you're pretty quiet in class. How do you like it?"

"It's good. But—"

"What?"

"Oh, never mind. I like the professor, but not some of the students. Just—I don't know."

As Lydia rose to get off at her stop, Tony asked, "Want me to walk you home?"

"Maybe soon," she said. "My mom has some plans for me today." She smiled and left.

As Ivan opened the door to his office, he received a call from Dean Sullivan.

"What's with the Red, White, and Blue game, Ivan? A student complained that you were discriminating."

"They're not cutting me much slack, are they? Did the student seem honestly upset?"

"Frankly, no. He just said you were discriminating. What went on?"

Ivan described the card system, the point of isolating students, and then the hour-long threshing session to air out concerns at the end of the short exercise. "The students who seemed most concerned came up afterward and talked to me. I spent a lot of time defining isolation and letting kids share their experiences. I really can't imagine what—"

Sullivan said, "He didn't seem that sincere. But I have a feeling I'll hear from him again."

CHAPTER 18

THE SUPERVISORS START TO WORRY

January 2009, Phoenix

The events unfolding under the instigation of Sheriff Bardo—a midnight raid at a city hall, the arrest of the "mask" women and the clappers in the auditorium, and more sweeps that looked like racial profiling against Latinos—bothered Asa Johnson. And then there was the three-helicopter arrest at the home of a county school official.

In his church, Johnson had come to know many immigrant families, mainly from Mexico and Central America. They were very tight-knit families, and the fathers were hard-working. They seemed to share the same faith. Therefore, he felt it was wrong to paint all immigrants with one "illegal" brush. And some of the arrests of activists—annoying as those people were—seemed to go beyond the proper boundaries of law enforcement. Was he, Supervisor Asa Johnson, becoming a softie?

When Johnson met with the other supervisors in their private conference room, he began candidly. "Folks, I hate to admit it, but some of those activists may have a point. It looks like Bardo has moved funds illegally. He's obligated to spend money for jail services but shifted it to cover his sweeps instead. And he's not providing clear records. We definitely need to insist on getting records we should have requested sooner."

Marcia Henderson, the predictable Democrat, agreed. Even the Chair, Ken Murdoch, nodded. "I'm all for law and order, Asa, but there has been too much weirdness. And we've been committed to the Court Tower project for years. With reduced funding from the 2008 recession, Bardo can't question that."

———

Sheriff Bardo was pissed. It wasn't that Bullard, Strong, and Snyder hadn't come through for him. They'd done fine. There had been the arrests of *Dirtbuster* editors, then "Mr. ACLU, and a bunch of activists in December. Then there was the midnight raid on Mesa City Hall and the investigation into several judges for alleged "racketeering and conspiracy to commit fraud" for their alleged financial involvement in the Court Tower matter. He knew that when he announced his investigations, the judges would have to recuse themselves from virtually every case brought by the County— *me and Shatigan, which means they can't mess up any more of my prosecutions. But now, the Board of Supervisors is demanding financial records from the MCSO! So what if the laws for MCSO require monthly reporting? I'm The People's Sheriff, not the subordinate to a bunch of lackeys and bureaucrats.*

Bardo called Bullard in and closed the door. "You know, Sid, something's been bothering me recently. The Board of Supervisors is getting too aggressive in their efforts to investigate our budget and funding. We need the money for the sweeps. We needed the money to staff that BOS auditorium and the BOS offices when we had to arrest those activists. And we have required secrecy as if we were the CIA or the FBI. It's time to fight back. Some County Supervisors have been too nosy for my taste—especially Asa Johnson and that smart-aleck Marcia Henderson. Let's contact Shatigan before he leaves office to run for Attorney General and draw up some preliminary charges. We need to investigate the hell out of the BOS. Both of them must have some shady business dealings."

Immediately, Bardo called Shatigan. "Robert, we need to investigate Asa Johnson—again!"

Since both Johnson and Shatigan were elected officials of Maricopa County, the Prosecutor from Yavapai County had already looked over the charges and stated quite firmly that there was "absolutely no evidence" to support any of the allegations. Yavapai refused to re-prosecute.

Bardo was determined to move ahead. "We need to do this again. But this time, we need a little more 'shock and awe.'"

Asa Johnson answered the phone at his office.

"Supervisor Johnson? This is Sheriff Bardo."

Johnson was surprised.

Bardo used a most conciliatory tone. "Mr. Johnson, we've had some, er, misunderstandings in the past, but I believe we can clear them up. So, I need you to come to my office in the morning to discuss the MCSO financial situation. Can you be here at 9 am?"

At exactly 8:55 am, Johnson pulled into the underground parking garage, on time for his appointment. He stepped out of his car and shut the door.

Suddenly, lights blared from the cameras of over a dozen members of the press. Twenty Kevlar-jacketed Deputies emerged from the darkness and surrounded him. Bardo stepped forward, in full uniform, directly in front of the cameras. "Asa Johnson, you are under arrest for ninety-five counts of corruption, conspiracy to defraud the government, and racketeering under RICO statutes. Deputies, cuff him."

With cameras whirring and light bulbs popping, Deputies Strong and Snyder grabbed Johnson by both arms, forced his hands behind his back, cuffed him, and paraded him past the media into the underground tunnel leading directly to the Fourth Avenue Jail.

CHAPTER 19

MEXICO AND THE BANDWAGON

Mid-June 2010, Cronkite Auditorium

State Representative Pat Marcos waited by the classroom door for Ivan. They entered together. Students filled every seat. They quieted down as Ivan and Marcos walked to the lectern.

Ivan asked his assistants to pass out worksheets. "Class, my TAs are handing out a study guide to aid you while you listen to each of our guest speakers. The list of questions will help you detect propaganda tactics. For example, do they try to marginalize any group? Do they scapegoat an individual who may not be responsible for the problem? Do they appeal to authority? Do they appeal to fear? You have the complete list of propaganda tactics in your notebooks. Now, please welcome Representative Patrick Marcos from our Arizona Legislature," Ivan said, flashing Marcos's career bullet points behind him on the SmartScreen.

"Thanks," said Marcos.

"Have at it." Ivan motioned to a TA to dim the lights.

Marcos began. "As you know, Mexico and the United States share a long history and a long border. Hispanics lived in Arizona long before the Anglos arrived. My great-great-great-great-grandfather arrived with Coronado, a Spaniard who brought Mexicans with him. The only folks preceding my ancestors were Native Americans, who were not pleased with the arrival of Spaniards or Mexicans. Some of my Indian friends say, even today, 'There went the neighborhood.'"

A ripple of laughter filled the room.

Marcos gave a short review of American and Mexican history and geography. Then, he showed a map of the United States and Mexico boundaries dated 1830. After recounting some of the wars fought by Mexico and the US, he placed the 1870 map next to one from 1830.

Students gasped with surprise as many became aware of the dramatic shift of power and possession of western lands over forty years. What was now California, Nevada, Colorado, Texas, Arizona, and New Mexico had belonged to Mexico.

"There is currently an imbalance between the U.S. and Mexico. While goods from each country flow abundantly from one to the other, the influx of humans to work has been almost exclusively from Mexico into the United States. The most recent time Congress has passed an immigration law was the 1980s, under President Ronald Reagan. At that time, many immigrants living in the U.S. without documents gained a path to citizenship."

Phil raised his hand. "Wasn't that amnesty? Just giving them citizenship even though they came here illegally?"

Jonah interrupted. "But they came here to work!"

"But it was still illegal to come here without going through the process," said Susan. "Some folks say they are suffering like people under the Nazi regime. But in the Holocaust, Hitler rounded up Jews, Poles, and others and slaughtered them. The Mexicans coming here do not have the same complaint of a repressive regime. Do they?" *Good grief. Do I actually agree with Phil on something?*

Karen Young remained silent. She only needed to distribute handouts and flick the lights. *But,* she thought, *Phil is right. All the jobs go to Mexicans. No wonder we whites have increased unemployment.*

Tony spoke up. "It's not just that things are bad in Mexico. Many immigrants have been here for a long time, for generations. Legality wasn't even an issue when they came. I think Reagan did a wise thing, letting people already here apply for citizenship."

Marcos acknowledged them. "You're all correct. For about one hundred years, there hadn't been much bother about immigration. People came—and went—across the border, both ways, or lived here already. It worked well. In 1984, President Reagan signed the North

American Free Trade Agreement. NAFTA was supposed to foster freer trade of goods among Mexico, the United States, and Canada. Mexico sells more goods in the United States. The U.S. sells more goods in Mexico. But NAFTA did not allow more Mexicans to come to the U.S. to do work others didn't want, like picking crops. The 1910 immigration quotas, favoring northern Europeans, were kept in place. However, throughout the United States, undocumented workers still do much of the agricultural labor because the businessmen and farm owners want it that way."

Phil asked, "Why not call them illegals? They are taking jobs away from American citizens. What part of 'illegal' do they not understand?"

Tony argued, "I'm getting tired of the illegal mantra. First, most American citizens don't want to do agricultural work! It's too hard. Plus, I've known many families, citizens of Latino heritage, who came here generations ago, grew up in the fields, then their kids went to school, bettered themselves, and went to work. Calling everyone illegal all the time marginalizes them. A lot of them have worked hard and become good citizens." *Like my grandparents.*

Marcos added, "Immigration laws, like most laws, change. What might have been legal or illegal yesterday could change tomorrow. For example, in the 1950s, here in Maricopa County, the law prohibited black children from attending school with white children. Finally, in 1954, the U.S. Supreme Court decided in a famous case, *Brown v. the Board of Education,* that segregation of public schools was unconstitutional—or illegal." He paused. "I hope that addresses some of your concerns. In 2002, the Arizona Legislature, recognizing the value of immigrants, asked Congress to pass a comprehensive immigration law that included provisions for Latinos to work in the U.S. and to allow them to return to Mexico and sometimes have a path to citizenship. However, that same year, the first major anti-immigration citizen's group put Proposition 200 on the Arizona ballot, sponsored by Senator Sylvester Hamelin. A seventy-percent majority voted to deny undocumented immigrants employment benefits."

Karen Young looked up—*my Uncle Sylvester.*

"In 2004, when I entered the Legislature, another bill, Proposition 300, was passed. It stated that anyone who could not prove citizenship would not receive the in-state student tuition benefit, even if they could prove residency." Marcos paused.

Lydia squirmed. *Proposition 300 applies to me.*

Marcos continued. "In 2010, Senator Hamelin and the new Tea Party both pushed for Senate Bill 1070, which would make it a violation of Arizona law simply to be present in Arizona illegally, and would require all law enforcement officers to question a person if there was reasonable suspicion about their status."

Tony demanded, "What's an example of 'reasonable suspicion'?"

Jonah exclaimed, "The state is racist! The police could stop any person who looks Hispanic."

Marcos responded, "That's the problem, isn't it? Latinos fear the police will stop them because of the color of their skin. My wife and son were stopped at the border, returning from a vacation in Mexico. They were forced to get out of the car at gunpoint and were given a pat-down by immigration officers."

Alicia was startled. "Just because they were Hispanic?"

Marcos replied, "Yes."

Phil said, "The officers probably suspected something."

Marcos switched topics. "I hope you will research two other points this summer. First, the alleged abuse of funds by Sheriff Bardo, and second, the Court Tower construction project. Sheriff Bardo directly ordered new surveillance equipment for almost $500,000. State law required him to clear a purchase in that amount with the Board of Supervisors before making the deal. He didn't. Under the same statute, the Sheriff is not legally permitted to use funds allotted to the jails for any other expense, such as deploying a SWAT team to conduct a sweep for illegal immigrants. Under Arizona law, Sheriff Bardo may have misspent millions of dollars." Marcos paused. "Second, the new Court Tower building project had been in the planning stages for several years. There had been no significant opposition to the project since the need was obvious. But as soon as the Board of Supervisors voted to allocate funds toward it in the fall of 2008, they simultaneously pulled back funding on several of the Sheriff's requests. Within weeks, Sheriff Bardo began an official investigation into the new court project. He obtained subpoenas from a judge to demand thousands of documents. His Deputies, in full uniform, including weaponry, interviewed dozens of people at their homes."

Alicia said, "The power of investigation is huge! Who did Sheriff Bardo investigate?"

Marcos answered, "Several Superior Court judges, their staff, other County employees, the Board of Supervisors, and some attorneys."

Tony asked, "But aren't the judges supposed to be part of an independent judiciary?"

Marcos continued. "The timing was precise. In the last two years, Sheriff Bardo and County Attorney Shatigan have brought civil and criminal charges against almost every official who had participated in planning the Court Tower project and had coincidentally reduced funds for Bardo's budget. In order to avoid a real or perceived conflict of interest, the County Attorney from Yavapai County was asked to continue the investigation because Mr. Shatigan, the Maricopa County Attorney, was too closely allied with Sheriff Bardo to appear capable of making a fair and objective evaluation of the facts. After several months the other County Attorney returned the file, saying there was no probable cause for any charges. Since he has always been a vigorous prosecutor, you'd think he'd support Mr. Shatigan. But he said that Bardo's investigation and Shatigan's civil and criminal charges were an abuse of power. Ultimately, a judge threw out the entire set of charges."

Jonah interjected. "Bardo and Shatigan are the real criminals."

Marcos smiled and then summarized, "My friends, keep some fundamentals in mind. First, every elected official has a constitutional obligation to carry out the responsibilities of their office without bias and without targeting a political opponent. Second, the power of a civil or criminal investigation is enormous, and no one should do it for revenge against a political rival."

Marcos asked the class for questions and comments.

"I didn't realize how much territory the United States gained from Mexico after the war in 1846. I guess it wasn't like Spain or Mexico had much of a population living in the desert." Susan looked thoughtful.

Tony added, "The issue of investigation seems to keep coming up. Have you been investigated?"

"Not that I'm aware of," said Marcos, smiling. "But can you ever be sure?"

After Marcos left, Ivan asked the students, "Did Representative Marcos use propaganda?"

Nazrin said, "I think Senator Hamelin was trying to get everyone on board, to pressure them to agree with him to sponsor legislation."

Jonah added, "That's like when I was in high school. I'd try to get my parents to let me stay out late after the school dances. I'd tell them everyone else was doing it."

The class laughed—they all understood very well the concept of "Bandwagon."

CHAPTER 20

STRONG ON TRIAL

Summer 2009, Phoenix

Deputy Sheriff Paul Strong sat next to his attorney on the prosecution side of the courtroom, waiting for the "mask" trial to begin. He felt decidedly ready to take the witness stand against those four women who, in December of 2008, had worn the ridiculous animal masks in the lobby of the Board of Supervisors' office. He and Snyder had arrested and jailed all four for their disruptive behavior. Furthermore, Assistant County Attorney Harold Tanner had decided to press forward to the full extent of the law. The prosecution had provided disclosure to the defense in the form of the DVDs from the BOS lobby, documenting the full demonstration of the thirty masked activists, the departure of twenty-six, and finally, the arrest of the four women.

The courtroom filled early. Approximately fifty people sat close together in rows intended for about thirty. As the judge entered the courtroom, the bailiff called, "All rise." Strong rose with the assemblage and, with a tap on the arm from Tanner, he sat down.

A veteran of the office, Tanner had conducted every size and shape of criminal trial. His specialty was sex crimes, so it was odd that Shatigan had plucked him from a significant pornography prosecution in Superior Court to handle this insignificant misdemeanor case in Justice Court. But these recent arrests of activists were high profile and politically potent. Shatigan wanted his best prosecutor. "*It is a day like all days," in the words of the immortal Walter Cronkite,* thought

Tanner, *"filled with the events that alter and illuminate our times." And I am here. But I don't want to be here.* Tanner preferred to prosecute rapists and pedophiles. *And frankly, these little cases are BS*—Bardo and Shatigan were playing with fire, as far as Tanner could tell, with flimsy evidence and invalid stalling tactics.

The judge ordered everyone to be seated. Tanner patted Strong's arm, and they both listened as the judge gave opening remarks about courtroom protocol. He then motioned for the prosecution to examine his first witness. Strong would be Tanner's only witness. Direct went smoothly. Strong mentioned the masks, threats to public safety, trespass, and disorderly conduct. Tanner ended his questions, reserving the right to return.

Each of the defendants had separate counsel. One by one, the first three attorneys took their potshots at Strong, and one by one, he fended them off.

Then, finally, the fourth attorney, the only woman, approached the witness stand. Defense attorney Emily Hartwell led her cross-examination with, "Let me review with you, Mr. Deputy. You said the women were trespassing?"

"Yes."

"Yet they were on public property, during hours when the offices were open to the public?"

"Yes. But security called us to the office, so we asked the women to leave."

The defense asked, "Because they were activists?"

"No. It was the masks they wore, the threats, and also the disorderly conduct."

Emily set up her equipment. "Let's look at the video provided by the Board of Supervisors. Your evidence. The people are leaving."

Strong said, "Yes. And they all have masks on."

"And now they are taking them off."

"No, they're still on those women."

"Let's rewind," said Emily. "Where are the masks?"

"I could have sworn—"

Emily paused the DVD. "And now the four ladies. What was disorderly about their conduct?"

Strong grunted, "They were wearing masks."

"Your prosecution video, Mr. Deputy Sheriff, taken by the property security office, seems to say they weren't."

Turning red, Strong blurted, "They were disruptive!"

Ms. Hartwell stated calmly, "In your video, the women all look pretty quiet."

"No, they were planning to disrupt the offices."

"Could you read their minds?"

"But they had no business being there!"

"Didn't you say this was at 10:00 in the morning, during regular government business hours?"

"I saw them with masks!"

"Where?"

"I was sure!"

"Mr. Deputy Sheriff, did you watch the video?"

"Uh, most of it."

Emily turned the DVD on again. "Did you see this part here," she pointed to the screen, "where the defendants sat down and removed their masks?"

Strong struggled. "They were wearing masks, your honor—"

"Thank you, Mr. Deputy Sheriff," said defense attorney Hartwell. "No further questions." She returned to her desk and sat down.

Strong took out a handkerchief and mopped the sweat trickling down his cheeks and into the collar of his shirt.

On re-direct, Tanner tried to prop up his client. "When the women were part of the crowd, did you see them with masks?"

Strong sighed with relief. "Yes."

Tanner said, "The prosecution rests."

The judge said, "The defense does not need to present its case. This case is dismissed. There was no trespass, and there was no disorderly conduct. In fact, there was no probable cause to arrest."

CHAPTER 21

SUSPICIONS

Mid-June 2010, Phoenix

After the talk by Pat Marcos, Karen Young called her uncle, the State Senator. As a TA in Professor Wilder's class, she sat through every lecture, her expression noncommittal. She had access to all the class records, names, assignments, and even grades. She would do her job of distributing handouts, flipping the lights, and grading some papers. She would also honor the confidentiality rule required by her position as Teacher's Assistant. Even though tempted, she would not take a class list of students. That would be wrong. But her uncle had asked her to call him if she encountered anything suspicious. The talk by Representative Marcos fell into the "suspicious" category.

"Ah, my favorite niece. To what do I owe the honor of this call?" Senator Hamelin favored Karen because she responded like a protégé, not like his son, who preferred petty crime over politics.

"Uncle Sylvester, Representative Marcos was a guest speaker in Professor Wilder's class today. He talked a lot about Mexican immigrants. Almost as if they were legal. I thought you should know."

———

Ivan returned to his office with a sandwich, soda, and two local daily newspapers.

Sullivan rang. "Ivan, what did you say that caused Senator Hamelin to call and harangue me today? He said you were one-sided and let only the pro-illegal side speak in your class. What the heck is up? He was furious!"

"He called today?"

"Yes, less than ten minutes after your class let out."

"Egad," whistled Ivan. "Who keeps his number in their cell phone address list?"

"You have a point, but I have to worry when a member of the Senate Judiciary Committee that oversees funding for the state universities makes a personal call. What went on?"

"Pat Marcos was here. He talked about Mexican-U.S. history, fairness in government, the Court Tower project, and stuff like that. It's on tape if you want to listen."

"No, I know Marcos. But could you find a way to let Hamelin speak to the class? He's likely to introduce legislation to cut funding for the universities if we don't coddle him a little."

"Didn't know he cared. Of course, he can come. Do you have his phone number? I'll call right now."

Phil met Harry on the north side of the building in the parking lot, away from other students. The traffic on Central Avenue provided white noise.

"Harry, I think I've got an idea," said Phil, looking around.

"Spill it, Phil. What's up?"

"Have you noticed how about two rows of students in the middle of the classroom all look Mexican? They might be illegal. What do you think?"

"Keep going."

"Wouldn't he have a class list in his office? If we could get that list—"

Harry said, "We could look at all the Spanish surnames."

Phil added, "My dad may be able to get someone in security to go into Professor Wilder's office. Then the MCSO will have the names of all the illegals. Like that Rivas girl."

Harry grinned. "Good idea! The department secretary may also have a list. I'll wander over there. I think one of the guys at the front desk from security can help. I'll tell my dad so they can coordinate."

Ivan dialed Senator Hamelin's office immediately. Having heavy hitters present their views to the class would be good exposure and training in analyzing propaganda and power. Hamelin had been the author of numerous bills and laws intended to squeeze undocumented immigrants out of the state. He was the chief legislative architect of the controversial SB 1070.

"Senator Hamelin's office. How may I help you?"

"This is Ivan Wilder, Professor of—"

"Oh, yes, we know who you are."

"I understand Senator Hamelin would be willing to come to speak to my class about immigration issues."

"He certainly would."

Ivan suggested a date and time.

"The Senator will be there," said his secretary.

Lydia waited by the front desk for Tony. He had deferred to her when she hesitated to walk home with him the other day. *In class, Tony's voice grows more intense when he asks questions. I don't always agree with him, but I like that he thinks about everything.*

Tony arrived, smiling.

They walked to the light rail together.

"My mom says come on home and get acquainted," Lydia said, smiling. "She probably made fresh fish tacos in corn tortillas. She's pretty traditional. She wants to know who my friends are, and she likes to cook."

"Thank you, that sounds good."

When they arrived at their stop, they headed for Lydia's house.

Tony was startled as they approached the housing complex, a cluster of small separate adobe-style two- or three-bedroom units. "Oh! This is—" He stopped. *This is one of Dad's rentals. Most of the tenants don't have papers.*

"What, Tony?"

"Oh, nothing. Just—"

When they reached her unit, she opened the door to the multi-colored living room.

"What terrific colors!" exclaimed Tony.

"My dad picked them. The landlord said we could paint what we wanted, as long as we return it to white if we leave. It's not a big place, but it's colorful." Lydia set down her books. "Mom? I'm home. I've brought a friend."

"Ah, *m'ija!*" *Señora* Flores gave Lydia a warm hug. "And thees ees your new *amigo* from your *clase?*" She extended a hand to Tony.

"Hi, Mrs. Flores. I'm Tony Mendez. Yes, Lydia and I are in the same class together. She was nice enough to invite me to stop by."

"Antonio Mendez?" *Señora* Flores looked puzzled. "Ees your father, ees hees name Ricardo Mendez?"

"Yes. Richard Mendez. Do you know him?"

"He ees our landlord. He talked to me once about his son Antonio. He ees very proud of you." She nervously wiped her hands on her apron.

An awkward silence hung in the air.

"He has been very nice to us." *Señora* Flores continued. "Come, seet down. We have tacos for a snack. Eet has been a long *clase,* no?"

They sat at the dining room table and chatted about the food, the class, and the city. Lydia kept quiet. Her mother seemed a little too friendly. After Tony left, she asked her mother what was going on. "He seems like a nice boy, *mi angelita.* But now I worry, too. Hees father, Mr. Mendez, he know we no have papers. I hope they no tell nobody."

CHAPTER 22

LINING UP THE OPPOSITION

Mid-June 2010, Cronkite Auditorium

Having just secured a speaking date with Senator Hamelin, Ivan called the Sheriff. If ever there was an elected official who grabbed any forum available, it was Bardo. Mr. "Toughest Sheriff in America" could have one hundred students as a captive audience and complete freedom to push his point of view.

"MCSO. May I help you?"

"Yes, I hope so. Professor Ivan Wilder here from the downtown ASU campus. I'm teaching a course this summer. I hope Sheriff Bardo will address my class on the uses of power from a Sheriff's perspective. May I speak with him?"

Eleanor Jones knew the Sheriff wouldn't take a direct call from anyone except confidants. "I can take a message. What date and time did you want this speaking engagement to occur?"

"Would one day later next week work? It will be the fourth week of the summer course, and I want the students to have as many important figures come to class as possible. Mr. Bardo is at the top of my list of speakers we want to hear. I have over one hundred students from journalism and public policy backgrounds."

"That's fairly short notice," Eleanor replied.

"I know," answered Ivan, "but I'd really appreciate it if he could address this class before SB 1070 goes into effect. I think he'll appreciate this group of talented students. One of his Deputies, Mr. Strong, has a son, Phil, in the class."

"I'll see what we can do, Professor Wilder. I'll be sure he gets the message. Thank you for your call."

Next, on a gamble, Ivan dialed the office of the County Attorney. Shatigan had recently resigned to run for Attorney General. The receptionist gave Ivan a new phone number since the former County Attorney was now stomping the campaign trail. Ivan left a voicemail that he hoped was enough of a lure for a bite. Shatigan was causing quite a stir, what with controversial prosecutions, and now leaving a messy situation at the county level to run for statewide office. *The students will be interested in hearing from an elected official, an attorney, who is also the subject of numerous ethics complaints.*

Finally, Ivan dialed the defense attorney who Jonah recommended. He remembered her from the TV coverage of those 2008 arrests and subsequent statements to the press. She was short, somewhat plain with thick glasses, and quite sure of herself despite having to defend activists against a seemingly unbeatable Sheriff—a female David against the mighty Goliath, Sheriff J. Edgar Bardo. She'd won a few.

"Law Offices," said Emily Hartwell, as her own secretary. She had spent eight years at the Attorney General's office representing Child Protective Services before going solo. She'd picked up adoptions and guardianships and inadvertently slid into defense work. In her late 30s, she had acquired a reputation as a go-to attorney for activists against the Sheriff.

"Is Ms. Hartwell there?"

"Who's calling?"

"Ivan Wilder. I'm a professor at ASU downtown. I'm teaching a summer school government-journalism combo course—"

"This is Emily Hartwell."

"Ms. Hartwell? Hello. Do you have a minute?"

"Yes, Professor Wilder." *What a surprise. I wonder why he's calling.*

"Call me Ivan. I called because one of my students suggested I ask you to speak to my class. Weren't you involved in two or three cases where the defendants were jailed but acquitted on First Amendment grounds?"

"Yes. You may call me Emily."

"Emily. Hi. I've heard rave reviews from Jonah—you represented him in his court case."

"He's pretty courageous."

"And outspoken. I'm wondering if you'd give a presentation in my class in the next few weeks."

"About what?"

"Mainly those two cases. Aren't they affectionately known as the 'mask' case and the 'clapping' case?"

"There's one more."

"What's the other one?"

"The supervisors give the MCSO *carte blanche* for spending. An activist protesting their lack of oversight was arrested on the public plaza for trespass. I call it the 'shackles' case."

"I hear you have footage from the actual arrests. And Jonah says the prosecution footage shows an abuse of power."

"I think so."

"I'd like you to show the videos and facilitate a discussion on whether there was an abuse of power. I know attorneys have an hourly fee—"

"There's no charge. I'd love to come. When?"

"Within the next few weeks. But I need to warn you. Senator Hamelin will be speaking next week. In addition, Sheriff Bardo may also speak in the next week or two."

"Super! Both sides. Please schedule me to talk after the Sheriff. You can give the students a day to process what the MCSO has offered them. Do you have audiovisual equipment?"

"Of course."

"I'd like to come over and check it out before I speak. My DVDs are key evidence. In the 'shackles' trial, the equipment didn't work. So, I'm obsessive-compulsive about knowing it will work for me."

"How about this coming Monday? My class runs from 9:00 am to 1:00 pm. Students usually split right away. Would you be able to come by right after that?"

She checked her calendar. Monday afternoon was clear. "What's the room number? I'll be there."

After giving Emily directions, Ivan decided he'd had enough for the week. He packed some reading, flipped off the lights, and locked the office door behind him.

CHAPTER 23

EMILY IN HER ELEMENT

Fall 2009, Phoenix

Emily's "clapping" trial for September occurred in the same courtroom as the "mask" trial. Tanner caused months of delay, re-filing the case with added charges and making excuses for failure to disclose documents promptly. Only five of the fifteen people clapping for the Latina speaker in December 2008 had been charged. Five defendants, four wearing the notorious red T-shirts, the fifth person translating for the speaker at the lectern. Five defense attorneys, all working *pro bono*, were outraged, even more so after viewing the footage provided by the prosecution. And Tanner had not even offered a plea deal. Shatigan had made it clear to Tanner: Bardo wanted to drag these damn activists all the way to trial. Tanner's job was to get convictions.

Even if Tanner had offered a deal, the defendants would not have accepted it. Four had been hauled out of a public meeting, humiliated, manhandled, and thrown in jail merely for clapping after a particularly compelling speaker. The fifth had been cited the following day after translating for the speaker and leaving promptly at the Deputy's command.

A new judge was presiding. It had begun with the "mask" trial judge, but the prosecution had used its one-time motion to change judges. What they got was a judge who was a stickler for the rules.

Emily sat on the left side of the room the four other defense attorneys in front of the bar, separating them from the general audience. All five defendants sat in the first row behind her, looking quite spiffed up for the occasion. Emily smiled at her client. He wore a three-piece suit, better dressed than his fellow defendants, an elegant cut above everyone else in the courtroom. She looked over to the right. Tanner sat at the desk with his first witness, Ken Murdoch, Chairman of the Board of Supervisors.

As criminal cases go, this was simple. Tanner put on his first witness—the namby-pamby Supervisor who, without informing his fellow board members, had authorized Bardo's Deputies to impose authority to keep the peace.

"Mr. Chairman," Tanner began, "are you the Chairman of the County Board of Supervisors?"

"Yes."

"And were you the Chairman of the Board on the morning of the arrests in question?"

"What morning?"

Tanner rephrased. "On Wednesday morning, December 8th in 2008, when the defendants were arrested."

Mr. Chairman responded. "Um, well, I believe that was a morning when I was chairing the meeting."

"And," Tanner continued," did you see the defendants disrupting the meeting, those defendants in the front row over there?"

Chairman Murdoch mumbled, "Um, well, I believe I recognize some of those people. And um, er, there may have been some disruption. There was so much going on. I can't exactly remember. Yes, maybe, wait, maybe somebody was disorderly."

Gritting his teeth into a determined smile, Tanner asked his witness again, "Did any of these defendants cause a disruption, a disturbance of the peace, on that morning, during the public comments section?"

One of the defense attorneys rose. "Objection. Leading the witness, Your Honor."

Emily could have sworn she saw the inklings of a smile curl around the edge of the Judge's otherwise non-committal mouth.

But the Judge said, "Overruled. Continue."

Tanner tried again. "Was there a disturbance of the peace?"

The Chairman's face puffed into an indecisive blur. He gazed blandly at Tanner. "Yes, sir, yes, I believe maybe some of these defendants may have caused some kind of a disturbance. There were the Deputies arresting them, and I gaveled for them to sit down, and then I called the ladies to the lectern, and someone was yelling at me, and, well, I can't remember. That's just it. I don't remember." He stopped.

Tanner looked at the floor to control his frustration. Finally, he turned to the Judge. "That will be all for now, Your Honor. I reserve the right to recall the witness."

The defense team then took turns eliciting an equally incoherent cross-examination from this elected official who seemed incapable of saying "yea" or "nay" about anything. How could he be running our government? It was a complete waste of a morning in court for the defense team.

After the lunch break, Deputy Sheriff Paul Strong stepped into the witness box and swore "to tell the truth, the whole truth, and nothing but the truth, so help me, God."

Tanner hoped this trial would go better than the last. But, by God, Bardo was making arrests on flimsy evidence, Shatigan was pressing ridiculous charges, and then he was inappropriately taking the cases to trial. *Frankly, it's bullshit.* He longed for a sick, twisted sex felony where he could show videos that made the jury retch. He could convict perps and put them away for a long time. To Tanner, the present case was immensely insignificant. He led Strong on direct. "Did the four defendants stand in the auditorium without express permission?"

Strong spoke with decisiveness. "Yes."

"Did they clap loudly?"

"Yes, very loudly."

"Did they shout?"

"Yes."

"Did the Chairman gavel them to sit down?"

"Yes, but they ignored him. They were disrupting the meeting."

"And the other defendant: did she wave her arms trying to rouse the crowd to make a public disturbance?"

One of Emily's fellow attorneys stood to object: "Leading the witness, Your Honor."

The Judge said, "Overruled. Continue, Mr. Tanner."

Tanner repeated the question.

Strong smiled, remembering how silly this lady looked when she turned to the audience.

"Yes."

Tanner asked, "Have you watched the video from the Board of Supervisors on this event?"

"Yes."

"Now, Mr. Strong, you have been with the Sheriff's Office for how many years?"

"Sixteen years."

"Tell us your history with the office."

Strong outlined how he'd started at a lower position and earned his way, through training and experience, to become one of two key Deputies under Sid Bullard at the top of the enforcement chain—akin to an "expert witness."

"Have you been in situations like this before, arresting people based on their disorderly conduct?"

"Disrupting a public meeting?" Strong wanted to be sure he was talking about the clappers at the meeting.

"Yes," Tanner clarified, "a public meeting."

"Yes, I have."

"And in your professional opinion, were these defendants disrupting the public meeting of the Board of Supervisors?"

"Yes. Absolutely, yes."

"And was it your job to take action to restore peace and decorum in that public meeting?" Tanner looked encouragingly at Strong.

"Yes. We had a letter from the Chairman to Mr. Bardo for our office to enforce law and order."

Tanner concluded, "Your Honor, I reserve the right to call the witness for further questions."

The defense team was hopping mad. As each of the first four took their turn on cross-examination, they railed at him, made accusations, and hurled aggressive questions. The Judge, ever the stickler on the rules of procedure, interrupted frequently to remind the defense that this was a cross-examination, not a Star Chamber inquisition.

It was almost 4:00 pm. The Judge decided they would end for the day and return in the morning.

At home that evening, Emily took a break by watching the local news—it did not cover the case. As the newscasters droned on, she slipped into a semi-doze with old images surfacing of litigating in Juvenile Court to protect children against abusive parents. When the news ended, Emily came to, turned off the TV, and pored over her notes. She re-wrote questions for cross-examination and then put in a good night's sleep.

The next morning, the Judge called the courtroom to order at nine o'clock sharp. This City Court usually handled DUI, domestic violence, and public disturbance cases. Very few cases went to trial because the defendants would plead out, and there was usually no audience. But for the clapping case, over sixty people wedged themselves in on the benches. More stood in the rear by the door. The Judge called Strong back to the stand.

Emily approached. She was much shorter than the other attorneys. Not particularly "pretty" in the classical sense, she felt that most mornings were "bad hair" days with her frizzy auburn bob that she pinned, two clips per side, to gain control. But it was clean. As was her tailored navy court suit. Maroon-framed rectangular glasses screened the intensity of her nut-brown eyes. She would not offend court decorum. Or stand out as a typical beauty. Or get the attention of any hot guys in the courtroom. She approached the witness and began. "Good morning, Mr. Strong."

"Good morning."

"I want to be sure you can pick out my client in the courtroom. Do you see him?"

"Yes. Your client is over there." Strong pointed accurately to her client on the front bench between two others.

"He's the attractive young black man, yes?"

"Yes," confirmed Strong. "In the good-looking suit. I wish I could dress that well."

A smile. Not a smirk. Emily smiled both at her client and at Strong. "Thanks for noticing." She paused. "Mr. Strong, I am going to show video footage of the Supervisors' meeting on December 8th. But first, I will show you some footage of a public hearing in the summer of 2008, six months before our case, also taken by the Supervisors' video cam. I want you to tell the Judge whether clapping and shouting occurred and whether it was disruptive."

Emily moused the DVD to the day in June of 2008 when a blousy blonde at the lectern of the BOS auditorium railed against "dirty, tuberculosis-ridden illegals who were making Americans sick" and then praised the Sheriff for trying to rid Arizona of their ilk. Then, Blousy asked, "Everyone who supports the Sheriff, stand and clap." A burst of noise erupted onscreen as about fifteen people—almost identical in number to the "clapping" day six months later in December—rose, clapped, whoo-woo-ed, and cheered. The camera zeroed in on the table where three out of five Supervisors also stood, leaning over their table, smiling, and clapping. The BOS Chairman, the one Emily saw as the mumble-jumble witness yesterday, almost fell onto the table, saying to the crowd, "I know I should call the meeting to order, but I just had to clap."

Emily asked Strong, "Was that disorderly?"

"No."

"Now, Deputy Strong, here is the footage of December 8th. Let's watch as the speaker stops talking, and then about fifteen people in the auditorium rise and clap." She rewound it. "Let's run that again. Did you hear any cheering or shouting?"

"Yes, there was yelling."

"Let's replay your video. Tell me when you hear it."

The tape ran from the end of the speaker's words, through the several seconds of clapping, to the moment when the Chairman gaveled, and everyone sat down.

"Did you hear cheering or shouting or yelling?"

"The Chairman was telling them to be quiet," said Strong. "It went on for several minutes. They were disobeying the Chairman. They were disrupting the business of the meeting."

Emily looked at the Judge. "Let's look again at the moment of the arrest. Can you identify my client?"

"Yes."

"Now, after the speaker concludes, my client is one of fifteen people who stands and claps, correct?"

"Yes."

"Now, the Chairman gavels for them all to be quiet, correct?"

"Yes." Strong took a deep breath. *I don't see what her problem is.*

She paused. "Let's time this. Do you have a second hand on your watch?" Upon an affirmative nod from Strong, Emily ran the video until the four red-shirted defendants sat down with hands in their laps. "Mr. Strong, the second hand on my watch gave that whole episode four seconds from start to finish. What did yours say?"

Lips pursed, Strong muttered, "It was five seconds."

"Granted, Mr. Strong. Five seconds. Not quite a few minutes, was it?"

"No."

"Let's look at the arrest again." She replayed the video. "Now they are all seated, including my client, correct?"

"Yes."

"With no shouting, correct?"

Strong mumbled, "Correct."

"With their hands in their laps?"

"Yeah."

"Now we see that you are coming down the center aisle, correct?"

"Yes."

"You are wearing the brown shirt, correct?"

"Correct."

"And is the Protective Services Captain coming with you in the white shirt?"

"Yes."

"But neither of you is wearing a white hat, are you?"

Huh?

Emily caught a glance of the Judge scowling at her. *I couldn't resist.* She continued. "And so, you asked my client to leave?"

"Yes." *What was that about the hat?*

"In the video, aren't there two other Deputies with you?"

"Yes."

"As you ask the defendants to leave, aren't you also blocking their way?"

Strong remembered that day. "They could have gone out the other direction."

"But one of the defendants did, didn't she?"

"Yes."

"And wasn't she arrested right at the lectern after being called to speak?"

"Yes, but she was disruptive."

"And she was on Sheriff Bardo's list of 'activists' to apprehend, wasn't she?"

"Yeah, but—"

Emily held back a smile. *That was a lucky guess!* "Mr. Strong, I am most concerned about my client. You saw that he was Black, didn't you?"

"Yes."

"But you didn't arrest him because of his race since that would violate his constitutional rights. Isn't that true?"

"No, that's not why I arrested him."

"Did you see his red T-shirt, the same as the three others?"

"Yes."

"But you didn't arrest him because of the T-shirt since that was his right under the First Amendment freedom of expression clause. Isn't that correct?"

"Right."

"Did you recognize the two women seated next to my client who had been arrested the previous Monday in the public lobby, who had been wearing masks?"

"Yes, when I came upon them, yes."

"But you wouldn't have arrested my client because he was sitting with them since that would violate his right to freedom of association, correct?"

"Correct."

"Then, Mr. Strong, if you didn't arrest him for any of those reasons, and if he was sitting down quietly when you came up to him and the others, why did you arrest him?"

Strong balled his fists tight under the witness table. "It was, it was—it was the totality of the circumstances!"

"I see. No further questions. Thank you, Deputy."

Tanner did a quick re-direct to prop up his star witness and rested his case. One of the other defense attorneys rose to make a motion to dismiss for the prosecution's failure to prove the case.

"Sit down!" ordered the Judge.

After a startled silence, a few audience members began to clap.

The Judge shouted, "There will be absolutely no clapping in this courtroom!"

Emily could barely contain a smile. *What a delicious irony, no clapping in the clapping case!*

The Judge then gave his verdict from the bench. "I find the defendants all to be innocent." He then turned to Strong and Tanner. "You should be ashamed! I was confused when I heard you made accusations of disorderly conduct yesterday. So, I went home last night and watched the videos—your evidence, Mr. Tanner—three times. Mr. Strong, when the Chairman called that young lady to the lectern, the other Deputy should have backed off. And you, Mr. Strong, should never have pulled the others from their seats. There should never have been an arrest—it violated their First Amendment rights. And Mr. Tanner, you should never have brought this case to trial." He took a breath, pulled himself up to his full-seated height, and pounded the gavel twice, hard, against his desk. "Case dismissed, with prejudice!"

Bardo got Shatigan and Tanner together on a conference call.

"This is ridiculous! Tanner, you're the best in Shatigan's shop. Yet two cases slipped completely through your fingers—that one about the masks and the T-shirts. What the hell???"

When Shatigan had handed Tanner the perp cases, there was always a stack of seedy DVDs or other evidence that made convictions a snap. Here, there was nothing to go on. Tanner was a lifer in the Country Attorney's office. Shatigan was already eyeing higher office—he'd be gone in a year.

Tanner told Bardo, "Tough cases, with the evidence we had."

Shatigan tried to smooth it over. "Hey, Harold. Just the witnesses. And those rotten DVDs. Not all your fault."

Not all my fault? Tanner fumed.

Bardo interrupted. "We need to get that Judge. What's his name? McClennon? McNelly? McIntire? Whatever the hell it is, and the other Judge for the guy in shackles—Dunmire—we need to start an investigation now! Robert, write up some papers that look like a Grand Jury has deliberated on these guys. We want them out of commission, and they'll have to 'recuse' themselves on any case we bring on any of them. Let's announce an investigation into their racketeering and corruption over the Tower projects. I'm tellin' ya, all of them have dirty hands."

CHAPTER 24

A VALENTINE'S DAY GAME

February 2010, Phoenix

It was now certain that the Arizona Legislature would pass the anti-illegal immigrant Senate Bill 1070 by April. Senator Hamelin, the architect of virtually every anti-immigrant piece of legislation introduced, spoke at every opportunity lambasting "the illegals desecrating the State of Arizona." As Republican leader of the Senate, he lobbied the Governor with dogged persistence. Known in most circles as "Hamelin's Bill," SB 1070 aimed to remove immigration decisions from Federal control and place them squarely with the State of Arizona. Most legal scholars thought the bill was, for the most part, unconstitutional since immigration was a national matter, but scholarly opinion seemed irrelevant in local political circles.

In the fall of 2009, Bardo began using the Tent City Jail located at 33rd Avenue and Durango to isolate all inmates without documents. With record numbers exceeding thirty thousand, the January protesters stomped up to the legal boundary of the Durango Jail to register their complaint.

A mere half-dozen black-shirted anarchists made a mess of an otherwise peaceful demonstration. They threw rock-filled plastic soda bottles at the horses of the equine police. While the anarchists felt self-righteous, the assault terrified the horses and resulted in arrests that would bring valid convictions. The irresponsibility of six black-shirted left-wingers, beaten back by dozens of black-shirted Deputies, tarnished the day for the thirty thousand participants who marched peacefully for hours until they finally arrived across from the Tent City Jail. A rousing contemporary Latino band greeted them.

———————

Political prognosticators felt confident that governor Alice Middleton, her finger to the political wind, would sign the bill into law at the end of April 2010. They expected protestors to demonstrate at the capitol on the day she signed. Self-designated patriots in patch-covered motorcycle vests would show up to support the Governor.

———————

Jonah Whalen, in February 2010, was depressed. As an organizer of medical volunteers for several pro-immigrant demonstrations, he was unsure at this point in his life what he would do next. It could be that what ultimately happened on Valentine's Day triggered his decision to take a summer course at the Cronkite School of Journalism. But, for now, he needed some action. And it needed to be different. On the first Sunday in February, he responded to an invitation from Arthur Smith, known to his friends as "Jester."

An eldercare worker by day and an artist by night, Jester had observed an explosion of culture in downtown Phoenix during the past decade. Interest in the arts had surged. Artists showcased their work on the first Friday of each month, from September through May. Gorilla Graphics published a map of all venues for each first Friday. Upscale galleries staged "events." Startup art studios found homes in abandoned warehouses. Bank buildings displayed art exhibits. Trinity Episcopal Cathedral's vestibule provided a venue for painters and photographers. The Herberger Center hosted numerous theater groups. Metropolitan Arts Institute, a charter high school, presented a "First Friday" of multi-media student creativity. Assorted guitarists, fiddlers, and drum circles played in vacant lots.

Human and cultural diversity increased, too, aided by the influx from south of the border. In boom times, it worked for everyone: more people paid into local enterprises, and more little businesses sprang up. The Latino addition made it more fun with its Mexican food and celebrations: *Cinco de Mayo*, the 17ᵗʰ of September, *Día de los Muertos*, taco stands, and folk dancers on the plaza.

The Latinos weren't alone. Margaret Hance Park hosted an Irish cultural center. An annual Chinese cultural festival delighted families in the center of downtown. A Japanese Aikido dojo had also become part of Phoenix in the 1990s.

Finally, the number of young people mushroomed, with most students at ASU's new downtown campus. Even the stuffy Chamber of Commerce enjoyed the uptick. As the buzz grew, some people moved into downtown apartment lofts. Folks walked over from the Willo and Encanto neighborhoods. After many decades of outward growth, the center of Phoenix was reborn like the mythical bird after which it was named.

Not all the explosions were friendly. The 2001 assault on the World Trade Center in New York, followed by the American invasions of Iraq and Afghanistan, seemed to produce an overarching anxiety about terrorism and things foreign. A fearful and ignorant citizen, enraged at "terrorists," had murdered an innocent, legal Sikh immigrant at a local gas station. A growing backlash against the Spanish-speaking presence had become both hostile and popular. Sheriff Bardo milked the Anglo tribal angst to its fullest, conducting raids by night and targeting Hispanics and their allies by day.

It was time to do something new. Something different. Something fun. Jester invited Jonah to nibble carrot cake and sip lattes at Carmen's Gypsy Cafe on the back patio of the Firehouse. The aroma of caramel coffee brought elegance to the unkempt backyard.

"Dammit," said Jester, poking a plastic spoon across the checkered tablecloth. "Nothing we've done so far has worked. Let's go, New Age!"

Jonah crossed spoons with Jester. "What do you have in mind?"

Jester grinned. "I have an idea for a new game—"

Thus, Jester and Jonah conceived "Urban Capture the Flag." Jester laid out the game plan. "The rules will be the same as for traditional Capture the Flag. There'll be Team A, with a yellow flag, and Team B, with a red one. Each will have a side, a flag, and a jail.

Each team will guard their flag. Team A will try to find and steal B's flag and run it back to safety on A's side. If B catches A in B's territory, B can put A in jail. A will then have fewer team members on the field to find B's flag. The same goes for Team B. And so forth, except—we'll play it in the heart of downtown."

Jonah broke a smile. "This little adventure is a far cry from the school playground."

"Indeed," said Jester, "that's the plan. Not only not at school, but not a daytime sport."

Carmen put their drinks on the table and asked, "At night? Won't it be illegal?"

"And when did you start caring, my dear?" retorted Jester. "But it will, in fact, be legal. Just unconventional. We'll set the boundaries downtown, in the heart of Phoenix, between 11:00 pm and 1:00 am."

Jonah grinned. "I know! Let's make the battlefield surround the Wells Fargo bank building, the HQ of the MCSO. We'll remind passers-by about their evil emperor on the twentieth floor. And we'll drive the Saturday night security guard a little out of his order-loving mind."

On Saturday, February 14th, 2010, a love-fest for the cause of freedom erupted. Jonah, Jester, and thirty others assembled on the bank building corner at 11:00 pm. Most of them were young and had donned the dress of their philosophical forebears of the '60s. They were the new Hippies.

Jonah headed up Team Yellow. Carmen and Jester captained Team Red. Jefferson Street was the southern boundary, with Adams on the north and Washington smack dab in the middle. The east-west boundaries ran from 2nd Avenue across Central to 2nd Street. There were enough buildings, parking lots, alleys, streets, garbage cans, and nighttime pubs to divert and confuse. They ran around like schoolchildren. Then, after a while, Jonah strolled toward the bank building, right in front of the security guard, waving from the middle of the street.

"Hey, you can't do that!" yelled the guard. "You're on our property!" But in point of fact, it was not his property, not management's property, not even the property of the county. That patch of concrete belonged to the City of Phoenix. Jonah and a few pals danced a jig just outside Mr. Guard's territorial clutches.

The Reds captured several Yellows, who then escaped from the Reds' jail. Then some Yellows captured even more Reds who also escaped. The whole thing was so much activist capture-the-flag fun.

Jonah jogged back to the flag post. Dang! One of the Reds had climbed to the top of a parking garage, grabbed hold of a nearby streetlight, slid down into Yellows' turf, snatched the Yellow flag from its dumpster, and scurried safely back onto Red turf. The Reds won.

The thirty-two players formed their respective team lines right in front of the bank's security guard, just out of reach of the cameras, and passed each other in two rows with congratulatory high-fives.

Nothing outwardly changed. A call from MCSO brought four Phoenix police cars to the corner of First and Washington, red and blue lights flashing. By the time they arrived, all Urban Capture the Flag revelers had dispersed. On Monday, the activists would still need to boycott the building. But for two hours in the middle of Saint Valentine's Saturday night, freedom held sway in the heart of downtown.

CHAPTER 25

CROSS-CURRENTS

Late June 2010, Cronkite Auditorium

Ivan headed straight for the auditorium, skipping the usual stop in his office. He focused immediately on the words of the Fourth Amendment on the SmartScreen:

> "The right of the people to be secure in their persons, houses, papers, and effects, against unreasonable searches and seizures, shall not be violated, and no Warrants shall issue, but upon probable cause, supported by Oath or affirmation, and particularly describing the place to be searched, and the persons or things to be seized."

Ivan asked the students, "Does anyone know, historically, why the Fourth Amendment was such a big deal to the Founding Fathers in the late 1700s?"

Tony suggested, "Didn't the British soldiers take over colonists' homes during the Revolution?"

"Exactly. The Fourth covers numerous rights regarding 'person, papers, and effects'—a catchall phrase to cover things the Founding Fathers didn't spell out in excessive detail."

"I notice it says 'unreasonable' searches and seizures," added Susan, "but are reasonable searches okay?"

Jonah jumped in. "That subpoena to seize the records of the *Desert Dirtbuster* was unreasonable!"

Phil argued, "But they must have been doing something wrong!"

Tony quoted the Fourth Amendment: "There has to be 'probable cause' that the person did something wrong, broke some law. Something specific."

"And the cops—or the Sheriff—" Jonah added, "have to go to a supposedly neutral body, like the grand jury or a judge. If the cops don't have a strong suspicion of a specific crime beforehand, they shouldn't get to go on a fishing expedition."

"Well, I have nothing to hide," quipped Phil.

Tony responded, "That's not the point. The government shouldn't even go into your home if they don't already have some evidence. They can't just pick on people. More folks than we realize might have something, even something minor, that they don't want others to know. It's just not all the business of the government."

Ivan wrapped it up." Tomorrow, Senator Hamelin of the State Senate Judiciary Committee will speak to us. Thursday, Sheriff Bardo will give you his view on the world. Next week, Ms. Emily Hartwell, the attorney who defended Jonah, will show us some raw video footage of the arrest. Be on the lookout for whether and how each uses propaganda in their presentations."

Tony caught up with Lydia and sat together on the Light Rail, but she was silent. As the train curved east from Central Avenue to Washington Street, he finally asked, "What's up, Lydia? Have I done something wrong? I thought we were friends."

Lydia looked out the window. She crossed her legs away from him and folded her arms around her books. *He knows about me.* "I'm not sure we should be friends, Tony. We're so different. Your father—" Words failed her.

"What about my dad? Just because he's your—" he lowered his voice so no one nearby could hear. "Just because he's your parents' landlord doesn't mean we can't be friends."

Lydia steeled herself. She'd come to like this young man. He was smart, and he'd been very polite to her *mamacita*. She liked having someone to ride with, someone to walk her home. "Tony, I don't think you understand. Maybe you should talk to your father. Things aren't what they appear. Just— I need some space." She became quiet and got off at her stop without saying goodbye.

Ivan wolfed down lunch at El Portal, had a quick smoke (beginning to hate the taste), and darted into the men's room behind the bank of elevators at Cronkite. He tucked in his shirt afresh, checked the mirror for rogue hairs, slicked down a few strays, and popped a few mints. He told himself he was not making any extra effort. As he reached the auditorium door, a short, thirty-five-ish woman set down her briefcase and greeted him.

"Professor Wilder? I'm Emily Hartwell. I was afraid I'd miss you. Did you forget our appointment?"

"Sorry if I kept you." Ivan shook her hand. "Had to catch a quick burrito." He unlocked the door and stepped aside to let Emily pass through.

She scanned the auditorium as the lights came on. "Is it all right if I put my laptop on the desk?"

Ivan scooped up some papers to make space. "They've provided the latest," he said, pointing to the battery of plugs, cables, outlets, and the screen. "Your presentation should work, Ms. Hartwell. Let's give it a try."

"Have you seen any footage of the trials I conducted?" she asked. "We were very successful with the prosecution's disclosure."

"No, but I've read about them. There seem to be three major ones—the guy who the cops hauled off the plaza in shackles, the case of the women at the Supervisors' office, and the arrest of the four people in the public meeting. Right?"

"Yes." She did not smile to acknowledge his awareness but continued her thought. "They will be instructive in exposing the abuse of power issues that you need to address in your class."

"We don't 'need to,' Ms. Hartwell." Ivan had expected to feel friendlier toward her. "However, you're right. Abuse of power is a major concern. It'll fit right in if that's what you're talking about."

"I don't have to talk that much, Professor Wilder," Emily answered. "I want to show the video footage of these separate arrests, the footage provided to the defense by the prosecution. I believe it will speak for itself."

"Well, okay. Let's boot up and see if your DVDs show up on the big screen. I'll feel a lot better, too, if it all works. As they say, a picture is worth a thousand words. Do you want me to dim the lights?"

"Sure, thanks." Oblivious to his mood, Emily slipped one disc into her DVD compartment, then fast-forwarded to the number on the screen she appeared to understand. There, for all the world to see, stood Stan Beltran on the public plaza, in his now famous three-piece suit, being handcuffed and ankle-shackled by police—an image requiring an explanation. "That one works," she said, ejecting it. "Let me try a few more." Emily ran two more DVDs, and as soon as she realized they worked with Ivan's apparatus, she would pop one out and go on to the next. "I don't want you to know the whole story before we begin next week," she quipped with a smile. "Don't you want to view the evidence with fresh eyes?"

She's lightened up. Good. "Yes, that'll be a kick. Representative Pat Marcos spoke to us last week. Senator Hamelin is speaking to the class tomorrow, and Sheriff Bardo will be here on Wednesday. So, you'll be our fourth guest."

"I'm glad I follow them. Marcos is even-keeled. Good historian too. As for Sheriff Bardo and his crew, I think the DVDs will speak volumes."

They walked out together. Ivan couldn't help but notice that her dark eyes had flashed at the thought of showing off her side of things. *Nice. She has spunk. And she's put together well, too—tailored, not too flashy.* He hadn't noticed a woman in four years. She was a little younger *—how much? But the ring finger suggests she's still single.* He felt awkward. "So, I'll see you on Thursday, Ms. Hartwell. Arrive early if you want. Any questions?"

"May I take the whole morning, Ivan? The footage isn't that long. It's just that we have to replay it several times for the students to get the full impact."

"Fine. And if you have any questions between now and then, be sure to call me. You have my number?" Ivan noticed that she wasn't calling him Professor Wilder anymore.

"Yes." Emily recited a number from memory.

Ivan walked her to the front glass door of the building. "Emily, maybe we can have lunch after the class and de-brief."

"I'd like that."

CHAPTER 26

A MORNING SWEEP

May 4th, 2010, Phoenix

Just before 8:00 am, Snyder stood by his MCSO sedan and surveyed the parking lot of a nondescript factory building. He was awaiting orders from Bardo. The blazing sun had not yet scorched the pavement. But, noted Snyder, the "heat" was here in full force—MCSO vans and sedans, the SWAT team, and a host of Deputies. Even Sheriff Bardo had arrived, looking like "Mr. Everycop" personified—same short-sleeved, tan shirt—like we're all a team.

Several dozen of MCSO's finest fanned out in the strip mall parking lot on West Van Buren, waiting for the night shift to get off. Monday night, coming into Tuesday, guaranteed a full house of illegals due to exit at 8:00 am.

The business park was ordinary—a spread-out collection of block buildings and a warehouse with a small office attached. Swamp coolers on the flat roofs signaled a lower-class operation, where the personnel within were not deemed worthy of conventional air conditioning. The inside would harbor illegals working under the worst conditions in town—conditions that union-organized American workers recognized as substandard after decades of union efforts and workers' rights litigation.

Bardo and his team were here on a tip from the immigration hotline the Sheriff had set up months before for irritated neighbors, disgruntled fellow employees, and even business competitors to call in and allege that the owner hired illegals with forged social security numbers. One phone call could put the company out of business in a day.

Strong and Snyder flanked the Sheriff as they entered the building unannounced. SWAT officers backed them up outside. Bardo, fully in his element, demanded that the manager line up all employees and have them checked for documents. Strong noticed that everyone in the place except the manager looked Hispanic. There were sure to be illegals here, people who smuggled themselves across the border with a *coyote* from Mexico. These illegals forged documents or stole someone else's social security number or driver's license to make money here.

Bardo and Strong began to process each employee, handing them off to backup SWAT members who would cuff the arrestees and escort them to an MCSO van. As they did so, Snyder flipped open a laptop. Then, taking each individual's identification, he searched the federal E-Verify System for social security numbers and the Arizona Department of Motor Vehicles site for valid driver's licenses. Within the hour, they'd arrested twenty-four people suspected of using false IDs. They'd turn at least ten over to ICE (Immigration and Customs Enforcement)—the federal enforcement guys who didn't seem to care that most of these workers were breaking the law. ICE focused their efforts on the dangerous felons, not the petty criminals.

As SWAT Deputies cuffed workers without proper ID and took them to the vans, a woman screamed hysterically at Bardo. "Coward! My husband did nothing wrong!" Then she turned toward the press.

"Damn!" said Snyder. "How'd they get here so fast? And isn't that Beatrice Milagro, the community radical, with her?"

"I'll go over and ask," said Strong. He made his weight and uniform count as he moved through the crowd toward the women.

Screamer yelled at Strong too. "You're taking my husband! He hasn't done anything wrong," she cried. "He just wants to work."

"Ma'am," Strong interrupted, "you'll have to show me your ID. Unfortunately, your husband appears to possess forged identification papers. If you cannot prove you are here legally, we must take you in too."

"Keep your hands off her," asserted the petite but immovable Milagro. "If you try to touch her, that woman over there"—she pointed to a short, plain Anglo woman in maroon-framed glasses— "that woman is an attorney. Therefore, you do not have reasonable cause to search her."

Strong backed off.

The hysterical woman quieted down, reached into her purse, and produced a bona fide Arizona driver's license—a sure mark that she was a citizen or at least a legal resident.

Strong returned to Snyder. "What's with that Milagro woman? And how did the hell that Heart Attack attorney know to get here?" He remembered Emily from cross-examination in the clapping trial.

"Stay clear of her—for now. But I'll remember to ensure that Bardo gets a file on her if there isn't one already."

They watched the Kevlar-vested SWAT Deputies shove two dozen Latinos into two vans destined for booking at the Fourth Avenue Jail. From there, the men would be transferred either to ICE or to the Tent City Jail that Bardo had set up to segregate men without documents from other inmates. According to the Sheriff, that made transport easier.

Back in the staff kitchen after the sweep, the receptionist washed dishes after brewing another pot of java as Strong and Snyder washed their doughnuts down with coffee. "We nabbed twenty-four today," said Snyder. "That makes over three hundred arrests of illegals, from thirty-two sweeps, and about two hundred of them on identity theft—fake or stolen IDs. Not bad for a morning's work, eh?"

Strong finished munching a chocolate éclair and wiped its cream off his chin. "What about the other ones?" he asked Snyder.

"Some of them were just ordinary legal residents or citizens with no offenses we could find," said Snyder. "Just got caught up in the sweep. But some others had outstanding warrants for traffic violations and other misdemeanors. A few had felony warrants. So virtually all of them, illegal or not, had done something wrong."

CHAPTER 27

TRASHING THE FOURTH

Late June 2010, Phoenix

As Ivan approached his office, the door was ajar. Inside, the mess of locked file drawers pried open, boxes knocked askew, and papers scattered on the floor stunned him. He called Sullivan. "Sir, I've been burglarized. Could you come over and take a look?"

Sullivan arrived in minutes. His mouth fell open. He let his gaze move slowly, deliberately, around the room. Then he said, "Ivan, this looks like a planned hit. My first impression is that the burglars intended to produce shock and awe—to intimidate you. It's a real mess. Do you know if anything at all is missing?"

"There was hardly anything to take. News clippings, papers to grade, course materials—" Ivan struggled to imagine anything worth taking.

Sullivan pondered. "The University has changed in recent years. In 2006, the Legislature passed a law prohibiting illegal aliens from paying the lower in-state tuition. To us, the decisions about fees are confidential within the University. The Registrar's office is more strictly protected than it appears and is locked tight as a drum when people leave at the end of the day. In the past few years, we have received complaints at all ASU campuses, and even some anonymous threats, that we don't have a right to provide in-state tuition to 'those Mexicans.' Unfortunately, people have sometimes been crass enough to target that one group when it's just as likely that our Canadian neighbors to the north will overstay their visas. Have you heard anything about it?"

"It's scuttlebutt among the faculty, but I hadn't thought—"

Sullivan suddenly remembered. "Did you recently get an updated class list from the Registrar?"

"Yes, but why?" Ivan asked. Then he realized, "Oh! It would have shown all the Spanish surnames." He stopped. "But that shouldn't be so important. It doesn't indicate legal status. The only mark I noticed was an asterisk for every journalism student."

Sullivan reminded him, "Remember how several years back we eliminated the custom of posting students' names on the bulletin boards? Many students, and their families, raised privacy concerns. So now, a class list is not available to the public."

"The list wouldn't reflect a lack of legal documentation but would have all Spanish and other foreign-sounding surnames. It could be something someone might want." Ivan looked at his inbox and rifled the papers on the floor. "It's definitely not here."

"Then I suspect this was a job to steal that information. If someone is after Latinos, the class list would sure help them out."

"Why would they target my office? Doesn't every class have a variety of students?"

"Think, Ivan. We know the son of a Sheriff's Deputy is in your class. I also learned that one of your teaching assistants is the niece of Senator Hamelin. There may be other links to power. I think they are targeting you, personally."

"But how would they get in? I had locked the door, but it was open when I arrived. There was no forced entry."

Sullivan speculated, "There are only three keys to your office—yours and two master keys. I own one, and the other is in the locked security office. It feels like an inside job. Still, we have to call the Security team first."

A pale, middle-aged man with the beginning of a dark afternoon shadow arrived quickly and dusted for fingerprints around the door and on the desk. "Professor, can you think of any reason someone would want to break into your office? Anything of value? Any test answers, stuff like that?"

Sullivan looked at Ivan. *Don't tell him everything.*

"As I told Dean Sullivan, the summer has just begun. I only have a few graded papers and some news clippings. But there'd be nothing anyway. I don't keep test answers. I give essays."

The security officer glanced at Ivan and then questioned Sullivan. "Sir, has Professor Wilder been involved in any radical activities, questionable political stands, that sort of thing? Would he know who the illegal students are in his class?"

Ivan interrupted. "I'm here. You can ask me. And no, I'm a professor, not an activist. But why would it matter anyway? What you are suggesting would not be a crime."

Shadow addressed Sullivan. "The line is not always that clear, sirs." The pretense of deference did not go unnoticed by either Ivan or the Dean.

Sullivan interrupted. "Professor Wilder is certain that he locked his office when he left for the weekend. Whoever broke into the office must be stopped. We think someone may know—" He caught himself mid-thought and stopped.

"Any names?" asked the officer.

"Not right now. Make your report, get it to us, and I'll forward further information as soon as possible."

When the security officer left, Sullivan turned to Ivan. "It's as if that guy could sympathize with whoever broke in. He was too quick to get to the illegal question. I'll get the locks changed. The senior security chief has been here since the building opened. I think he's reliable. I'll check."

"Thanks, Mitch. Yeah, let's change the locks."

"So, you're sure the class list is missing?"

"It's not in the inbox, and I can't find it on the floor."

"Damn! Can you think of anything else you did to aggravate security? Anything you should tell me? I need to know as much as possible to stay on your side."

"Come to think of it—I've written several blogs about freedom of the press and assembly. And this spring, I went to the capitol to observe the student demonstration when Governor Middleton signed SB 1070. People were taking videos of everything. Do you think the Sheriff really has a file on me?"

"Yes, he keeps files on anyone who isn't in lockstep. But the County Attorney is the one who wanted to bug your classroom. So, they're probably working together. Ivan, I have some friends on the university board, at city hall, and in the business community. Some of them may have ideas—normal people, businessmen, even conservative politicians, think it's getting out of hand."

"Wouldn't Shatigan, or Bardo, for that matter, need a warrant if they want to conduct a search or set up a bug or wiretap?"

"You should know. Yep, based on probable cause. And when Shatigan's people asked, they didn't have it, so I said no. There was nothing they could take to a judge."

When Richard Mendez arrived home, Tony cornered him. "Dad, what do you know about Lydia Flores? We're in the same class at Cronkite, and clearly, she knows her stuff. I went to her house the other day and met her mom, and today, all of a sudden, Lydia froze me out as if I had leprosy. She said to talk to you."

Mr. Mendez was a handsome man at five-foot-eight with the chiseled features of Spanish heritage. He took a beer and a soda from the refrigerator, handed Tony the soda, poured some corn chips into a bowl, and grabbed a new jar of salsa. Tony watched him stall for time. His father poured the salsa into a smaller bowl and placed everything on the dining room table. "C'mon, sit down," he said. "First of all, Son, this conversation needs to be confidential. It goes nowhere, understood?"

"Sure." Tony was puzzled. "But why?"

"The Flores family have been my tenants for almost fifteen years. They are some of the best tenants you can have. Clean and careful, they fix their plumbing, electrical—stuff like that. Mr. Flores is very handy. He even does maintenance work for me on some of my other apartment units."

"Okay."

"They have never caused me one moment of trouble. They've never missed a rent payment."

"Okay."

"You know I have a heart. There are some hardship cases where I let the rent go by for a few months. But I am not a pushover for deadbeats. If I think someone is trying to skate, I'll evict them. I've gone to court several times. Anglo, Black, Hispanic—it doesn't matter—if they're trying to pull one over on me, I kick them out."

"I know. I've heard you talk about some of them."

"There have even been some who've paid the rent with cartel money. At first, I was naïve. I rented to some folks who had the money. Then they'd run drugs out of their back window and trash the apartment. I'm better at spotting them now. Sometimes I worried that your mom would become a widow over some of the tenants I took to court."

Tony hadn't seen this side of his father before. But it fit in with the conservative slant—he was anti-crime and he cut no slack for slackers or criminals.

"So, Dad, what does this have to do with Lydia?"

"Except for her brother Jesus, who was born here, the whole family is undocumented. They are in Arizona illegally, so they live under constant fear that Sheriff Bardo could round them up and refer them to ICE for deportation."

"Oh! So that means that even Lydia—?"

"They brought Lydia north when she was about two years old. She's never been anywhere but Arizona. They don't travel. They've never tried to go back. For all I know, they don't have much in the way of relatives south of the border."

"So that's why she blew me off. All this time, she's been sitting quietly in class because she doesn't want anyone to notice her. I bet she especially doesn't want Phil to realize who she is."

"Who's Phil?"

"His father works in the Sheriff's Office. He's always spewing stuff about the illegals."

"And she's one of them. You hit the nail on the head."

"But why doesn't she apply for citizenship, Dad? Why haven't her parents applied?"

"That's a tough one. I'm not entirely sure. I used to get on their case about it. Mr. Flores holds two jobs—fake ID and pays into social security, even though he'll never see a dime. Lydia's mother cleans some houses for cash. They are models of good citizenship. But they never applied."

"Why not?"

"Turns out, if Mexicans can't prove they are here legally—which is a lot of people—they have to return to Mexico and await the processing of their application on the other side. For Mexicans and most Latinos, that process takes ten years before their application for re-entry becomes active. Imagine leaving everything they know in the U.S. for ten years. It would kill their family to do that."

"Would this happen if Lydia applied?"

"I don't see why not. As the law stands now, she's just like everyone else."

"But isn't Lydia a candidate for the DREAM Act, where adults brought here as children have a preferential path to citizenship, even if their parents don't?"

"Looks like it."

"Dad, from what I know, the DREAM Act would let her get a green card if she joins the military or goes on to higher education. She's already at ASU. She'd be the perfect candidate."

"Tony, she would. But it's not entirely true. The political climate has taken a dive these past few years. There must be a lot of fear because politicians who used to work together don't anymore. Since the economic downturn in 2008, many whites are afraid—Latinos too. Some of my tenants who had jobs paid their rent on time, and caused no trouble, have left Arizona because of Bardo and now SB 1070. Hell, the police could stop even you and me, claiming we look illegal."

Tony smiled sideways. Dad had never cursed in front of him.

"Anyway, Son, where Lydia's concerned, you have your work cut out for you. If I were in her shoes, I would hardly trust anyone. Her parents think I'm okay, but what if I changed my mind? Think about it. They are so much at our mercy."

"Does *Somos Republicans* have a stand on immigration, Dad?"

"Funny you should ask. We've always supported the Chamber of Commerce's position of letting immigrants come to work in the U.S. because it helped businesses bargain over wages—right to work, not padded with union benefit packages. And, honestly, immigration seemed to be a stimulus to the economy. More small businesses started up with more consumers at all our stores. It appeared to be good for everyone, especially the business community. But some of us have had second thoughts. The more recent undocumented workers jeopardized jobs for folks who've lived here a while and worked their way up. The illegals work for less, and they don't complain. Meanwhile, many of our Chicano friends feel that underlying the current political climate is a fundamental racism that bodes ill for all of us. That's why *Somos Republicans* will push for comprehensive immigration reform, and they hope the court will strike SB 1070 down. I didn't expect I would come to think that way, but things are very unpleasant right now."

Tony felt he'd somehow gone from being just his father's son to a fellow adult in less than half an hour. "Thanks for talking to me about it, Dad. I feel older and wiser but not so happy."

"Well, take care with how you relate to Lydia. I've known her for a long time. She's a lovely young lady. She has done exceptionally well at school and has never gotten into trouble. I wouldn't like anyone in our family to cause trouble for her. I only want the best for the Flores family."

CHAPTER 28

THE PIED PIPER

Late June 2010, Cronkite Auditorium

It wasn't quite a swagger. Senator Hamelin lunged doggedly toward the lectern, chin out-thrust, an odor of righteous certitude rising off his hulk—like steam from Chernobyl.

Ivan spoke. "Ladies and gentlemen, I would like to introduce Senator Hamelin, President of the Arizona Senate. Senator, welcome to Cronkite's class in Power and Propaganda."

Hamelin plopped his notes in front of him. He looked at the crowd over his half-glasses, perched low on a bulbous nose. His two plain-dressed aides had positioned themselves in front of each entry door to the auditorium. One kept his hands folded tightly across his chest, armed against the unpredictable. The other held a mobile phone and seemed to be entering information. Satisfied with his security detail, Hamelin curtly nodded to Ivan and began. "I hear you people have listened to Representative Marcos's spiel on immigration. I'm here to give you the facts. We have an invasion going on, and we need to push back against this wave of illegals coming into Arizona."

Invasion? Thought Susan. *That's misleading.*

"The bottom line is that those people who come here illegally are felons—criminals! The Federal Government has done nothing—nothing—to rid us of this scourge. So, the sovereign state of Arizona has taken matters into its own hands. We have passed a law requiring everyone to produce IDs at the voting booth, so illegals can't commit voting fraud. We've passed a law that would require them to pay higher, out-of-state university registration fees if they can't prove they are here legally. Some of them may even be here at ASU."

He paused, ice-blue eyes glaring over the tops of his spectacles, toward the middle of the risers, where over a dozen Hispanics sat together. "You need to remember—Arizona is under siege. You are not a citizen of the United States. You are a citizen of the Sovereign State of Arizona. We will make laws to rid ourselves of those vermin. We will get them out through enforcement and attrition. This year, we've passed Senate Bill 1070, which gives us two powerful tools to get them out of our state. First, we've made it a state felony for them to be in Arizona illegally. Second, we have required law enforcement to question any individual if he reasonably suspects the person is here illegally."

Feeling defensive, Tony started to bristle. "How does an officer 'reasonably suspect'?"

Hamelin looked at Tony and paused, assessing his haircut, clothing, skin color, and English. "I know what you're thinking. You think it's by their skin color. No. I'm not racist. But usually, an officer can tell."

Alicia, flushed with fear and anger, burst in. "Is it the accent? Is it people who speak Spanish? Or is it people who speak English as I do, with an accent? Because I am a citizen. I am not illegal!"

Taken aback, Hamelin answered, "No, not if you speak English. But the police—they know. The Federal Government has filed an appeal to stop SB 1070. It's their *jihad* against Arizona—a *jihad!* We'll go beyond the activist lower courts." Flecks of spittle landed near the sandals in the front row. "We'll go all the way to the Supreme Court."

Nazrin interrupted. "Senator Hamlin, you are misusing the word *jihad*. That is an Arabic word for a Muslim holy war against the infidel or, more commonly, a spiritual struggle. It does not fit anything that the United States government does. As a Muslim, I feel deeply uncomfortable with your use of that word. In the deep religious sense, a true *jihad* is a beautiful thing of spiritual power!"

Hamelin glared at Nazrin and then, looking away, jabbed his finger across the lectern. "I'll tell you. People who come illegally, even if they are children, are illegal. And if illegals get here and have kids in Arizona, the children are merely anchor babies. Their parents brought them or had them here to get an anchor to legal residence or citizenship."

Lydia cringed inwardly. *He'd go after my brother Jesus!*

Hamelin continued. "The Fourteenth Amendment of the Constitution was never intended to apply to illegal aliens." He shook his fist for emphasis. "We need to toss the anchor babies back across the border."

"Any last thoughts, Senator Hamelin?" asked Ivan.

"Yes." Hamelin glanced at Ivan, then stared straight at the two rows of Hispanics on either side of Lydia. "I believe my duty is to the rule of law. And I play hardball." He glanced at the aide with the mobile phone, who punched in some notes.

After an awkward moment of silence, Ivan chided the class. "Let's give the Senator a hand. Thank you for coming today, Senator Hamelin, and taking the time to share your views. You can be sure that your words will impact the future leaders of Arizona government and journalism."

As the students flowed out of the auditorium and down the hall, Susan caught up with Nazrin. "Hi, Nazrin. Isn't that your name?"

Nazrin nodded.

"I'm Susan Goldstein." Susan noticed a flicker of surprise. "I just wanted to congratulate you on how you came back at Senator Hamelin on his improper use of the word *jihad*. You put him in his place."

Nazrin's uncertain flicker changed into a smile of relief. "Thanks! Do you think so? I was a little nervous, but my parents have taught me to stick up for myself."

Susan added, "He needed someone to put him in his place. You know, we in Judaism have a similar concept to *jihad*. We call it God wrestling. It's like when you feel deeply and closely connected to God, and you may be struggling over something, and yet God remains a mystery."

Nazrin stopped, turned to Susan, and grabbed both her hands. "Wow! You get it. We Muslims hear ideas about the spiritual struggle from an imam. But your God wrestling is like our *jihad*. And *jihad* is not a political term that some senator can use however he wants. I'm glad you spoke to me."

"Nazrin, I know we only know each other from class, but I think we may have things in common, and I feel I could learn from you. Could we get together for lunch soon and get better acquainted?"

"You think you don't know much? Even though I've been through public high schools, there are days when I feel clueless. Some of the imams preach such bigotry. How about tomorrow?"

CHAPTER 29

ANTELOPE DANCER #1

Thursday, May 6th, 2010, Phoenix

Bullard called Strong at home at 6:00 am. It was mandatory to be at the office by 7:15. Bardo had called Snyder and two other officers—men he could trust and who gave cash to the "Re-Elect Bardo" campaign. There was something Bardo wanted them to do. Grumbling as he drove to work, Strong listened to the local news.

"Yesterday in the park, two-hundred-and-thirty-seven Hispanic families were gathered for a *Cinco de Mayo* festivity when Sheriff J. Edgar Bardo's Deputies made a sweep," the announcer said. "They took one-hundred-and-seven men and women and left the others, including all the children, and marched them into vans to be taken to the Fourth Avenue Jail. Immigrants' rights watchdog Beatrice Milagro asked if the MCSO would identify the children left at the scene without a parent or guardian. A spokesperson for the Sheriff responded, 'We're just enforcing the law.' Now, here's the weather."

That was yesterday, thought Strong—he and Snyder had coordinated the sweep. *This is today.*

It was early, 7:20 am. Bullard had told the receptionist to brew two pots and bring a bunch of donuts. The four men were in the kitchen, holding their coffee mugs, having a first round. "This better be good," Strong murmured to Snyder. "They've stopped paying overtime, so technically, we shouldn't even be here."

"Men," began Bullard, "thanks for showing up early like this. Sheriff Bardo appreciates it."

Never mind that it was mandatory. Bardo was the toughest Sheriff in America, and Strong loved him for it. Bardo had *cojones.* He knew how to be tough on crime, tough on criminals, and tough on illegals. Strong liked him a lot. And he'd earned his niche near the top of Bardo's pecking order.

Bullard told it like it was. "The Board of Supervisors has subpoenaed the MCSO's financial records. The Feds are continuing to investigate racial profiling in the sweeps. It doesn't help that the ACLU won a lawsuit against the Arizona DPS over racial profiling outside Flagstaff. People are suing Sheriff Bardo like crazy: the guy in the three-piece suit, the masked women, and the rowdy red-shirts. People roughed up while in jail. Judges! Three County Supervisors, especially the one we threw in jail! The Feds are questioning activists about possible MCSO abuses of power. Those ne'er-do-wells are presenting themselves as victims, of all things. What a crock! But of all of them so far," he continued, "the two most insidious activists are the guy called Rafe with a video cam and the Milagro woman from Guadalupe who is on the Internet the second—the second, mind you—another sweep is announced. How the hell does she get her info? She has activists and lawyers on the scene practically before the SWAT team arrives to alert those damn illegals about their rights. She shows up in her slick little SUV just as things begin to happen." Bullard paused to let the men remember their irritation, even humiliation, at the hands of the petite Beatrice Milagro. "She documents every arrest by the deputy's name and badge number. She has info that could give the wrong idea about Bardo's efforts to rid the county of these leeches who bring in disease and drugs and run up the costs at schools and hospitals. They don't even try to speak English." Bullard gulped in some air and then paused to take his swig of coffee. "Frankly, though," he said, preaching to Bardo's choir, "our success rates were pretty high. Usually, sixty to seventy percent of those caught in a raid have been illegal. Most of the others have committed some crime, so we have arrested very few honest citizens. You've probably noticed a few regulars at each event, right?"

The men stood by the kitchen table, backs straight, legs slightly spread, clasping their hands in front of their crotches.

"Here's why. And let me remind you, you are under oath to serve the office you swore to uphold. That includes secrecy and loyalty. I'm talking about the Milagro woman."

All four Deputies had experienced personal frustration at the hands of this tiny, attractive Latina. Every one of them was in her files.

"So, gentlemen, Sheriff Bardo wants her neutralized."

Strong's jaw dropped. *Neutralized is a movie term for snuffing out the enemy—a bit too far, even from the toughest Sheriff in America, for a woman who hasn't committed a crime.*

"You wonder where I'm going with this," Bullard said, nodding. "I understand your concern. But the Sheriff and I have discussed it thoroughly. So, your orders come straight from the top. We are not planning to take a human life, though, on occasion, a man is tempted." He stopped, the corners of his sagging mouth turning up ever so slightly as if surgically face-lifted.

The Deputies smiled surreptitiously. Talk around the locker room had always focused on getting her in private to show her what a real man could do. In jest, of course.

At least Strong thought it was in jest. He wasn't sure about Snyder.

However, Bullard was going in a serious direction. Feet shuffled, hips shifted. "We need you four men. Only you. We need absolute confidentiality." Bullard continued, his voice dropping. "Even if you ever think you know, you do not. Understand? Even though you will be the only ones in on the operation, we need you men not to know. Not to have heard any of this discussion this morning. If anyone questions you, all we discussed was a strategy for peacekeeping when SB 1070 goes into effect on July 29th. Understood?"

Eyelashes twitched in relief. The Deputies nodded in unison.

"You should feel no qualms about today's plan. Sheriff Bardo and I have decided to call it Operation Victim-Witness. Catchy name, eh?"

Strong had downed two cups of coffee with his glazed doughnut and felt the pressure. Unconsciously, he moved toward the men's room.

"Strong, don't rush off. You are essential. You have done outstanding work on plenty of our most recent ops. And Snyder and you two others." He filled in the directions.

Snyder and Strong drove an unmarked car to an MCSO covert location in South Phoenix. It was a nondescript slump-block residence, the windows silvered with aluminum foil against the sun and snoops. It looked like any house on the block—with parched weeds scattered among the desert rock in a dirt-bare front yard. The driveway ended in a carport with a side door to the kitchen.

Snyder handled the keys. They entered the kitchen and locked the door behind them. He checked the front door—deadbolted. Curtains covered every window inside the aluminum sheeting pasted against the glass. Assorted furniture from the Salvation Army, set askew on the stained shag rug, made the living-dining area look like a flophouse for crackheads. From four sets of clothing piled on the kitchen table, they donned uniform shirts and pants from "Tim's HVAC," a non-existent refrigeration company. Lightweight black leather gloves completed the outfits.

They exited the back door, jumped into the unmarked sedan, then drove to a nearby warehouse in a run-down commercial/industrial park on Broadway. They pulled up by the dock-high loading area behind one of the buildings. A truck with the "Tim's Heating and Cooling" logo on the side stood at the ready. Strong and the other two got in. Snyder took off in the sedan. They all knew the address, but it was Snyder's job to scout Milagro's home on the edge of Guadalupe and watch her leave. He'd call them after she was out of sight.

They hadn't gone as far east as the I-10 when Snyder called. "She's just left in her SUV and is around the corner. Time to move." Within minutes, they were at the house in their HVAC-labeled van. Snyder picked the lock. Strong stood beside him, pretending to wait for someone to answer the door. They entered quickly and moved with dispatch through the living room into what seemed to be her bedroom. Nothing. They checked the living-dining area and the other two bedrooms. Aside from some Native American artwork and jewelry on the dresser, they found nothing.

Frustrated, Strong said, "She has a desk in her bedroom, and nothing's on it."

Snyder ventured, "What about her closet?" Bingo! A computer sat on top of a crate next to a stack of CDs. Snyder seized the laptop. The other two men picked up the CDs. Strong noticed a cell phone and grabbed it. *Maybe it has the photos of all of the MCSO Deputies from the sweeps.* In less than five minutes, they were in and out. Milagro's contact records, names and cell numbers, and information on any deputy involved in every action were now in MCSO's possession. Soon the men had changed back to regular uniforms and reconvened on the twentieth floor of the Wells Fargo building. Snyder had put the goods in lockup at a separate location.

Strong tapped on Eleanor's window. "Hey, Ma'am, fix another pot of coffee, now, thank you." Eleanor hurried to the staff kitchen, where the guys sat at the lunch table munching sandwiches from the ground floor lobby's snack shop. The men kept grinning at each other, ignoring Eleanor as she cleaned the coffee pot and set up a new supply.

Snyder opened the conversation. "Gotta say, that Milagro is h-o-t, HOT! Those photos of her in her wedding dress—" He chuckled.

"Shhh," Strong cautioned. "Never know who's listening."

Indeed, the door opened. Bullard swung his girth toward them but decided, after all, not to sit at one of the undersized lunchroom chairs. "Done?"

"Done," said Snyder, nodding at the others. "Very well done. She'll be one pissed lady when she gets home."

"And nervous, too," grinned Strong.

"Enough said," noted Bullard. They scarfed the sandwiches and left the staff kitchen with their personalized ceramic mugs re-filled with coffee.

Alone in his office, Strong picked a small object from his pants pocket. He moved aside the nondescript paperweight received by all ten-year MCSO veterans to make room for the new item. *Something the missus would like if she were still alive.* Standing less than three inches tall was an exquisitely sculpted, authentically painted figurine, the traditional Yaqui deer dancer of the Pascua healing ceremony.

CHAPTER 30

BOMBARDO

June 30th, 2010, Cronkite Auditorium

As Ivan entered the auditorium on Wednesday, a young woman stood waiting for him. Ivan recognized her from the Hispanic-dominated middle rows.

"Professor Wilder, you said you would invite some guest speakers to the classroom. I think you would like— My aunt knows a lot—" She clutched her books to her chest.

"Could you tell me a little bit more?"

"Her name is Beatrice Milagro. We both live in Guadalupe. There has been harassment by the Sheriff's Deputies. There have been unfair arrests. There has been discrimin—"

A large group of students burst into the auditorium. They fanned out and climbed up the ramp on both sides of the room to take their seats.

"What is your name, Miss—?"

"Lydia Flores. Would you call her, Professor Wilder? She can tell your students how it really is under the Sheriff's rule." She pressed a card with a phone number on it into his hand. "Please."

"I'll—" Ivan took the card, looked on the other side, and saw the name. "Beatrice Milagro, you say?"

Lydia nodded and moved away, taking a seat midway up the auditorium on the same side as his desk. She was inconspicuous and surrounded by other Hispanic students on each side and in the row behind her. Ivan quickly slipped the card into his back pocket as the classroom filled.

At precisely 9:00 am, two flak-jacketed Deputies from MCSO accompanied J. Edgar Bardo down the hall from the security desk and knocked on Ivan's classroom door. Ivan let them in, relieved that Bardo honored his commitment. *If their purpose is intimidation, those two bodyguards have outdone themselves.*

Bardo approached the lectern. His two bodyguards, guns and tasers at the ready, stood on each side of him like lesser flags.

Ivan introduced him. "Sheriff Bardo, thank you for coming to speak today. You are addressing some of the leaders of tomorrow in both journalism and the political world." Bardo looked away vaguely, shook Ivan's hand, wiped his palm on his pants, and said, "I hope they found my website. It lists all our programs. We run an extensive operation." Bardo mentioned a few programs without a smile.

"From the information we left with your receptionist," said Ivan, "the class expects you to speak about the official duties and the activities of the Sheriff. Does that include operating the jails, reporting on spending, and conducting sweeps on illegal immigrants?"

Bardo began. "Lemme say this at the outset. I am the elected Sheriff. I'm doing what the people voted me to do, and that is to enforce the law. I will continue to do that. I do not take orders from the Federal Government. So, you want to know about the County Jail? I'll tell you. It isn't the Ritz Carlton. I say to the inmates, 'If you don't like it, don't come back.'"

Tony spotted propaganda techniques right away. *Saying he's the elected Sheriff, that he will enforce the law—that's an appeal to authority. Saying he doesn't have to answer to the Federal Government is misleading.*

Bardo continued. "Many people ask about the Tent City Jail and how it's hot in the sun. Like today, the end of June. It'll go up to one-hundred-and-twelve degrees. But I say it's one-hundred-and-twenty degrees in Iraq, and our soldiers are living in tents too, and they have to wear full battle gear, but they didn't commit any crimes—so shut your mouths. People complain about pink underwear for these guys. We found that a lot of them stole the underwear. So, we dyed it—a big drop in theft. No coffee? Green bologna? Remember, these guys are in jail for a reason. We try to make it feel like it should. Tent City is a concentration camp."

Alicia kept spotting propaganda. *"For a reason" sounds like a glittering generality, marginalizing all inmates.* Some people in the jails were not yet convicted, merely awaiting trial. Others were serving short sentences for lesser offenses.

"I have to set priorities," said Bardo. "They're always trying to cut my budget. If I have to do a sweep on illegals at a job site or a City Hall, or in a neighborhood, I'll do it. You wanted to know about the budget? My main duty is to enforce the law. It costs money. It is the job of the Board of Supervisors to fund my office so I can do my job. I'm doing what the people elected me to do. I don't have time to send the BOS an invoice for every new van or crime sweep. Remember, the public is my boss, not the Board of Supervisors. I have the highest approval rating of any elected official in Arizona. I serve the public. I'm gonna keep serving the public. Any questions?"

"But, Sheriff Bardo," interrupted Susan, "haven't you demanded records from several officials? One newspaper article said you are using politically motivated criminal investigations and making expensive demands under the Freedom of Information Act. If they are abusing power, aren't you?"

"Excuse me, ma'am, but there's no such thing as abuse of power in the Sheriff's Office. When I investigate or make arrests, I'm not abusing power. I'm doing my job."

"But," interrupted Jonah, "there were a lot of cases where it looks like judges found defendants innocent or threw cases out because there was no probable cause to make arrests."

Bardo scowled. *Who is this punk?*

Jonah continued. "Aren't you going to have to settle some damages claims?"

"Well, mister," Bardo replied, "you raise an interesting point. Because the County is telling me I have to go to mediation. Some of the Supervisors shouldn't have voted on the mediation because we are investigating them. They should have abstained. I have a file on every one of them."

Nazrin entered the fray. "Why do you need a file on everyone? What you're describing sounds like the secret police in my parents' old country, Iran, where the Ayatollah persecuted all political rivals. And now, with President Ahmadinejad, it's even more oppressive."

Bardo retorted, "Well, ma'am, we are enforcing the law. All the people who come here illegally are breaking the law. It's my job to arrest them and have them deported."

Even as hands waved for more questions, the time was up.

Ivan said, "Thank you, Sheriff Bardo, for addressing us today. Class, let's give a round of applause."

As Bardo and his aides opened the door and stepped into the hall, everyone could hear the lively music of a rock band. The trio stopped in their tracks. Ivan looked past Bardo and down the hall. A local four-piece band, The Hayseeds, had set up in the lobby by the security desk. Playing guitar, mandolin, fiddle, and bass, they blasted protest songs. Activists and other students surrounded them, chanting distinctly, "Bom-bar-do, he must go, Bom-bar-do, he must go," bursting into raucous applause as the song ended.

School security officers ringed the protesters, creating a safety barrier between the rowdy rockers and the Bardo trio. Bardo frowned. Huddling with his black knights, he grunted. The three guests headed down the hall in the other direction for an obscure exit out the back of the building.

The front lobby was clearing after the impromptu band concert. Phil watched with irritation as Jonah ran down the hall to give a big hug to the leader of the band. Harry caught up with Phil just outside the building. "Phil, I got the class list from the secretary's office. Lots of Spanish names. Illegals! You can give it to your dad for a sweep."

Phil felt a plan forming, and he would be part of it. "Great, Harry," he said. "There's no school tomorrow, so I'll catch you Monday. I'm sure Dad will want it."

Tony felt a rankling irritation over Bardo's speech. *That guy must have said, "I enforce the law," half a dozen times. That's just a propaganda technique. And calling folks illegals—as if we're all illegal if we're Hispanic. He's marginalizing a whole group of people because of the color of our skin. I wonder what Lydia thought.* Moving quickly out the glass doors, he tried to catch up with her. But she hurried away and mingled with a large group of Latinas, sitting among them on the train.

The Sheriff and his bodyguards drove directly to the County Attorney's office before returning to the 20th floor of the Wells Fargo building. Since Shatigan was planning to leave office and run for Attorney General in the fall, Bardo needed to be sure they were in sync on their investigations.

In the elevator, a nondescript civilian wore a name badge indicating that he was with the County Attorney's staff. He said, "Good Morning, Sheriff."

Bardo returned the greeting. "Say, I don't know you. Hayes? What do you do for Shatigan?"

"I'm a social worker. I'm with the victim-witness program, assisting children who've seen or experienced crimes. I calm their fears and prepare them as witnesses."

As if he hadn't heard what the man actually did, Bardo said, "A social worker? A social worker? Waddya think you're doing, coddling victims? I'm the victim here."

The civilian did not respond. As they reached the fourth floor, Bardo said to his two black-vested guards, "Let's get off here. I don't hang around with social workers."

Back at MCSO headquarters, Bardo called Bullard into his office. "How did 'Mission Wilder' go?"

"Good," said Bullard. "We seized the updated class list. Not as good as registration cards, but there were over a dozen Spanish surnames. And we wreaked havoc on Wilder's office. Shock and awe. A good beginning."

"Excellent! And Bullard, tell Strong to have his kid get the name of the long-haired hippie who sits near the front. I'm sure he'll know who I mean—the one who runs his mouth off."

———————

In the evening, Eleanor Jones called Beatrice Milagro at home from her home phone. They had attended the same church for years, Our Lady of Guadalupe next to Tempe, and served on the ladies' altar guild together.

Beatrice's phone rang. The electronic voicemail asked for the caller to leave a message. Eleanor spoke with restrained urgency. "Beatrice, this is Eleanor. I have something I think you should see. Please call me—at home."

CHAPTER 31

A DVD IS WORTH A THOUSAND WORDS

July 1st, 2010, Cronkite Auditorium

The day after Bardo spoke, it was Emily's turn to address Ivan's class. She patted her hair in the ladies' room and pulled her jacket down to smooth out the wrinkles. *I have no reason to pay attention to that sort of detail; this isn't trial court. Still—* She entered the auditorium a few minutes before the students arrived.

Ivan greeted her and ushered her over to the video equipment. Everything worked. Shorter than Ivan by ten inches, with dark eyes behind thick maroon-framed glasses, Emily looked like a spinster schoolteacher in the making. But she knew her DVDs. Ivan picked up a lavender fragrance emanating from her jacket, enhanced by the summer heat. He kneeled to untangle the cables on the floor, noticing maroon toenails that matched her glasses frames.

To Emily, Ivan seemed like the kind of professor who had earned his rep by fostering provocative discussion in the classroom. He'd written several "My Turn" Op-Ed pieces in various newspapers. She'd asked around and heard that Ivan occasionally got in the crosshairs of some politicians. But he was still an academician.

Soon the auditorium was bustling with students getting settled. Ivan escorted Emily to the lectern. "Class, some of you already know that Ms. Emily Hartwell, a defense attorney, has defended our very own Jonah Whalen and three others in a case where the MCSO arrested them in the Board of Supervisors auditorium. We have discussed freedom of assembly and expression. Ms. Hartwell

169

has been kind enough to bring us live footage of this and two other arrests. Use your worksheets as a guide. Be on the lookout for First Amendment issues and whether Ms. Hartwell is using propaganda." He smiled at Emily. "I've prepped them to analyze every guest speaker, Ms. Hartwell. Be on your toes."

Emily smiled back. "I look forward to the challenge, Professor Wilder." As Ivan retreated to his desk, she popped the first DVD into her laptop. "I will be showing you footage from three arrests in 2008. I was a defense attorney in all three trials. We'll have time for a few questions during each scenario. This first case is affectionately known as the 'mask' case. You can see about thirty persons wearing masks crowded into this area, the public lobby on the tenth floor of the County Supervisors office building. Can you also see about thirty officers in tan and white shirts? The white-shirted men are from the County Protective Services division. They don't have the authority to make arrests. The tan shirts are from the Sheriff's Office—they do." Emily ran the video until most demonstrators removed their masks as the Deputies herded them into the elevators. Then she pushed re-play. An officer was asking everyone to leave.

She paused the video and asked the class, "Can members of the public wait in this lobby at ten o'clock in the morning on a weekday?"

Susan read from the relevant section of the statute. "Members of the public may be in public offices during hours of operation on weekdays, from nine to five, Monday through Friday."

"Watch what happens next." Emily rolled the video, rewound it, and paused as four women removed their masks and sat in the four lobby seats. "Have they removed their masks? I ask because, as you know, in many armed robberies, robbers wear masks to disguise themselves. Masks can be a danger to the public. Are they masked, talking, shouting, or waving their hands?" The video showed no movement and indicated no sound. "Keep looking." She continued the footage as one of the Deputies approached the four women and said, "You have to leave. You have no business being here."

Startled, Phil said, "Hey, that's my dad arresting those people!"

"He's the one who arrested us, too, on Wednesday!" Jonah said impulsively. Then he stopped, uncomfortable with his proximity to the story about to unfold.

Emily asked, "Do you mean the officer speaking to the seated Anglo woman?"

Phil cleared his throat. "Yeah. He told me about them. They were all wearing masks and stuff, trespassing and disturbing the peace."

Emily rewound the footage until the large group disappeared into the open elevators, leaving the four women and about eight officers. "Let's take another look." She let the video run, and the class watched as each woman removed her mask, placed it by her side, and sat in a chair. She let it roll as Strong told them they had to leave, said they had no business there, insisted that they were trespassing, and finally motioned to four Deputies to help. They took the women's arms, put handcuffs on them, and escorted them into the elevators. The video ended. "Did you see them wearing masks?"

Phil hedged. "No. But they were before!"

"But as they were sitting and waiting, were they wearing masks?"

Tony kept his eyes on the image on the screen. "No. They'd taken them off."

At Emily's request, one of the TAs flipped the lights back on. "Ladies and gentlemen, would it make any difference to you, thinking about the First Amendment right to petition your government for a redress of grievances, whether they were petitioning a Supervisor to get a traffic light in their neighborhood versus whether they were questioning the Sheriff's management of his taxpayer-funded budget?"

Tony said, "Everyone has a right to try to get the government to listen, don't they?"

Susan had Googled the criminal statute. "You're only trespassing if you're in a public place when it's not open for business, which it was, or if you're causing a disturbance, which I didn't see them doing."

Emily let the students talk amongst themselves while she changed the DVDs. Then the TA dimmed the lights again. The class quieted as soon as she ran the next clip. It showed a loose-bloused blonde lady at the lectern of what again appeared to be a public space. The class could hear the woman say, "They all come across the border bringing tuberculosis and murdering innocent citizens. The Sheriff is arresting them and getting them deported. Everyone who supports the Sheriff, stand up and clap!" As the tape rolled, approximately fifteen people stood and cheered. Sounds of "Woo-woo!" proved the DVD sound system was alive and well. The camera panned over to the table of the five Supervisors, three of whom had risen to their feet. The students could hear the Chairman say, "I just had to clap!"

Emily then forwarded the video to a new segment where a Latina woman approached the lectern. She spoke in Spanish about how, even though she was an American citizen, she was afraid the Sheriff would arrest her. Another Latina woman translated. As they finished, fifteen people in the audience gave a standing ovation. Immediately, the Chairman gaveled for everyone to sit down and be quiet. The fifteen sat down and stopped clapping.

"Did you notice, class, that the clappers merely applauded and did not make any vocal sounds?" Emily asked.

Many students nodded.

"If anyone has a second hand on your watch, please time the number of seconds from when the Chairman gavels to when everyone is quietly seated." Emily re-played the same section.

Several students timed it at five seconds.

"Compare them to the blonde lady. Who would you say was disturbing the peace?"

Jonah said, "Is there really a question? The blonde and her crowd of rowdies!"

Phil remained silent.

Emily continued. "Notice how the Chairman calls two women to the lectern for public remarks. "It works like this. You enter this public auditorium and fill out a card with your name before the public comments section begins at 10 am. You give it to the officer of the day, and after the Supervisors' official business, the Chairman will call you. You can speak for about two minutes."

Like forensics investigators, the students watched intently as the Chairman called one woman to speak. They looked on as deputy Snyder cuffed and removed the woman who had approached the lectern after the Chairman called her name. They heard the Chairman call another woman's name when the first woman did not appear at the lectern. The students stared as Deputy Strong, an officer in a white shirt, and two other uniforms marched down the center aisle and motioned the other woman and two men to step into the aisle, simultaneously blocking their way.

Some students gasped when the three were also cuffed and arrested, even after the Chairman had called the woman to speak. They heard the Chairman calling the women's names. Then, they heard Deputy Strong say, "You're not speaking. You're under arrest." Ivan's students sat dumbfounded while they watched Deputy Strong march the four people out of the room in police custody.

Alicia's raised her voice in alarm. "They were arrested because they oppose the Sheriff! That happened when I lived in Venezuela. It is not supposed to happen here in America!"

Tony recognized his classmate. "Hey, that's Jonah! What were you doing there? Wow, man, bummer! And Phil, isn't that your father again? He looks the same as the guy who arrested the mask women!"

Jonah shook his head slightly and slunk down in his chair.

Phil said nothing. Cold anxiety choked him. The room was still.

Susan broke the silence. "For an arrest to occur, the statute requires that they make a disturbance and intend to disrupt the meeting. Ms. Hartwell, why did the Deputies pick on these four, not the other ten or eleven people who clapped? I didn't see any disturbance until the Deputies made the arrests!"

Emily paused the video. She read from a court transcript of when the Judge said, "Mr. Deputy Sheriff, you should be ashamed! There was no disturbance. You should not have made an arrest. Case dismissed, with prejudice!"

As a group of students burst into applause, Jonah held his face in his hands. Phil had put his head down into his arms folded on the desk.

Emily let the applause peak and fade. "I have just a few seconds of my last video," she said. On the screen, a dark-haired, clean-cut man stood on the public plaza outside the County courthouse. She pushed the pause button. "This was another activist, Stan Beltran, who had just spoken in the fall of 2008 inside the Supervisors auditorium. He wanted the supervisors to question the financial practices of the Sheriff's Office, which they had not done in over a year. Then they asked him to leave. He left as requested." Emily continued. "What is the Arizona statute regarding the Sheriff's responsibility for funding?"

Susan read a law that required the Sheriff to provide a monthly accounting to the Board of Supervisors.

"Thanks. You may want to cover all the responsibilities of both the Supervisors and the Sheriff another time. But for today's purpose, if a citizen asks the Board to demand a monthly accounting from the Sheriff's Office, do you think that would be within his First Amendment rights as a taxpaying citizen?"

The students watched the DVD. Two Sheriff's Deputies approached the man in the three-piece suit as he stood quietly with some friends on the plaza. First, they grabbed his arms and cuffed his hands in front of him. Then they placed shackles and a connecting chain from his legs to his wrists as they placed him under arrest. Finally, they force-marched him off the plaza.

Emily paused the video and asked the class, "What did you notice, ladies and gentlemen?"

Phil's voice wavered, "Wasn't he trespassing?"

Jonah argued, "No!"

Tony asked, "If he was trespassing, wasn't everyone else on the plaza trespassing too? Why single him out from about fifty people around him?"

At Emily's request, a TA put the lights back on. "Class, you have hit on the heart of the matter. Suppose an elected official, such as the Sheriff, is required by the Arizona and U.S. Constitutions, and by his oath of office, to impartially and without bias enforce the law. Can he justly arrest one man doing nothing different from the others— except to question the Sheriff's official conduct?"

There was a chorus of "No!"

"I submit to you, ladies and gentlemen of the Power and Propaganda jury, that using elective office to arrest even one person without probable cause, simply because you don't like his or her views, is an abuse of power, even if a majority of people who elected the official think it's okay."

———————

Asa Johnson convened his fellow supervisors in the conference room. So far, Bardo had brought charges against Marcia Henderson—practically destroying her business by false allegations—and also against Ken Murdoch. But, of course, Johnson had been released from jail after his attorney appeared and the jailhouse judge affirmed the complete lack of evidence.

"Friends, I never thought, when Bardo got elected and continued his campaign against crime and illegals, that we would come to this point where we have been abused simply for doing our duty."

Ken fidgeted, ever avoiding confrontation.

"But," continued Johnson, "I've noticed that several others have sued the MCSO for violation of civil rights—those 'mask' and 'clapping' activists, a Mexican who was here legally but jailed, and the families of the unfortunate inmates who died from MCSO abuse or neglect."

Marcia added, "He ruined my business, Asa—and yours!"

Johnson laid his hand gently on her arm. "I've spoken to my attorney. He believes all three of us have valid civil rights complaints against Sheriff Bardo. Shall we proceed?"

CHAPTER 32

FOOD FOR THOUGHT

July 1ˢᵗ, 2010, Phoenix

As the students left class, Jonah hugged Emily. "Great job," he said, pounding her back in admiration.

"That was quite a presentation, Emily," Ivan added. "You were really in a zone, weren't you?"

"Yes. These guys should never have had to endure any of that."

"Say, you don't have to return to your office just yet, do you? Want to catch a bite of lunch?"

"I'd love to." They walked a few blocks to the Fair Trade Café on Central.

"Mind if we sit outside?" Ivan asked. "I smoke."

"And here I thought you were such a nice guy," Emily quipped. "Sure, if I can sit upwind."

They chose the mesh-metal seats at a glass-topped table in the shade, shielding them from one-hundred-and-five degrees in the direct sun. A string of spray misters cooled the dry heat, extending the livability of outdoor seating in Phoenix during the summer.

A slender young man came to take their orders. Ivan had met him before and knew him to be a recent graduate from architectural school still seeking "real" work. "Hi, Dave," he smiled. "How are things going?"

"Great, Professor W," said Dave. "Say, I have a collection of photos and drawings on exhibit inside. Take a look after lunch."

"I looked at them the other day when I was in for a sandwich. Nice presentation. Good photography and creative design. You're on your way to becoming an excellent architect."

"Not in this job market. But thanks for noticing. May I take your drink orders?"

"Iced tea with lemon, please," said Emily.

"The same," said Ivan. Then, as the waiter walked back inside, Ivan lit up. He inhaled, exhaled quickly, blowing the smoke away from Emily, and said, "I really should stop. They tax these things for a good reason, and I'm sure I contribute to global warming."

"And you have to sit outside, even in the summer. If I hadn't enjoyed your class so much, I might have—" Emily didn't finish her thought. Instead, she focused on her work. "Perhaps one day, some of your students will be new clients for me."

Without a smile, Ivan stared at the pedestrian traffic in the sunlight. "Given this political climate, you are probably right. Oh, I bet I can guess your politics from you being a defense lawyer."

"Really? So, what do you think?" Emily asked. "Am I a Democrat? Or a Republican? Libertarian? Would it surprise you that I think Bill O'Reilly is both smart and handsome—for an older man?"

Ivan laughed. "An older man? When you removed your jacket, I thought you might have a Fox News tattoo on your arm."

Emily stared at him. *A Fox News tattoo?* She relented. "Touché. But let's not talk about me anymore. Tell me about you. How well do you let your students get to know you? I'll bet you have to appear as unbiased as a reporter in this kind of journalism class."

Back on safe turf, Ivan relaxed. "I guess you'd say I'm always in favor of a robust debate and thorough analysis. Then it's really up to them."

They ordered from the organic menu.

Emily gave the lemon in her iced tea another punch with the long spoon and sipped slowly.

After lunch, Ivan paid the bill for them both. "Your video footage gave everyone food for thought, even my wannabe Deputy Sheriff—his dad is one, you know. Maybe you caught that during the presentation."

"I did. Those two always work together—Strong and Snyder. That kid's dad made most of the arrests in all three cases. I did the cross on him in two of the trials."

"Maybe that explains the kid's reaction. He did not look happy. I'm sure that his story is not over yet."

As Emily picked up her briefcase, Ivan said, "Let's have lunch together again sometime."

Phil felt strange, unsettled. The videos from two years ago showed a story very different from what his father had described. And yet his dad had just said yesterday someone in security had gotten hold of Professor Wilder's class list, with names of Hispanics. He smiled with relief when Harry appeared.

Harry said, "El Portal?"

They walked quickly around the corner and caught a quick burger and fries.

Harry spoke first. "That woman lawyer was a sleaze—like she was trying to undermine law and order. What did you think?"

"Yeah. I didn't like her."

"Say, Phil, guess what? I picked up a copy of Wilder's class list from the department secretary's desk. She seemed pretty clueless. I don't even think she'll miss it."

"Wow! And my dad said that someone in security had managed to get into Professor Wilder's office and get a copy too. So we're rock solid. What next?"

"If you tell your dad, and I tell my dad," said Harry, "they'll put their heads together and talk to their bosses. Then they'll figure out who's illegal. Phil, I wouldn't be surprised if you and I get to see a sweep before our very own eyes."

"Yeah!" said Phil. But he still felt bummed about the footage of his dad right there in class with everyone watching.

"Say, Phil," said Harry, "I meant to ask you. Did your father say anything about the mask and clapping trials? I think my dad was the prosecutor on both of them. He seemed pissed. He seemed to think Mr. Shatigan, the County Attorney, had done something wrong."

"I dunno, Harry. My dad said that Mr. Bullard and Sheriff Bardo had ordered them to enforce law and order. What do you think?"

"To tell you the truth," Harry replied, "I think that lady lawyer is a dyke. I think she gets her lesbian rocks off trying to make people look bad."

"Yeah!" Phil said in response. *But I think she kind of liked Professor Wilder.*

For several days Lydia had avoided Tony. Today, Tony hurried out of the auditorium and waited for her in the hallway.

"Lydia, can't you just listen to me? I don't think you're being fair. I talked to my father, and—I want to talk about it with you." Tony tried his best not to be belligerent or begging. It was tough finding a middle ground.

Somehow, it worked. Lydia slowed to match his pace. "All right. But not here. What if we stop at the Chinese place for lunch in Tempe? It's quiet."

"Super. I'll treat." Tony kept pace with her, and they caught the Light Rail. They got off at Lydia's stop and walked a few blocks to a strip mall. A golden awning framed the restaurant's red front door. The hostess ushered them to a high-backed leather booth near the back. Today, after the rush of lunch hour, it was quiet.

After their order arrived, Tony slid his plate over and sat as close to Lydia as he could without appearing rude.

She raised her eyebrows, surprised.

"I don't want anyone to eavesdrop. Okay?"

Lydia nodded. "Okay."

"Look, Lydia, I know some crazy things are going on around town these days. I talked with my dad about your situation, and, well— I know."

The relief washed through Lydia like a cleansing rain. Surprising even herself, she laughed and then used her chopsticks to pick up a piece of broccoli. "What? You tink Mexican girl she no can yooza dee chop-esteecks?"

"I'm glad you have a sense of humor! You've been pretty serious so far. Anyway, I just wanted to say I'm not one of them. Whoever they are. My dad's a Republican, and I'm pretty conservative too, but we don't seek out trouble, especially not for good people. I just wanted you to know that."

"Thanks, Tony. I appreciate it. In class, I just don't know who to trust. The girls around me—well, we're all in the same boat, so we stick together. But that kid Phil. I don't want him to know my name or that I exist. I don't trust him at all!"

"Well, I hope we can be friends, ride the Light Rail, maybe do some stuff on the weekends."

"I'd like that."

———

Sullivan called. "Ivan, come on over. I've found out something you should know."

Ivan put a note on his door in case students showed up for office hours. Minutes later, he found himself yet again in the Dean's office.

"First," said Sullivan, "I checked with security. There was a new kid on staff, one of the guys who sometimes mans the front desk. The MCSO had recommended him. He was on duty that weekend. Our chief officer confronted him. It turns out that he was working inside the school to get information for Bardo. They took the class list from your office and did all the damage on purpose. Shock and awe. See? I told you. Meanwhile, the department secretary also can't find the hard copy from her tray. We may have at least two folks with sticky fingers. And the senior security guy has suspicions about the fellow with the five o'clock shadow."

"The only tip from the list is Spanish surnames. Maybe some other foreign names too. No one would be that crude—"

"Ivan, do you know why they targeted you over any other professor at Cronkite, or at the entire ASU downtown complex, for that matter? Why hit on you alone?"

"What?"

"I frankly think they trashed your office more to intimidate you personally than to find stuff."

Ivan sighed. "You may have bitten off more than you wanted to chew by giving me this class, Mitch."

"You're right. It is more than I want. But you, too, have bitten off a big chunk, agreeing to teach it. We're in this boat together, whether we like it or not. Free press and academic freedom go hand in hand. Cronkite must stand for that. At least now you and I have the only keys to your office."

CHAPTER 33

SURREPTITIOUS PLANS

July 1ˢᵗ, 2010, Phoenix

Jonah and Jester went to Carly's for a sandwich and beer after an afternoon training session for the upcoming rally on July 29ᵗʰ, the day SB 1070 would go into effect. They'd played Urban Capture the Flag in the spring. Since then, work, school, and life had kept them busy. But now, they desired a new creative pursuit. They sat at one of the tables with a view facing Roosevelt Street.

"Looks like some top leadership is coming in," said Jonah. "Sam Aguilar will be there. He's been around for years. A real rock among the Latinos and Native Americans."

Jester asked, "But what about you, J? You're only medical."

"About twenty of us in the health community have formed a coalition, the Purple Cross. The Red Cross and local emergency ambulances don't help inside the demonstration. So we do. We wear white armbands with a purple cross. We provide first aid to anyone hurt in any action."

"Great."

"What about you, J? Capture the Flag was such a hoot, but it's so 'last year.' I can't imagine you're just running in low gear for July 29ᵗʰ."

Jester maintained an air of mystery. "Let's just say it'll involve a bigger flag."

Snyder slicked back his hair in the men's room in a neighborhood bar. Darker than most of the guys at MCSO, with brown eyes and black hair, Snyder looked the part. You might think he was Mexican if you didn't know he was the grandson of a "black" Irishman with some Italian mixed in. Having grown up in a heavily Puerto Rican neighborhood in the South Bronx, he could turn a phrase *en español*.

On this particular afternoon on July 1st, Snyder decided to shoot pool with some *Mexicanos* in South Phoenix when a hot tip surfaced. He had just stepped out of the men's room, surveying the half-dozen green-felted pool tables under faux-Tiffany lights. He approached a swarthy loaner at the bar and invited him to play a round. According to this fellow pool shark, "A hundred and fifty Mexicans are going to meet tomorrow at *Centro de Amistad*, the agency that coddles illegals. It has to do with how you can get legal papers, citizenship, or something like that."

"How do you know?" asked Snyder, leaning casually against his cue stick, awaiting his turn at the table.

"Because I've been the janitor there."

"Why would you rat on our own people?" Snyder stepped up to the table and took his turn, sinking an odd-numbered ball into the corner pocket.

The source heated up. "Well, dammit, I'm legal. And besides, they just fired me because I supposedly harassed some women workers. What's wrong with a little fanny pat?" the source quipped, patting the edge of the pool table.

Snyder reviewed the details again. The source gave the same account as the first time. It sounded solid. Snyder smiled inwardly, feigning a lack of interest toward the *hombres* hanging around within earshot. He left after the game and took off in his car. Since his news had to do with operations, he called Bullard.

"Office of the Sheriff. May I help you?"

"It's me, Snyder. Put me through to Bullard."

"Mr. Bullard told me to hold his calls this afternoon."

"Tell him it's me, Snyder! Tell him I have an inside scoop on a sweep he could do tomorrow morning."

"But—" Eleanor Jones balked. Snyder rubbed her the wrong way.

"Just tell him. He'll want to talk to me. Hurry up." Snyder waited as she put him on hold.

"Mr. Snyder? Mr. Bullard will speak with you. Let me put you through." Another click, a pause, then a pick-up click.

"Snyder?"

"Yes, sir. I've got a lead. There is going to be a huge crowd down at *Centro de Amistad* tomorrow. Do you know them? They cater to illegals. Tomorrow morning they're hosting a meeting with hundreds of people to talk about how you can get around the immigration laws and get citizenship papers. We could round up the whole bunch."

"How do you know the source is legit?"

"The source works there." *Or at least he did.* "He's Mexican himself, I'm sure of it. But he's legal. He heard them talking about it in the main office. The meeting is tomorrow at 9:00 am. Do you think we should have a SWAT team on it?"

"Come on in," said Bullard. "It sounds good. Will I see you within the hour?"

CHAPTER 34

"OH, BEAUTIFUL"

Friday, July 2ⁿᵈ, 2010, Phoenix

Early morning temperatures ushered in the July 4th weekend in the high seventies, expecting one-hundred-and-ten degrees by noon. But in Arizona, as they say, it was a "dry heat."

Congressman Valenzuela pressed down his lightweight suit as he emerged from his car at 8:30 am when it was already ninety degrees. Wiping sweat from his neck with a handkerchief, he approached the chain-link fence outside the community center. At night, young men used this court for basketball. By day it served as a playing field for children whose mothers took English classes or job training at the *Centro de Amistad.*

This morning, a hundred and fifty people would have their special day in this court. The risers, usually stacked outside the chain-link fence for fans, were now arranged inside. The ceremony would begin at 9:00 am. Valenzuela knew that these attendees and their families would be on time. This day was the day they had all been waiting for, had been working for, and had studied for—and they had all passed the test. One hundred fifty people would be sworn in as new citizens of the United States of America.

As predicted, the risers inside the fence filled by 8:45. An overflow of friends and relatives stood to either side. Valenzuela walked to the podium facing them. The Stars and Stripes waved from above one side of the dais, and next to it, slightly lower, the copper star and sunset stripes of the flag of Arizona. The director of the

Centro was already seated on the platform, as was Federal District Judge Dmitri Ivanovich, who would give the oath.

The band from Excelencia High School gathered under the east basket. At a sign from the director, they began with "Oh Beautiful for Spacious Skies" to warm up the crowd and settle them down. A mix of older people and young adults, families and students, laborers and professionals were all present to become citizens or celebrate a loved one who had earned the right to naturalization.

A young woman in formal Navajo dress approached the microphone. The band director gave the student musicians a nod. In clear and delicate strands, backed up by strings and a wooden flute, she sang the national anthem—first in Navajo, the language of her birth family, and then in English, for the country of her birth. Everyone assembled rose at the first note and remained standing, hands on hearts, hats by their side, for the duration.

When she ended, the crowd waited. They were not at Chase Field; these were not the Diamondbacks. No raucous applause signaled, "let's get on with the ball game." No, this was a far grander, far more profound moment than the one coming up in the afternoon about ten blocks north of this run-down, overused basketball court in the shadow of the air-conditioned baseball dome.

Valenzuela acknowledged several local dignitaries from the community for their various roles in supporting newcomers and protecting civil rights. Mayor Stewart gave a short speech about diversity and the multinational heritage of Phoenix and the Valley of the Sun. Then the Congressman introduced Judge Ivanovich to administer the oath of citizenship. The Judge asked everyone to rise as he called their names—involving twenty languages—until the entire hundred and fifty people stood attentively in eight rows facing him.

"This solemn moment is a joyous moment for all of us," he began. "I was in your shoes many years ago. As a small child, I came to the United States as a refugee from totalitarianism in the Soviet Union. I was welcomed in a community like your own. And with the opportunities of public education, the support of my surviving family, and some effort on my part, I was able to complete law school, serve with the Judge Advocate General of the United States Army, enter the private practice of law, and, finally, become a Federal Judge here in my beloved state of Arizona."

The Judge then highlighted three stories of individuals from within the assemblage, their three countries three continents apart, each with a unique language and culture, and each one following a different path to citizenship. After a pause, he said, "Now is the time for saying the oath of allegiance. Will you all raise your right hand and repeat, phrase by phrase, after me?" He led everyone in their new language of English.

> "I hereby declare, on oath or affirmation, that I absolutely and entirely renounce and abjure all allegiance and fidelity to any foreign prince, potentate, state or sovereignty of whom or which I have heretofore been a subject or citizen; that I will support and defend the Constitution and laws of the United States of America against all enemies, foreign and domestic; that I will bear true faith and allegiance to the same; that I will bear arms on behalf of the United States when required by the law; that I will perform non-combatant service in the Armed Forces of the United States when required by the law; that I will perform work of national importance under civilian direction when required by the law; and that I will take this obligation freely without any mental reservation or purpose of evasion; so help me God."

Judge Ivanovich stated each phrase and paused, with the crowd repeating after him in unison, until the conclusion. Then, he looked up from his script at the assembly.

There was a momentary hush. Congressman Valenzuela and Judge Ivanovich looked out over the crowd. Many wept. Finally, it was the Judge's honor to say to the hundred and fifty before him, "I now declare you citizens of these United States of America!"

The crowd burst into applause, followed by tears and embraces.

They had all been so engrossed in the occasion that no one noticed the squad cars from the MCSO silently surrounding the entire property of the *Centro*. With the sudden sound of helicopters thwap-thwapping overhead, Strong and Snyder burst through the gate, followed by over twenty men in black, with bulletproof vests, black masks, and guns drawn. "You all are under arrest!" shouted Snyder.

At first, everyone was in shock. Then, realizing the enormity and danger of the blunder, Mayor Stewart stepped off the speaker's dais and strode toward Snyder, shouting, "I demand to know what you are doing here!"

"We're here to arrest all these illegal people," Snyder said, spitting the word, "who are present on Arizona soil without proper documents. We're taking them in." Snyder began to wave his Deputies toward the crowd.

Judge Ivanovich limped forward, propped up by a four-pronged cane. His septuagenarian frame had suffered from the years, but his mind and commanding presence had not. "Mister—I do not know your name. But I am a Federal Judge. The people you see here are all citizens of the United States. We have just sworn in a hundred and fifty newly naturalized citizens. They have studied; they have worked. Some have already served in the Gulf War, Iraq, or Afghanistan. You have made a grave mistake. Now tell your masked monsters to get out of here and call off those damned helicopters. That's an order!" He leaned over his cane, close to Snyder.

Snyder snapped back, "We're here to enforce the law! We know they are illegal—"

The Judge stood up as straight as his arthritic back would allow. "You are wrong. They are citizens. And I have to power to bring in the United States Army. Do I make myself clear?"

"But we had it on good authority that they were coaching illegals—" Snyder blustered.

"You had bad information. If it weren't your Fifth Amendment right to keep silent, I would demand a public apology from you to every person here. You have terrorized them. You have violated their right to a dignified ceremony!" And with that, the Judge thrust his chin right up into Snyder's face and forced him to back up.

The crowd sat, or stood, immobile, watching twenty flak-jacketed Deputies beat a hasty retreat. They watched as the helicopters circled up and away. They remained silent as the Deputies found their squad cars and stepped on the gas. And, still stunned, they waited.

Mayor Stewart took the mic in hand. "My fellow Americans, what you have witnessed today is the very thing we must fight against. There is evil afoot in this county that would abuse power and deny the rights of our citizens and visitors from other lands. I apologize on behalf of the State of Arizona and the City of Phoenix. But you are citizens. You have just sworn to uphold the Constitution against enemies foreign and domestic. Therefore, you have the right, and perhaps even the responsibility, to file a complaint with the United States Commission on Civil Rights against the shameful conduct of the Office of the Sheriff. My office at City Hall will stand ready to support you. And I believe that Representative Valenzuela will do the same."

The Congressman nodded.

Concluding, the Mayor said, "Now, my fellow citizens, let's go into the community room where Bavarian pretzels, Greek *baklava,* Jasmine tea from Thailand, and Mexican chips and *guacamole* await you. Again, congratulations, and welcome to Phoenix, Arizona, and to these United States of America."

CHAPTER 35

A GOOD MECHANIC

Sunday, July 4th, 2010, Fossil Creek

Ivan rose at 4:30 am. Early dawn brought buildings from shadow to sunlight. He'd spent Friday and Saturday posting assignments, grading papers, and surfing the Web. He packed the Wrangler with lunch, water bottles, and a freeze-dried dinner. The back seat of the Jeep already housed jumper cables, road tools, two gallons of gasoline, the Mexican blanket Marti had bought in Nogales, and a tarp. He headed east out of Phoenix on McDowell Road through the Arizona National Guard HQ and the Papago Peaks. He turned north from McDowell and then drove east on Indian School Road, named not after the Salt River-Pima Indians through whose land he was now going but after the now-closed boarding school for Indian children in central Phoenix. Church and governmental representatives brought Native American children from distant reservations so they would get a "proper" education, which often included the forceful elimination of speaking in their mother tongue from the hallways and playgrounds. He swung south off Indian School onto Mesa Drive and entered Route 87, heat waves shimmering on the Beeline Highway as he headed northeast toward Payson.

The Jeep climbed gradually through the Mazatzal Wilderness until the last saguaro cactus on the southern slope of an unnamed mountain until prickly pear, jumping cholla, and creosote bushes replaced them on the north. Ivan stopped briefly in Payson for coffee, a doughnut, and a cigarette. He then headed northwest, over the

East Verde River crossing, until he reached the town of Strawberry. From there, he took the 708, a dusty dirt road to the west, and soon arrived at a small parking area on the mesa above Fossil Creek. Dry limestone glared hot and barren, save for occasional shoots of broom snakeweed and buckwheat.

Exiting the Jeep, Ivan stretched, took another smoke, and hauled out his backpack. He descended toward the creek, noting the almost instant change in climate from barren desert to scrub oak, piñon pine, and desert holly trees with their little red berries still intact. He reached a rock outcropping and paused. Hundreds of feet below him, the riparian strip of the Fossil Creek stream bed cut a serpentine path through the rock. From its eastern origin at Fossil Springs in the Mogollon Rim, the creek flowed westward toward Camp Verde. Below, massive cottonwoods and sycamores proclaimed the presence of water underground.

Ivan reached the creek in about one-and-a-half hours. Walking upstream, he encountered the towering cottonwoods and willows mixed with Texas Mesquite and box elders. Virginia Creepers, Arizona wild grape, and occasional poison ivy tangled close to the trail. Fossil Creek, unlike its title, bubbled lush and welcoming as it flowed into pool after pool of cool water gushing from underground springs.

Hot and sweaty from the hike, Ivan was relieved to find a spot unpeopled by other weekend hikers. He slipped off his boots and socks, removed his hiking shorts and T-shirt, and stepped carefully into the small green pond. Edible cress growing in lily-pond clusters dotted the edges. The middle of the pool was chest-deep. His feet felt for smooth mud between the pebbles. He dunked under completely, then, emerging with a splash, he combed his hair back with his fingers and laughed to the trees encircling the pool. Cupping his hands, he drank the fresh cold spring water. The aroma of mesquite bushes hung in the air as he dressed, tugging his clothes on over his wet skin. A slight breeze chilled him despite the heat.

After lunch, he headed back up the trail. A willow flycatcher, startled by his movement, flew out of a mesquite tree. Ivan looked up to see a bald eagle coasting on air currents. It was the hottest part of the day, and the sun shone relentlessly. The last half-hour of the hike was grueling.

Back in his Jeep, Ivan struck out toward Camp Verde on the 708, soon known as Fossil Creek Road. The road flattened about a half-mile beyond the creek's last access point. Stuck in the road stood a beat-up Honda Civic with a flat tire and a woman trying to remove the lug nuts. Ivan pulled up.

"Can I give you a hand?" he asked.

The woman rose from her crouch, smudging the grime across her sweaty cheeks. "Ivan! What a sight for sore eyes! Boy, could I use your help. I am so dumb!"

"Emily?" Ivan would not have taken lawyer Hartwell to be the wilderness type. *By the looks of the city car and flat tire, she isn't.*

Emily slumped against her car. "I've been struggling with this thing for a half-hour, and I can't even get the lug nuts off."

"Have some water."

"Thanks." She sat on the ground.

Ivan stood near her, blocking the sun to give her some shade.

"I've been working on an appeal brief all weekend. I had this fantasy of driving up to Fossil Creek and forgetting the city." Emily took another swig from the canteen. "I would take a few sips from a crystal-clear pool, but I haven't even reached the creek. Now it's late afternoon. Some break!"

Ivan brought another water bottle and began peeling an orange. "I hate to say I'm smarter than a lawyer, but I can change your tire. Call it brute strength. Mind if I take a look around?"

She waved a tired hand.

He took the booklet from her glove compartment, flipped to the flat tire page, and found the parts to a jack in her car's trunk.

While Emily rested in the passenger seat of Ivan's Wrangler, he made short work of her easy little Civic. He came around the Jeep's shady side and lit a cigarette, standing downwind with it in his far hand.

"Thanks, Ivan, thanks. I don't know what I would have done if you hadn't come along." Emily sounded grateful but exhausted. "But I don't know how you can smoke those things. Doesn't it dry you out on an afternoon like this?"

"Just a habit," he said. Paused. "Brings back memories. Still, it's just a dumb addiction. I'll stop someday."

"I shouldn't complain. You just saved my day."

"But you said you hadn't even seen the creek."

"Yeah. I dreamed I'd arrive and slip into a pool, enjoy the wilderness, drive to Camp Verde for dinner, and head home after all the traffic."

"Something both you and I seem to have forgotten is that today is July 4th, and being a Sunday makes tomorrow—Monday—a national day off. So, there'll be bad traffic tonight and tomorrow afternoon."

"Hunh!"

"You're feeling sad, aren't you?" Ivan ventured. "I don't mean to rub it in, but I just spent the day paddling in an upstream pool and laying under the trees. It soaked the city cares away. And all you've had so far is a bad trip."

"Tell me about it." She looked close to tears.

What? This is a different side of a tough and articulate defense attorney who went after the Sheriff and County Attorney with such incredible vigor. "Say, I have an idea. Since your car's fixed, let's caravan our cars back to the first entrance by the Creek—it's only a half-mile. We can park there. I have supplies in my Jeep. We can hike upstream. There are pools all along the way. We can have a freeze-dried supper, spend the night under the stars, and leave early in the morning. I'll follow you out in case of another tire problem. We'll beat the traffic." The idea of staying out for the night under the brilliant sky reminded him of years of camping with Marti and his sheer love for the Arizona wilderness.

Emily scowled out the windshield, then at Ivan. "Are you propositioning me?"

"What?" he snapped. "Maybe this is a bad idea! Forget I suggested it."

Emily gulped, caught off-guard by his anger. "I take it back. I didn't mean to be presumptuous. Besides, nobody ever hits on me anyway. It just came, like, well—out of the blue."

Ivan took a drag, inhaled, and exhaled slowly, thinking. Then he said, cautiously, "I'm confused, Emily. I was married for almost twenty years to the same wonderful woman, and we hiked and camped out a lot. I loved being with her and sleeping under the Arizona sky. I just thought, well, you hadn't even seen the creek or the stars. You'd missed everything."

"Oh. I had no idea—"

"I had just thought—"

This conversation was far more personal than Emily had expected. "Ivan, what happened?"

"She died. Four years ago. Breast cancer."

"Oh, I'm so sorry."

"So am I. I've just buried myself in teaching to keep my mind off her. I've hardly gone camping at all since she died. Emily, I tell you, if there's a God, He—or She—is there in the dark starry sky among the pines and mountains."

"I apologize. I didn't know. But, well—"

"What?"

"Could we start over? I mean, could we pretend I never said what I did? Ask me again if I'd like to see the creek."

Ivan looked out at the descending sun. He studied the Tonto National Forest around him, the haze of the Black hills west of the Verde River, and the jagged mountains of the Prescott National Forest. He took a deep breath. "You know, Emily, I wouldn't even know how to put the moves on a woman. But you are an intelligent, attract—" Stopping mid-sentence, he gently removed her dust-covered glasses, took the water bottle, dripped some water onto his neck scarf, and wiped the smudges off her face. "—an attractive woman."

"I'll take that as a compliment. Thanks." Emily managed a smile. She borrowed the wet rag to wipe her glasses and dried them on a clean corner of her cotton T. "So, if you're willing to re-state your original invitation, let's go back to the creek and find a fresh pool."

Ivan hesitated, then ventured, "Emily, trust me. I am not being forward. I think we've cleared that up. But now is the time for you to make the big decision. The moon is in its last quarter. You'd be able to see the Milky Way and the two dippers. I could carry the stuff from my Jeep so we could stay the night."

"Yes, why yes, Professor Wilder, thank you. I would like that very much," Emily replied. "Let me see if I have anything in the trunk that might help." As it turned out, her sports bag held a towel, one water bottle, fresh socks, and another shirt. "Do you have enough food?"

"It won't be Vincent's," Ivan said, referring to the classy French restaurant on East Camelback Road, "but I have freeze-dried beef stew and some granola bars."

They made their way along the trail, passing by the site of the old dam, and continued about a quarter mile until the creek opened up to a pool that spilled out from a four-foot waterfall. "Let's try here."

Emily took off her shorts and shirt. Ivan gazed discretely downstream. She stepped gingerly into the water. "Hey! It's perfect! Come on in." She sank to her shoulders.

"I spent most of the day in the water, so this is my break time," he called. He wasn't sure what other incompetence lay behind the veneer of "I know it all" she'd displayed as counsel for the defense.

As the sun dipped below the horizon, Ivan awkwardly tossed a towel to Emily as she emerged dripping wet from the pool. While she dried and dressed, he set up the camp stove for the beef "delight." As dinner heated, Emily stood nearby, silently enjoying the cooler breeze of dusk. Ivan spread the tarp on the ground, then covered it with the Mexican blanket for them to sit and share dinner.

"I have one Sierra cup and one plastic forky-spoon, so we'll have to dine consecutively," he said, offering her the first bite.

They sat together thus, wordless, motioning the cup back and forth and occasionally sipping from water bottles. Then, crunching the granola bars, they watched the early stars of the evening appear in the southwest. They eventually lay back on the rug to gaze. It was still a warm night.

"What if I get cold?" Emily finally asked.

"You get half the Mexican blanket. If you're cold, you can roll it around you. Or, you can lean against me. I could be cold too. Uh, oh. That was a joke. Don't want to be too forward."

"It wasn't. Maybe I'll need that extra warmth."

A Mexican spotted owl hooted in the distant shadows with the soft echo from a tree downstream.

It seemed to Ivan, as the sky darkened from cobalt to navy, with millions of suns from distant universes twinkling silently above them, that conversation was unnecessary. God's work was in abundant evidence.

Only at Brownie girls' camp had Emily experienced the vast stillness of a night in the mountains. She had forgotten. Its power and beauty came back to her. After a while, she finally spoke.

"Thanks so much, Ivan. This—" Emily paused, searching for the right words, "—this night by the creek is just what I needed."

"Good. You're welcome."

Ivan lay still, thinking of Marti. He looked deep into the Milky Way. He found a star, twinkling a little apart from the others, and he named it for her. While it was not the biggest or the brightest, it flickered gently in the firmament.

Morning found them back-to-back, each with their share of the blanket pulled around them.

They rose before dawn. Wordlessly, they gathered their belongings, bade a silent, visual *adieu* to the glen, and walked back to their cars. They tag-teamed along Fossil Creek Road through Camp Verde and stopped at Cordes Junction for McDonald's egg and sausage McMuffins.

Ivan lingered. He was enjoying the company of this odd, sometimes self-righteous, plain-looking woman. With her hair mussed up and dirt on her clothes, she didn't seem too young anymore. Somehow, sharing just the quiet and the sky had humanized her. He stirred his wooden stick around in the paper cup and said, "Okay if I get more coffee?"

"Me too? With sugar?"

As the dawn became morning, they studied their coffee, feeling the other person's presence.

Finally, Ivan said, "We should be getting on down the mountain. But just in case something happens on the road or comes up back home, shouldn't we swap cell phone numbers?"

"You can have mine, Ivan. But don't you remember? I have yours. I didn't forget it."

The drive back into Phoenix was uneventful. Very few cars dotted the southbound they arrived at Emily's apartment, Ivan parked on the street and accompanied Emily to the front door of the apartment building.

"Thanks again, Ivan. You were terrific." She squeezed his arm with appreciation. "See you soon."

CHAPTER 36

A TRAUMA BOND

July 5th, 2010, Phoenix

Pulling into his driveway, Ivan felt refreshed. It had been such a short escape but so complete. Suddenly, as he turned off the motor, two black sedans with the MCSO medallion pulled up and blocked his exit.

Snyder and Strong hopped out of one car and confronted Ivan. Snyder commanded, "Out of your car, mister. Are you Professor Wilder, the one with the class downtown?"

"Yes. What's up?"

Snyder snarled, "We have a bunch of questions to ask you about several of your students. We think you are knowingly aiding and abetting illegal aliens."

"I want my lawyer," Ivan blurted. He started to fish in his pocket for the slip of paper with Emily's phone number.

"No, you don't. Hands on the car."

Ivan slowly put his hands on the Wrangler. He knew anything was possible, considering what happened in Emily's film footage. He tried to maintain a sense of calm. "I don't know what you are doing here, but I have a right to counsel. Her phone number is in this pocket. And my cell phone is on my belt. I believe it is within my rights to consult an attorney before answering any questions."

They reluctantly motioned him to retrieve the paper. With his right hand on the roof of the car, he crossed his left hand over and, with two fingers, withdrew a slip of paper from the right front pocket of his shorts. He then put his left hand on the car, spread open the paper under two left fingers, and used his right hand to unsnap the cell phone from its holder. Finally, he dialed Emily.

"Hello?"

"Ms. Hartwell, this is Professor Ivan Wilder. There are two Sheriff's Deputies here asking me questions."

"Ivan, listen carefully. Don't do anything to provoke them. I'll be right over. You have the right to remain silent. Tell them your attorney is on the way and you will not speak without me present. Hold your ground—politely but firmly—on this. If they take you to jail, I'll bail you out."

Ivan shut his cell phone and repeated his rights to Snyder and the other deputy. They stood sweating in the driveway as the morning temperatures passed one hundred degrees.

In less than ten minutes, Ms. Hartwell arrived, in legal attire, stepped out of her car and approached them. "Officers, I am Ms. Emily Hartwell, counsel for Professor Wilder. Do you have a warrant?"

Snyder and Strong stared at her.

Strong told Emily, "We want to question him about several of the students in his class."

"It is Professor Wilder's right to remain silent. Professor Wilder, I advise you to say nothing. Gentlemen, unless you have a warrant for his arrest or to search his home, you are without legitimate business here."

Strong and Snyder looked at each other. This woman pissed them off. They'd seen her at sweeps. She'd cross-examined them both and made them look like fools. They canvassed the empty street. No cars moved; no dogs walked. Simultaneously, both men came to the same conclusion.

"Professor Wilder," smirked Snyder, "you are under arrest for aiding and abetting illegal aliens in a criminal syndicate in violation of the law."

Emily stood her ground. "You have no probable cause to arrest Professor Wilder."

"Arrest her too," Snyder told Strong. "Disorderly conduct and refusing to aid a peace officer." Two Deputies from the second car moved in swiftly and cuffed them both, shoving them into the back seat of Snyder's squad car.

Al Freeman answered his cell phone. "ACLU."

"Al, I can't believe it!" said Emily, barely suppressing her rage. "The MSCO was questioning Ivan Wilder, at his house, about aiding and abetting undocumented students. They didn't have a search warrant. I went over to represent him. They jailed us both. We're at the Fourth Avenue Jail. Can you bail us out?"

It was mid-afternoon by the time Freeman was allowed through jail security to bail them out. Even he was in disbelief. "What the hell happened, you guys? Are you sure you did nothing to provoke the fuzz? I know they are goons, but on a quiet holiday Monday morning, at home?"

"I swear, Al," said Emily, "I just told them Ivan had the right to remain silent."

"And that they had no probable cause to arrest me," Ivan added.

Al pondered the scene. "Was anyone around?"

Emily and Ivan spoke as if in a chorus. "Nobody. Not even a dog."

Freeman knew. "These charges are made up out of thin air. And we'll go after damages when it's all done."

"But you shouldn't have to spend your time on this crap!" Emily said, pounding the dashboard.

"Where do you want me to drop you?" Freeman asked.

"Let's go to Ivan's since both cars are there," said Emily, "and then if you want, Ivan, you can come to my apartment." She looked back over the seat to Ivan, who sat in the middle of the back seat. "Okay?"

Ivan nodded. "That'll be fine. I'm too numb to stay in my own house tonight."

Freeman tried to make a joke. "You guys ever hear of a trauma bond? People, like war buddies, are bonded for life because of what they have suffered together. Now you've got your trauma. Yesterday you were just a professor and attorney. Today you are co-defendants. Lucky you." He smiled.

Emily looked at Ivan. For a tall, strong hiker, he suddenly seemed defenseless. "Yeah, well, thanks, Al. So much for sick civil libertarian humor. How about you get another attorney to help Ivan since you'll defend me? Right?"

"Absolutely," answered Freeman. "Probably John McCormick. You know him?" He looked at Ivan.

"Yeah," said Ivan. "Sort of. He called me a few times after the *Dirtbuster* arrests and after your arrest too. Small world." He managed a wan smile.

<hr />

Ivan followed Emily into the living room of her modest one-bedroom apartment. She suggested he sit on the couch while she inspected each room. "Just checking, Ivan. I want to make sure they didn't hit my place when we were in jail. Ha, ha, that was a joke."

Watching her from the couch, Ivan admired her spunk. "Good for you, Emily, keeping your wits about you. Find anything suspicious?"

"No," she said as she headed for the kitchen. She took two delicately carved slender-stemmed wine glasses from the cabinet. "My very best crystal, to celebrate freedom as we never have before." Emily poured two full glasses of burgundy from a box and set them on the coffee table. Despite appearing casual, her hands shook. "Have some wine. It'll calm your nerves."

"Thanks." Ivan took his glass, clinked it with hers, smiled, and took a long, slow swallow.

"Stay there," said Emily. "I have some leftovers in the fridge. Let's stave off our drunken stupor with some food to sop up the house burgundy." She took a plastic container from the refrigerator, popped it in the microwave for two minutes, then divided it onto plates and handed one to Ivan. "Macaroni á la Hartwell."

Ivan smiled again, grateful for comfort food and Emily's competence around the house. They sat silently, still emotionally numb from the hours spent behind bars. Ivan studied the weave of the carpet. He noticed Emily's foot bounce back and forth against her crossed leg.

She took several big swigs of wine and toyed with the macaroni. Finally, she spoke. "This situation is outrageous! I still can't believe it! How can we ever stop them from making abusive arrests?"

Ivan kept staring at the rug. The weight of what happened to them kept sinking in deeper. "Emily, I don't mind saying I'm terrified. I'm still in one ugly adrenaline rush. I don't think I can sleep tonight. When those doors clanged shut behind me, and I wound up in a holding pen with over twenty other guys, I feared the worst. I've never—" He paused. "Nobody hurt me, but two guys went off on a screaming rant. The one urinal reeked. I was petrified." Ivan shuddered. "What was it like for you?"

Emily said, "They put me in solitary, with a camera on the cell, so they could watch me even when I went to the bathroom. Real pervs. Al couldn't arrive fast enough to save my sanity." Emily took a bite of her supper.

Ivan thought about his empty house and the possibility that the Deputies could return and arrest him again at night. A deep, wordless fear shook him.

Emily studied the silent figure of this man, roughly ten years her senior. He seemed helpless and fragile as an uprooted tree in a tornado. "Ivan," she said softly, "would you like to stay here tonight? What if they come back to your house?"

Relief flooded his face. "If that's okay with you. I don't want to go back there tonight. But could you drive me home in the morning in time for me to shower and change for class?"

"Sure." Emily brought a sheet and pillow from the closet to make up the couch for him. Then, sharing opposite ends of the sofa, feet touching in the middle, they continued venting for almost two hours, finally drifting into aimless chatter.

When Ivan finally fell asleep, exhausted, Emily retreated to her bed and set the alarm for 6:00 am. She dozed off to muddled dreams of sorting puzzle pieces and fending off pit bulls.

The following morning, when Emily dropped him off at his house, they shared a hug. Ivan said, "I don't remember being so scared since I watched Marti during her last few weeks at Hospice. I felt so helpless."

Emily clenched her teeth. "I hate them! I hate what they do! They throw innocent people in jail and then drag out a prosecution to trial, beating us down and defeating any opposition through illegal abuse. It was bad enough with the activists and Hispanics who happened to be in the wrong place at the wrong time. But with you and me, they totally trumped up the charges. I don't know where it'll end."

"Tell Freeman thanks. Now we'll be co-defendants. Trauma bond buddies. Ha ha."

CHAPTER 37

A PICTURE, A PATTERN, AND PARANOIA

July 6th-7th, 2010, Guadalupe

Beatrice Milagro took the messages off her landline. She rarely answered that phone. The raid in early May left a palpable feeling that someone had violated her privacy and safety. She listened to the voice messages.

"Beatrice? Hello, this is Eleanor Jones. I have something I think you should see. Can we meet somewhere?"

Beatrice wrote down the number and dialed. "Eleanor? This is Beatrice. Something I should see? Let's meet at the Church of Our Lady of Guadalupe during Wednesday afternoon mass."

The Church of Our Lady of Guadalupe was less than half full. Eleanor slipped into a pew about mid-section on the right side of the nave. She wore dark glasses, a frilly Mexican-flowered blouse, and a sunbonnet—dramatically contrasting her usual tailored, dowdy office outfit. She waited to choose this specific row until the priest, the acolytes, and the choir paraded from the anteroom, down the right aisle to the back of the church, across to and up the center aisle, settling themselves at the front of the church. The smell of sacred incense hung in the air.

The woman already sitting in the pew also wore a full sweeping dress. Her head was bowed, with a hat and diaphanous lace veil screening her face. It was time to kneel. Independently the two women adjusted their prayer cushions and knelt closer together than necessary for such an uncrowded pew. The priest began to intone a series of monotonous prayers. Eleanor carefully extracted a small piece of paper from her purse and slipped it under the other woman's knee. She casually fluffed her skirt in the hot, stuffy church, concealing the movement of the other penitent's hand to the knee and her subsequent removal of the paper. The prayers droned on.

Eleanor waited. Glancing sideways, she saw Beatrice bring the paper close to her face.

Beatrice read the words in Eleanor's handwriting. "Is this yours?" Then she flipped the paper over to see an imperfect yet adequate color photograph of a three-inch figurine: a miniature Pascua Yaqui Easter Antelope Dancer, with the antelope's head and antlers atop the dancer's masked face.

Eleanor heard an almost inaudible gasp, followed by the one word she feared and hoped to hear when Beatrice whispered, "Yes."

For the Propaganda and Power students, it was a day to catch up, return papers, and ask questions about specific news articles and propaganda terms.

Jonah approached with his laptop. "Professor Wilder, could I show you something?"

"Something you want to show me here? Or in my office?"

"Best in your office if you have a minute."

After class ended, Ivan hurried to the elevator to wait in his office for Jonah who arrived and he opened his laptop on Ivan's desk.

"You will appreciate this, sir. I have made a chronological chart of all the cases against day workers and activists since the arrest of the *Desert Dirtbuster* editors in 2007. There are now over twenty cases." He pointed to the spreadsheet on arrests.

Ivan winced.

"The thing is," said Jonah. "Two top Deputies, Strong and Snyder, have led every arrest. Mr. Tanner, Shatigan's jugular vein prosecutor, has taken every case to trial. And *every* case has resulted in acquittal, sometimes even before the presentation of evidence by the defendants. That means the judges in every case—several different judges—declared there wasn't enough evidence for probable cause to arrest any of us!"

The flow chart was precise in detail. The characters stood out in separate, coordinated colors. "Jonah, have you shown this to anyone else?"

"Just some of the co-defendants. But we can't do anything. So, I thought you'd have some ideas."

"I recommend you talk to Ms. Hartwell. I think your flow chart indicates a pattern of abuse. I can't see how anyone would deny it."

As Jonah left, Ivan considered what to do with this new information. It had all the trappings of a federal offense—a pattern of intentional civil rights violation. But right now, he needed to see Sullivan. He thought of Jonah and Emily and how their three lives were becoming indelibly intertwined.

Sullivan's door was ajar. "What's up?"

"Mitch, it's worse! I hoped to say I'd had a great weekend at Fossil Creek over the holiday weekend. But when I got back home on Monday, four MCSO Deputies showed up and blocked my driveway. I called Emily Hartwell to come over and represent me. But when she arrived, they arrested both of us. They charged me with aiding and abetting illegal aliens. Emily and I spent most of July 5th in jail until the guy from ACLU bailed us out. At least she knows someone in high places. I would still be inside if it hadn't been for her."

"Or, you might never have been there in the first place if it hadn't been for her." Sullivan chuckled.

It was Ivan's turn to be un-amused. "Either way, it's getting way out of hand. I don't know where to turn."

After class, Phil ate at a sandwich shop on his own. He was confused over the homework assignment that required an analysis of Senator Hamelin's speech for propaganda. Professor Wilder had provided a list of terms for different kinds of propaganda. He studied the notes over a ham and cheese sandwich. He thought he liked what Senator Hamelin said, but some comments didn't seem entirely accurate—like using the word "vermin." And then *jihad*. That Muslim girl had a valid argument. Later, at home, he looked at the list of propaganda terms again and wrote a first draft of his analysis of senator Hamelin's speech.

When his father arrived home, they decided to break away from burger joints and dined at the local pizza parlor. They took a booth in a quiet corner and ordered dinner.

"Thanks, Dad, for going to a new place."

"It's okay." Strong seemed preoccupied.

"Anything new you can tell me about, Dad, any new arrests?"

"Yeah. We arrested two activists over the July 4th weekend. Aiding and abetting illegals. Mr. Shatigan will be prosecuting. I hope the charges will stick this time."

Phil gulped his soda. "You know that guy, Harry Tanner, who I told you about? The one whose dad works for Mr. Shatigan?"

"Yeah, what's up?"

"Here's a copy of a list of names he gave me of students in the class who he thinks are illegals. Maybe they match the list the security guard got from Professor Wilder's office. There are lots of Spanish last names. Maybe it'll be another case for you. Maybe you can arrest these guys right in his classroom. Wouldn't that be cool?"

"Hey, Phil, you may have something here." Strong looked at the list. "Nice job, son. I'll show this to Snyder and Bullard. Don't be surprised if you see me there one day soon."

"And Dad, this other guy in class is an activist pain in the butt. They've arrested him before. His name's Jonah Whalen. Long-haired hippie. Third-row center. He's always pro-immigrant. Could you arrest him, too?"

Strong remembered Whalen. He had arrested four activists at the BOS auditorium. They were charged and tried, but all were found innocent. *It would be great to nab him for real.*

———————

After checking in with Emily to see if she had heard anything about being formally charged—she hadn't—Ivan went home. He cleaned out the Jeep from the Fossil Creek trip.

A knock came at the front door as he plucked a super-sized dinner from the freezer. Still spooked from the arrest, Ivan looked out the peephole. His neighbor waited on the porch—a rather odd, reclusive neighbor. He unlocked the deadbolt and opened the door.

Elwood Finbach held a DVD in his hand. "Hello, neighbor," he mumbled. "I don't know your name, Mister, uhhh. But I have something I think you should see."

Ivan stalled. "I was just about to start dinner—"

Finbach held his ground. "I believe you will want to see this, Mister Neighbor. Do you remember yesterday when you pulled into your driveway sometime in the morning?"

"Yes."

"And the Sheriff's black cars pulled up?"

A nod. "Yes, again."

"You know, Mister Mister, the government is after us. They're out to get us. I don't trust any of them—the whole lot of them. Some of them have alien chips implanted in their necks. None of us is safe. But I try to protect myself. I've strung concertina wire on top of the fence in my backyard and set booby traps at the gates. The oleander bushes around the yard are four feet thick. No one can get through them. I have coated windows so you can't see in, but I can see out. I often look out my window to see if anyone is there. Plus, I run videos of the street and the back alley 24/7 in case anyone comes to threaten me or try to break in. Anyone."

"And?"

"Those men who arrested you and the young lady, Mister Neighbor. I have every move they made on this DVD."

CHAPTER 38

GOING AFTER ILLEGALS

Mid-July 2010, Cronkite Auditorium

Former County Attorney Robert Shatigan parked the car and checked his hair and mustache in the rear-view mirror. Then, stepping out onto the hot asphalt parking lot, he waited in the blazing sun for the two bodyguards to exit their cars. Together they entered the building marked with the sign "School of Journalism." The men at the front desk nodded in recognition and directed them to the auditorium.

Ivan took notice of the threesome. "Ladies and gentlemen, this is Robert Shatigan, our former County Attorney, now running for Attorney General. Mr. Shatigan, please speak about illegal immigration and the conflicts between your office and other county officials."

Shatigan jumped right in. "I understand that Professor Wilder told you all to register to vote. That must mean you are all citizens legally present here in Arizona. Good. You can vote for me in the upcoming election. I will be the toughest on crime, from prosecuting every capital offense to demanding that all felons get a plea bargain for only their worst offense. People have wondered about the race issue in our office. Let's be honest. The reality is, and has been for years, that high crime rates have beset the African-American community. We cannot pretend they are not a problem. People call me a racist, but I am just being honest. This leads me to illegal immigration. If people come here without papers, they are here illegally. We should prosecute them. If arrested on charges, they should be denied bail, even on crimes for which citizens could make bail. Why? Because, even with a simple theft, they are likely to flee back across the border to avoid being brought to justice. I also oppose coddling those illegals arrested on DUIs. Why pay for the extra court interpreter and staff to run the DUI diversion program in Spanish? If you come to Arizona with the help of a *coyote*, you should speak English. "Do you know what a *coyote* is?"

Phil said, "The ones who bring the illegals—"

Jonah objected, "They're only hard-working people seeking—"

Shatigan interrupted. "Yes, the ones who bring illegals. Those people who cross into Arizona with a *coyote* are not victims. They are co-conspirators. They decided to come here illegally. We will prosecute everyone—the *coyotes*, the illegals, and anyone who aids them in their illegal enterprises. They are all criminals. Furthermore, we should challenge the laws that let children born of illegals here in Arizona get citizenship and free education. They are using hard-working citizens' tax dollars. We should not allow illegals to come here and have their anchor babies become citizens."

Ivan changed the subject. "Could you address the public corruption cases your office has initiated?"

"I have also been tough on public corruption. A judge obstructs justice when he holds a hearing when he shouldn't, doesn't when he should, or rules against me. Nobody is above the law. Wherever I see corruption, I am going to investigate and bring charges."

At Ivan's request, the students gave Shatigan a mild round of applause. He and his aides left the auditorium and closed the door behind them.

Susan, Tony, and Nazrin didn't realize it, but they had taken the same notes and had thought the same thoughts. *He says nobody is above the law, but he's acting like he is. He's appealing to authority as if he's higher than the judges. That destroys judicial independence.*

Suddenly, a loud pounding on both doors reverberated through the auditorium. Bursting through the doors, eight uniformed men in bulletproof vests with guns and tasers on their hips shocked

Ivan and his students. Six strode up the aisles while two blocked the exits.

"What's going on?" Ivan demanded. "This is my classroom. You can't just—"

A megaphone-loud voice smothered his words as Snyder demanded: "We have warrants for the arrest of an 'Alicia Ree-vass' and a 'Lydia Floors.' We suspect them of being illegally in this state. He spelled out their names. R-i-v-a-s, and F-l-o-r-e-s!"

Many students gasped audibly. Both girls were present.

Ivan moved toward Snyder.

Strong shoved Ivan against his desk and commanded, "Stay back, mister. We are enforcing the law."

By now, the six officers had reached Alicia and Lydia as they cowered between other alarmed students.

Alicia struggled to be heard above the commotion. "You cannot arrest me! I have rights as a citizen!"

Snyder barked more Spanish-sounding names and added, "Show us your papers! If you don't have papers, we're taking you in."

Alicia protested. "But I don't carry my papers. I am a citizen—"

Snyder motioned one of the Deputies to take her arm and remove her from the row. Meanwhile, Strong grabbed Lydia.

With tears in her eyes, Lydia surrendered.

A girl sitting closer to the front said to her, "I'll give your stuff to Professor Wilder."

Ivan called out in frustration, "You can't do that! You don't know who is who. You don't know if they have committed any offense."

But none of the Deputies paid attention. Instead, Snyder and Strong shoved Lydia and Alicia ahead of them while the other Deputies cuffed and marched the rest out of the auditorium. Tony was the only student with a Spanish surname who they left alone. His family was too well-known. In all, the list totaled twelve people with Spanish surnames.

Tony sat in shock. *No wonder Lydia was afraid! And I can't do a thing to help her.*

Finally, Susan spoke. "What is our country coming to? So, they can arrest anyone, even innocent people—even a citizen?"

An anguished hush spread through the auditorium.

Someone disrupted the silence, but he didn't identify himself. "You don't know they're citizens."

The students remained silent, still regaining composure from the disruption and arrests of their peers.

Ivan held the remaining students a bit longer. "I apologize to you all," he said, "on behalf of the School of Journalism, for what you just experienced. But unfortunately, all we can know now is that eight of Sheriff Bardo's Deputies, armed and alleging to have a warrant, have taken twelve of your fellow students from this room. When class breaks for the day, I will contact the administration and determine the status of each student. If any of you is sure of their names, or have any of their possessions, stop by my desk as you leave. I believe I know them all, but it happened so fast I'm not sure who the Deputies arrested. I know that every student here is registered to be in the class, and ASU deemed them eligible to attend class as either a tuition-paying or scholarship student. I will find out where the Sheriff's Deputies took them and if they have family who can bring them home. We'll see what happens next."

When Ivan dismissed the class, he took note of the fellow in the back who had said those chilling words. *So, he is the mole, the other shoe Mitch knew would drop.*

Sullivan was waiting in his office. "I already heard about it from security," he said, motioning Ivan to close the door and take a seat. "No, they didn't notify me in advance, and no, I would not have allowed it."

"Mitch, what the hell is going on? I feel like we're in a Nazi state!"

"They must have been working off the class list."

"You're right. The Deputies took only Hispanics and called out the names from the list—except Tony Mendez. But there's nothing—nothing—that says a Spanish last name equals 'illegal.'"

"Give me all the details you can," Mitch said, "and tell me anyone you suspect. I'll go to the University President. We'll call the Board of Regents. Then, we will contact the FBI and the U.S. Department of Justice. If anything else happens, I mean anything, let me know."

After Ivan left, Sullivan sank heavily into his chair, still reeling from the arrests. A soft knock on the door startled him. He did not expect anyone. "Come in."

A beefy red-eyed kid came in and stood by the closed door.

"Sit down, son. What can I do for you?"

"I'm Phil Strong, in Professor Wilder's class."

"Ahh." Ivan had mentioned him.

"Sir, I'm so sorry. I'm sorry about all those arrests. Sir, it was scary. I didn't know—"

Sullivan paused. "Yes, I suspect it was pretty terrifying for everyone, not just those taken into custody."

More silence. Phil fidgeted, wringing his fingers in a tight sweaty twist.

"Is there something you need to tell me?" Sullivan waited.

"Well, sir, um, I wish I hadn't done it. I mean, well, I got the names from Harry, who got them the department secretary, and my dad got the class list from the security guard, and he and Mr. Snyder did the arrests, and—"

"Phil, stop. That burglary of Professor Wilder's office, if that's what you mean, was a felony—a crime. You may say incriminating things. So—please don't go on."

"But Dean Sullivan, I just need to say I didn't think it'd look like that. I feel awful. I may have ruined—"

"Phil, please stop talking. The theft of the class list was criminal conduct. The sweep in Professor Wilder's classroom changes the course of action we at Cronkite will take. Let me remind you that Professor Wilder's class has only a week or so to go. So, any student who can't or doesn't attend his class this last week will have the opportunity to get credit if they turn in all their assignments."

"Oh."

"So, I need to let you know. You don't need to keep attending Professor Wilder's class."

Phil wiped both sweaty palms on his jeans. "Thank you, sir, but if it's okay with you, I want to keep going to class. Professor Wilder's a good teacher. He's even listened to me. I know they all hate me, but I owe it to him."

———————

As he slumped onto the couch at home, Phil felt his cell phone vibrate. He answered it.

"Phil, this is Harry. Cool coup today, agreed? Good intelligence on those illegals. Great job getting the info to the top."

"Uh, yeah, cool, Harry."

"Say, wasn't that your dad with the other one, Mr. Snyder?"

"Yeah."

"Cool! I bet my dad will be the prosecutor. We'll nail 'em, Phil. We'll help get all the illegals out of Arizona."

"Yeah, Harry. Say, I gotta go." Phil hung up.

CHAPTER 39

WHO IS SAFE?

Mid-July 2010, Guadalupe, Phoenix

The phone rang for the fourth time as *Señora* Flores stood at the kitchen counter making enchiladas for dinner. First, the Cronkite administration called to say that Sheriff Bardo's Deputies had arrested Lydia and eleven other students in Professor Wilder's class. They were in the Fourth Avenue Jail to be referred to ICE. Then, Professor Wilder called to express his concern. Soon after, Tony called. However, looking at the caller ID, she couldn't bear to pick up that call, wondering, *did he report Lydia?* But this fourth call was from Tony's father.

"*Señora* Flores, this is Richard Mendez, Tony's dad. Yes, I've heard the whole story. It's horrible. Tony wanted me to call. He's afraid you think he's somehow involved. But I know my son. That is not like him. He would not do something so despicable. Mrs. Flores, I called because Elias Bustamante, from one of the best defense and immigration law firms in Phoenix, has agreed to represent Lydia. He believes all the arrests stem from an illegal search. Mr. Bustamante is at the jail to see if she is there and whether the authorities will release her to his custody. If not, he will track her down at the ICE facility and follow this matter until she is free. There's no charge. And, *Señora* Flores, I am acquainted with Congressman Valenzuela and one of our Senators. They know me well. They know I do not ask for a favor unless it is important. I have asked that they process Lydia's case to give her a green card and a path to citizenship. I am determined to see this through to ensure that Lydia is safe and can stay in Arizona. I believe she'll be free to come home to you by tomorrow."

―――――――――

"Emily? Al Freeman. McCormick agreed to defend Wilder— *pro bono*, of course. We'll sue for damages later. And there will be damages. Say, Emily, we have another problem. We don't know if it's a pure civil liberties case, but the goon squad came to Wilder's class today and took twelve Latino students to jail. About half were women. They claimed that all the students were illegal. I'm sure one of the girls is a U.S. citizen, but she didn't have proof. The problem is some of the others are probably undocumented. One girl, Lydia Flores, is a poster child for the DREAM Act. She came here as a kid and has been pursuing a degree at ASU—until now. Can you help? I'll meet you there."

―――――――――

Ivan was almost asleep when his phone rang. The call display showed Hector's cell phone number.

"Ivan? This is Lupe. Lupe Muñoz. I'm sorry to call so late," she sobbed. "Ivan, something terrible has happened. Someone shot Hector! They tried to kill him!"

"What? Can you tell me what happened?"

"It's crazy, Ivan. Our neighbor, a man we have known for years, started an argument with Hector over SB 1070. He's never been friendly. But this afternoon, he yelled at Hector and told him to go back to Mexico, where he belonged. Then he pulled a gun and shot him! Ivan, you know us. Hector's family has been here for generations. Mine too."

"Should I come over? Is he in the hospital?"

"Can you come? He's at St. Joseph's Hospital. Ivan, I am afraid."

By the time Ivan arrived at St. Joe's, Hector had been transferred from Emergency to ICU. Ivan found Lupe and her eldest son Jorge in the waiting room. "What's the latest from the doctor?"

"He's in serious condition. But the doctor told me he thinks Hector will be okay."

"Did the police arrest the neighbor, Lupe? You can't go home with that nutcase on the loose."

Jorge filled in the details. "Someone called 911 right away. An ambulance came, and the police were there in minutes. Another neighbor who heard the shot ran out and gave my dad first aid. They helped stop the flow of blood. The man who shot him had walked back into his house as if he'd just ended a normal conversation. They arrested him and found the gun. They said they will ask the court to hold him without bail."

"Then you're safe to go home. But my God, that's crazy! Where'd that lunatic get the idea that he could just shoot someone he didn't like?"

Lupe sighed. "You read the news, Ivan. The country is full of hate right now. I guess I'm surprised it didn't happen sooner."

Jorge added, "What's even crazier is that our people have lived in Arizona way longer than he has."

They stayed another hour to see if Hector's condition had changed. The nurses finally indicated that Hector was stable and that they should be able to leave for the night. Lupe, Jorge, and Ivan walked together to the parking garage.

"Want me to follow you home?" Ivan asked.

Lupe gave a wan smile. "No thanks. Jorge is with me. We'll be fine. Thanks for coming so quickly. I was terrified. I don't know what I would do without—" she trailed off.

"I'll come again tomorrow when I finish class," Ivan promised. "Hector's my best friend. We've gotta let him know his teammate is pulling for him."

CHAPTER 40

BAD CIRCUMSTANCES

Mid-July 2010, Cronkite Auditorium

On Thursday, a palpable gloom hung over the auditorium. Alicia had returned to class. The once talkative Phil looked dazed and sat staring dejectedly at his notebook.

Ivan gave an update. "I've been in contact with the administration and the families of the arrested students. Some of them have been bailed out. Others are being held. Some, like Alicia, are citizens. Some are not. I'll let you know everything I learn. The assignment for next Monday is to write a paper analyzing the effect that SB 1070 may have on the State of Arizona and the people living here. A community activist, Beatrice Milagro, from the town of Guadalupe, will talk about her experiences. Her presentation will be your last chance to take propaganda potshots at politicos." He sent each of the arrested students a notice describing the remaining assignments and stated that if they could turn in the requirements, all of their work would count. A special administrative representative would settle questions about final credit. Grudgingly, Ivan did the same for Harry Tanner.

Lydia's absence subdued the Flores family at dinner. Lydia had a good chance of being released, but she was still in jail as of dinner time. Elias Bustamante had called. He updated Lydia's parents about the release of their daughter to his custody that evening. He would bring her home as soon as that happened. When a second call came in from Tony, Jesus answered and handed the phone to his mother. This time she listened.

"Mrs. Flores, I'm so sorry. When you see Lydia, please tell her I'm sorry." Tony stumbled over his words. He tried to say more, but he choked up. Still, he lingered on the phone.

"Tony?"

"That's all. I didn't understand why Lydia was so afraid. Now I do. Just tell her I hope I see her soon."

Early Friday morning, Ivan and Emily met in front of the downtown Superior Court building. They passed through security together and soon found Al Freeman and John McCormick.

"Nice to see you both," said Freeman, and the pair nodded. "Sorry about the circumstances."

They took a central court tower elevator up to the criminal section, soon arriving outside the courtroom of Superior Court Judge Dunmire.

"Do you have a copy of the charges?" Ivan asked McCormick, still in the dark about criminal procedure. So sharp on history, politics, and propaganda, he was on equal footing with all first-time criminal defendants: ignorant and afraid.

"It's simple." McCormick handed him a copy of the official complaint. "We go before the judge. The judge will read the charges and ask if you understand them. You'll say, 'Yes, Your Honor.' Then, he'll ask how you want to plead. You'll say, 'Not guilty, Your Honor.' I'll be right here if you have questions. I'm also here to cut you off if you are about to say anything stupid."

A short, dark-haired man walked by, nodded curtly to Freeman and McCormick, and entered the courtroom.

"That's Harold Tanner. Shatigan has been using his blockbuster attorney on all the political cases. He is supposed to meet with us to suggest a plea. But watch him today—he will not acknowledge your presence. And he will not offer us a plea. They plan to take this to trial, even if they lose. They aim to exhaust and destroy anyone they think is a political enemy."

"I don't even know—"

"Time to keep quiet, my friend. These walls have ears." McCormick nodded toward security guards posted in the hallway as he entered the courtroom with Ivan, Emily, and Freeman.

After court, Ivan explained the situation with Hector to Emily. "He was my best friend in high school. We were both on the Central High football team. He and his wife Lupe have always been friends to Marti and—"

"Go ahead, Ivan. It would be good for you to see them. Let me know if there's anything I can do." Emily slid her arm around Ivan's back for a side hug. "I'll catch you sometime soon."

Ivan drove over to St. Joseph's hospital. Hector had been moved from ICU to a semi-private room and was sitting up, tubes connected to both wrists. A thick gauze bandage protected his abdomen. Lupe sat in a chair on the window side of the room, holding his hand.

"Hola, hermano," Ivan said. "Hi, brother. How're you feeling today? It's nice to see a little color in your face."

"Mejor. Better. The staff people here are top-notch." Hector patted around the edges of his abdomen, making a few plastic feed lines sway between his wrists and the poles near the bed. "Somehow, the bullet missed my heart and lungs and went right through me. It missed the kidneys too. No major organ damage. I'll be going home in a few days." He paused, his breathing labored. "You?"

"Your instinct about security was right on target," Ivan said. "The new kid was a Bardo plant. He and a few MCSO Deputies likely raided my office one weekend. Stole the class list. He's been

225

fired and charged with burglary. We'll see if he names anyone who might have put him up to it."

Lupe asked, "Ivan, what's this I hear about you being arrested?"

"Let's get Hector home before we talk about which neighborhood is safer. I'm out, and I have a good attorney defending me. So it'll all work out. I have a pretty young co-defendant with me to make it tolerable."

Lupe smiled. *It's time.*

"Tell you what," Ivan said, "when Hector's home and feeling better, invite me over, and I'll make you some *chimichangas* from scratch. With all the trimmings."

"You?"

"Lemme see—stripping the beef, mixing the guacamole. I haven't cooked them since Marti—"

"Señor chef supremo, we'll see you in two weeks."

CHAPTER 41

BEATRICE

Late July 2010, Cronkite Auditorium

A week later, a petite dark-skinned woman approached the lectern in the Cronkite auditorium. The students silently sized her up, noticing a tidy package in a short-sleeved olive dress with her hair pulled back in a bun. At most, she appeared to be five-foot-three in high heels. If size mattered, she was the inverse—for a small person, she came with a big reputation.

Lydia Flores had entered with the speaker, Beatrice Milagro. She paused, looked into the audience, and caught Tony's eye. He opened his lips wide in a silent greeting. *Hi*. His cheeks flushed when she smiled. Hushed anticipation greeted Lydia as she returned to her seat. The students nearby smiled, welcoming her back.

Beatrice Milagro scanned the student audience, recognizing Tony. *Tia Beatrice* was Lydia's auntie and Tony's long-time neighbor. She knew Tony's father had helped Lydia.

The daughter of an American Yaqui father and a Mexican Yaqui mother, Beatrice was thus a full-blooded member of the Pascua Yaqui tribe. Her extended family members lived on both sides of the Arizona-Sonora border. She had made a name for herself by persistent tracking of the Sheriff's sweeps of Hispanic neighborhoods and job sites. She worked in tandem with a funny-looking Anglo guy named Rafe, who filmed all of the MCSO sweeps against Hispanics. They weren't lovers, didn't live together, hadn't known each other before an encounter at a neighborhood sweep, and they were by no means "an item." But no other two persons were more destined to spend time together than Rafe and Milagro.

Sources all over the valley would call either Beatrice or Rafe. Within seconds one contacted the other. They, in turn, spread the word via phone or email trees. The activated trees would spread the message further with information about the time and place of the upcoming sweep. By the time the Sheriff's Deputies arrived, ten or twenty observers would have appeared. Beatrice and her allies would take cell phone photos. Rafe caught ongoing action by video cam. Medical teams, attorneys, and the media would show up. How Milagro organized this show of "observers" mystified the MCSO—until the raid on her house and the confiscation of her computer, cell phone, and all her files.

"Ladies and gentlemen," Beatrice began, "I am now under constant FBI protection after the break-in and burglary of my home. But first, I want to tell you that the arrests here in this classroom last week were a completely unjustifiable abuse of power. If there had been an issue of illegal conduct or status of those arrested, the proper action would have been to contact the respective parties at their homes and serve warrants upon them—not make a group arrest! Instead, the Sheriff's goons chose to create a public spectacle to shame twelve innocent Latino students, intimidate you all and create a widespread impression of guilt without due process. Then, about two months ago, my home was burglarized in full daylight. Neighbors said an air conditioning truck pulled up, but the men removed a box of CDs and my computer. An ordinary burglar would take things of value for a quick sale—all my precious Native American artwork and Mexican gold and silver jewelry. But none of my artwork and jewelry—" she fudged a little, hoping that the one missing item could become evidence, "—were taken. This circumstance did not come about overnight. I am a full-blooded member of the Pasqua Yaqui Tribe. My people have inhabited the town of Guadalupe, nestled within the City of Tempe, for over a thousand years. Tribal lands, as people traveled from village to village, have always extended from here to what is now known as Sonora, Mexico. You are probably aware that the United States won the war with Mexico in 1848, creating a national border that had not previously existed between the U.S. and Mexico. Unfortunately, the Yaqui faced a peculiar dilemma. My ancestors have lived on both sides of this border, created in the mid-19th century. Some are Mexican citizens, while others of us are United States citizens. Yet we are all members of the same Yaqui tribe. The United States government has allowed unique tribal identification, with complicated restrictions, to Yaqui tribal members so that some may cross the US-Mexican border within tribal lands and visit family and friends." She paused, looking at her audience. "Does anyone have a question?"

Alicia asked, "What's different about Guadalupe than the other cities like Tempe and Phoenix?"

"Good question. The town of Guadalupe is about one-mile square. We are a small town, and we are virtually all connected by our tribal membership, even though some are married to Mexicans, Anglos, or members of other tribes such as the Tohono O'Odham and Pima-Salt River. I hope I am not confusing you." She paused. "We do not have the large, wealthy population or the commercial and industrial properties that provide a tax base to fund all our government operations. Therefore, the City of Tempe takes care of our firefighting needs. In addition, the Guadalupe Town Council currently has a contract with Sheriff Bardo to handle our police requirements. The problem is that the Sheriff's Deputies, who are supposed to protect the citizens against crime, harass the citizens of our small town. Their conduct is racially motivated. We are all at least partially Native American. The harassment began even before there was an immigration issue. In 2007, when a group of citizens was walking to a funeral at the church, MCSO Deputies stopped them, alleging that the group needed a party permit. I ask you, why would you need a permit to go to church? In April 2008, Our Lady of Guadalupe church held a large baptismal ceremony. The local archbishop presided. The MCSO's squad cars drove around the town, and its helicopters flew overhead. Twenty officers kept a command post near the church. Some children were so frightened they would not attend church to receive the sacrament. Does that make sense?"

Jonah said, "But I've heard a lot about the Sheriff picking on the people in Guadalupe. Is that true?"

Beatrice answered, "Yes. Since 2006, I have attended almost every sweep in the valley targeting Hispanic people. Sheriff Bardo says they are illegal immigrants, but most Latinos live here legally. Many of us are citizens. Sometimes the Deputies wear black ski masks to make arrests in broad daylight—just like gangsters. Why should they hide their faces? When my home was burglarized, rather than taking my valuable art and jewelry, the burglars took my computer, a set of DVDs with photos of all the significant actions taken by the MCSO, and the lists of every person in our phone bank. The only people who could have wanted this information were those in Sheriff Bardo's office against whom I had incriminating evidence. The Federal government must think there is something to my allegations because they have begun to investigate the case and to provide me with bodyguards. Sheriff Bardo says he is, and I quote, 'upholding the law.' But I think the day will come, not too far in the future, when the evidence will show he is the one breaking the law." Beatrice stopped talking and gestured to the students for more questions and comments.

Susan asked, "Were there any fingerprints in your home?"

Beatrice replied, "No, it was a professional job."

Tony asked, "Has anyone harassed the people on the phone list you mentioned since this burglary?"

"Yes. Several people have seen unmarked cars parked in front of their houses in the evening. When these citizens have called in, the police have said the car is from MCSO and has the right to be there."

Agitated, Phil argued, "You don't have any proof that anybody in the MCSO did anything wrong. You're just making wild accusations."

Beatrice held her ground. "I think there will be evidence. But no one else—absolutely no one—would want what they took from my home. It was a political hit job."

CHAPTER 42

ANTELOPE DANCER #2

Late July 2010, Cronkite Auditorium

Ivan nursed a smoke on the north side of the Cronkite building. Then, stomping out the half-finished butt, he headed south past El Portal and through the glass doors, thinking of Marti and Emily. *That cigarette is my last!*

It was Monday, the last week of summer school. Thursday, July 29th, would wrap up a two-month study of Politics and Propaganda, the same day SB 1070 would go into effect. Activists on all sides would again demonstrate and counter-demonstrate, publicizing their opinions of this hotly-contested law.

Ivan addressed the stuffy auditorium full of students eager to complete their summer school session. "As all of you should know from your avid study of the news, the Federal Judge has ruled on SB 1070. Until later this year, when the law will receive a full hearing, she has stopped several sections while letting others go into effect. For example, she temporarily blocked the section that requires an officer of the law to make a reasonable attempt to determine the immigration status of a person stopped, detained, or arrested if there is 'reasonable suspicion that the person is in the country illegally.' It will be your job to analyze why she came to that conclusion."

Jonah raised his hand. "Will her injunction hold up in the long run?"

Ivan replied, "We'll find out. The Judge also—temporarily—blocked a section that makes it a crime if a person fails to apply for or carry 'alien-registration' papers. Those are the grounds on which they arrested the students in our classroom. Another provision that the justice blocked allowed a warrantless arrest of a person when there is probable cause to believe they have committed a public offense that makes them removable from the United States. Finally, the Judge barred the clause making it a crime for illegal immigrants to solicit, apply for, or perform work. The six-page news spread in the *Arizona Republic* will allow you to read for yourself and analyze SB 1070 and the commentators' comments." Ivan paused and looked at his notes. "Before I tell you about your last assignments, does anyone have a question?"

Silence filled the auditorium. The students were still unsettled by the arrests of their classmates.

"Okay, then. First, analyze the Judge's decision about SB 1070 and see what propaganda you can detect in comments by the media pundits. Your second assignment is just for fun and extra credit. Offer predictions on how everything might turn out and why. Since it's only a prediction, there can be no wrong answers. Finally, if you choose, you can attend a demonstration and write about what you observe. Everything is due next Monday."

As the students exited the auditorium, Ivan asked Jonah, "Could you wait a minute?" After everyone had left, he said quietly, "You know the spreadsheet you showed me a few weeks ago? I spoke to Ms. Hartwell. She has an idea for it. Is it okay if I give your phone number to someone?"

"Sure, Professor Wilder. As long as they're not from the MCSO."

Phil avoided all the students and hopped the Light Rail north to his neighborhood. Walking through the mesquite-canopied streets, he thought about how much responsibility Professor Wilder had given all the students. It was way different than the remedial junk he had expected. His cell phone rang as he dropped his books on the kitchen table. He saw Harry's number come up on the screen. He let it go to voice mail and then listened to the message.

"Hey, Phil, it's me, Harry. What's up? Haven't heard from you. Call me, dammit."

At the Federal office building in downtown Phoenix, Assistant U.S. District Attorney Nick Montagne ushered a woman in and closed the door. "Have a seat, Ms. Jones. You said you had something important? And you did not want anyone in your office to know you were coming here? The office of Sheriff Bardo? What are you trying to keep secret from your employer, and why do you want to inform our office?"

Eleanor held her purse tightly on her lap. "Mr. Montagne, I am the receptionist for the Sheriff's Office. I make coffee and clean up for the Deputies." She paused, hesitant.

"And?"

"When I'm making coffee and washing dishes in the lunch room, the Deputies hardly notice me."

I wouldn't either.

"I overhear many conversations."

"What do you have to tell me?"

"Mr. Montagne, my friend Beatrice Milagro's home was burglarized under very suspicious circumstances. I heard the men talking about it in the lunch room. Beatrice said that the burglars took important documents on DVDs and her computer. Now they have the names and phone numbers of everyone on her contacts list, plus all the Deputy Sheriffs who made arrests and anti-immigrant sweeps. She told me that she filed a complaint with the U.S. Department of Justice and that this action violated her civil and Constitutional rights. She told me you were handling her complaint."

"What does this have to do with you?"

"Beatrice is a member of the Pasqua Yaqui tribe. She has a Native American art collection and some valuable gold and silver jewelry from the Mexican side of her family. She told me they took none of these valuable art and jewelry items."

"You seem to know a lot. Go on."

"Except for one small figurine of the Antelope Dancer, one of the sacred dancers at the Pasqua Easter ceremony."

"So?"

"The figurine is about three inches tall, and the dancer wears the head and horns of the antelope as part of his Easter ceremonial dance costume."

"Oh?"

"I have a photograph of it. Here it is." She handed him the little piece of paper.

Montagne looked at the photograph. "Yes, that's how she described it to me. Where did you get that?"

"I took this photograph in May."

"What! Where?"

"It was in the MCSO office. I saw it on the desk of Deputy Sheriff Paul Strong."

CHAPTER 43

PREDICTIONS AND MORE PATTERNS

Thursday, July 29th, 2010, Cronkite Auditorium

The last day of school. Tanner was gone, but eight Hispanic students had returned. Phil still showed up, looking glum.

As the students quieted down, Ivan began. "Class, today it's all about predictions. SB 1070 goes into effect today. You may be involved in demonstrations in the next few days. Just keep safe. Try out your journalistic skills by describing events of history as they unfold. Now for predictions. I'll flash the topic on the SmartScreen. Feel free to make your comments."

Ivan read the topic. "The County Attorney."

Susan said, "He'll lose the Republican nomination for Attorney General. There will be a bar complaint."

Nazrin disagreed, "Mr. Shatigan has a pretty face. He spoke the party line. He will get the Republican nomination and become the next Attorney General."

Ivan noted the next. "MCSO and Sheriff J. Edgar Bardo."

Alicia said, "There will be an indictment against the MCSO for racial profiling. Even the business community is concerned."

Jonah added, "He deserves it. And hey, do you remember the case when they arrested me? Last week after mediation, we won a settlement for five hundred thousand against the Sheriff's Office."

"I saw that in the newspaper," said Tony. "Good going, Jonah."

"You can thank my attorney, Emily Hartwell," answered Jonah.

Ivan said, "A decision like that is a big deal. Of the thousands of people charged with criminal offenses, virtually no one has a valid civil rights complaint."

Alicia said, "It restores my faith in the process. At least in your country—my country—we have a process."

Ivan took a deep breath and read the next topics. "The DREAM Act and Anchor Babies."

Lydia stood up. "I want to thank my classmates. You have been very supportive. Although I was in jail for a day, the ICE people, your Federal Government agency that handles immigration, let me go. I have lived in Arizona since I was two years old. I do not know any other country than America. The ICE officials said they permit me to stay here in Arizona while they process my case. I do not know what will happen. Even if I can't legally work, at least I can go to school. Maybe I can major in criminal justice and help support what is right here in the United States.

"I do not have documents. I am an illegal person here in Arizona. I hope Congress will pass the DREAM Act. Then I will have a path to citizenship. Although Senator Hamelin called my younger brother an anchor baby, Jesus is a citizen. He was born here."

Ivan read the last topic on the SmartScreen. "SB 1070."

Susan said, "My father thinks the Federal Government's prerogative of handling immigration will prevail."

Jonah commented, "The U.S. Department of Justice will find that MCSO did commit racial profiling and will bring a lawsuit to stop the sweeps against Hispanics."

Ivan posed one last question. "What do you think—what do you hope—will happen to the tone of political debate here in Arizona and across the country?"

Alicia replied, "If people can take a lesson from your class, Professor Wilder, we can have a lot better tone of discussion."

Tony added, "Here, everyone could voice their opinion. I thought some comments were really off the wall, but you respected all of us. I may have even changed my mind once or twice."

Lydia said, "I have changed my mind about some of my classmates. At first, I did not trust anybody. But a lot of you were really supportive during and after my arrest. That meant a lot to me. If you can do that, others can start seeing us as humans instead of just calling us names or scapegoating us."

"When I first came to class," said Jonah, "I thought it was easy. Almost all the folks I know without documents are just here to work. But now I realize that it's complicated."

————————

After class, Ivan's cell phone buzzed. He recognized the caller's ID. "Ivan here."

"Ivan? It's Emily."

"Hi."

"How did your last day go?"

"It was fun. The students were quite talkative. Several said how important it was that you brought your videos."

"Glad I could help. So, your class is done! SB 1070 goes into effect as we speak. Tomorrow there will be demonstrations all over town. I will be an official observer. However, you've been in your ivory tower almost all summer. Except for our oopsie with the thugs. Want to join me for a street-side view?"

"Name the time and place, Ms. Hartwell. I'll be there."

————————

Jonah did not recognize the caller.

"Jonah Whalen? This is U.S. District Attorney Nick Montagne."

"Federal?"

"Yes."

"Professor Ivan Wilder said you had a spreadsheet I should see. Could you come to my office? And, if appropriate, would you be willing to testify as a witness before a Federal Grand Jury?"

"What are you doing right now, Mr. Montagne?"

"Nothing that I can't rearrange."

Jonah hopped on his bicycle and rode went directly to the office of the U.S. District Attorney in less than ten minutes.

For the next two hours, Montagne reviewed Jonah's chart of arrests. He made copies of everything. "This is extraordinary! It corroborates all our other interviews—judicial staff and Supervisors from Maricopa County, and almost every case involves the arrests of Hispanics or pro-immigrant activists."

Jonah added, "Several Judges found the defendants innocent. They've all cited no probable cause for an arrest."

Montagne nodded. "A pattern is becoming indelibly clear."

CHAPTER 44

A BIGGER FLAG

Thursday, July 29th, 2010, Phoenix

All the major channels and print media were in attendance in the Sheriff's Office of MCSO on the 20th floor of the Wells Fargo Building. Reporters and video cams crowded the north side of the room, facing Sheriff Bardo, who stood with his back to the south window. Good thing it was a big room—for a big desk, behind which stood the big man.

It was time for the big 6:00 pm press conference. SB 1070 had gone into effect. Freshly shaved and showered in the twentieth-floor locker room, with a newly-pressed uniform shirt tucked obediently into his trousers, Sheriff Bardo collected his thoughts. He planned to continue with the sweeps despite the Federal Judge's injunction. *I'll show 'em I am the toughest Sheriff in America.*

Bardo's office took up the southeast corner of the twentieth floor, its chocolate-tinted ceiling-to-floor windows offering a panorama of South Mountain, the Papago Peaks, the Tempe "A" (from the hill near Arizona State University), and planes landing at Sky Harbor Airport. A construction hole to the southeast—a city block covering Washington to Jefferson (north to south) and Second to Third Streets (west to east)—allowed an almost unfettered view across the southeast valley. A two-hundred-forty-foot construction tower interrupted that view. Now, after the demolition of a city park overrun by vagrants, the big ditch heralded the arrival of yet another skyscraper.

From the air-conditioned office, Bardo, Snyder, Strong, and the reporters viewed the Papago Peaks cast off a deepening red hue as the setting sun brought hazy yellows and blues to the searing July sunset. Bardo was bursting with satisfaction from the events in recent weeks. His base seemed to love him more than ever, despite the call for an investigation of Snyder's disastrous blunder and the dismissal by a judge of all charges against Supervisor Asa Johnson.

Cameras rolled as Bardo opined that the Federal Judge's injunction "will not impact my Deputies. I'll be going ahead with—"

Snyder caught sight of a gnat inside the east window. No! It was something outside, over at the construction site. What? Bardo's words faded as Snyder, hypnotized by events unfolding on the crane, adjusted his vision. The "gnats" were humans! These guy-wire gymnasts slowly let themselves down from the crane's cross beam at either end, like spiders spinning their strands. In the distance, a plane headed for the airport cruised far below the men as they dangled freely on their cables. They hung about forty feet apart, sliding down from the crossbeam, more than two hundred feet above the ground.

Snyder stared. Above the two spidermen stood two other humans on the arm of the crossbeam. A police helicopter hovered overhead. There was no safety net. One slip and it could be splat, like a bug on a windshield. *What is going on???*

Suddenly Bardo's office buzzed. The reporters discovered the crane. All ten cameras facing directly south to catch Bardo's speech, turned in unison to the east, distinctly away from the Sheriff and directly toward the breaking news beyond the window.

Bardo looked around to see what everyone was staring at. *What the hell?* He sucked in a huge breath, blustering, deprived of an audience, as all the major channels swung their video cams toward the action and whispered about the incident starting to unfurl.

And unfurl it did. Slowly, as the arachnid acrobats slithered down their guy wires, dropping vertically from the beam, parallel to each other, a parachute-cloth flag unraveled between them. The flag caught in the gentle breeze and billowed out, thirty feet wide and forty feet tall, one-hundred-and-fifty feet above the ground. It hung, fluttering in the summer wind, directly across from the office of Sheriff J. Edgar Bardo. Emblazoned on the top half of the banner, STOP stood out in black against the white field. Just below STOP floated the word HATE.

Snyder stood transfixed as the actors, finally shimmying to the ground, shook their cables. The sign billowed. Snyder didn't realize that the high-wire acrobats were Jester and Rafe, two of the most determined opponents of the MCSO.

The two gymnasts passed the wires off to supporters and ran toward each other laughing, palms smacking in a big high-five.

Jester was right. It involved a bigger flag.

The buzzer on the front office door startled Eleanor. It was after 6 pm. She was sorting files while Sheriff Bardo gave his press conference. "Who is it?" she asked through the MCSO office announcement system.

"U.S. Marshals. We are here on a warrant."

She buzzed them into the waiting room and slid her window slightly open.

One of the uniformed men showed her a copy of the warrant.

"May I tell the Sheriff who you are here to visit?"

"No. But you need to direct us. We are here to search the office of one Deputy Sheriff, Paul Strong."

CHAPTER 45

ANTELOPE DANCER #3

Friday, July 30th, 2010, undisclosed location

The next morning, with half the Phoenix Police scattered around Phoenix monitoring demonstrations, Deputy Sheriff Paul Strong sat in a holding cell in an undisclosed location that served as the Federal Detention Center. The Marshals had taken him there for his protection. Although the burglary charge could be considered a state offense leading to placement in the Fourth Avenue Jail, locking an MCSO deputy in his boss's facility could have resulted in an overnight murder. Besides, there were federal issues.

A guard directed Nick Montagne to inmate visitor's window number three, shielded from onlookers on either side by a solid metal partition. A guard ushered Strong to a seat on the other side of the thick plexiglass window. Montagne picked up the phone in his left hand and motioned for Strong to pick up his. Then he placed his right hand on the thick glass separating him from the inmate, then spread his fingers wide in the greeting of families who, due to the arrest of a loved one, are deprived of the possibility of touch.

Strong looked at the hand. Then, with some hesitation, his left hand met Montagne's right, finger to finger, thumb to thumb. *Hello.*

"My name's Nick Montagne, U.S. District Attorney. How have they been treating you?"

Dark pockets sagged under Strong's eyes. Even though he could sleep alone in a double cell, the startling reality of the circumstances pummeled his psyche. "Not so good."

"Look, Paul—can I call you Paul?" Montagne asked.

Strong nodded.

"Paul, this must be a shock to you. You've been in enforcement for years—toeing the line, following the boss's orders. You thought you were enforcing the law." He waited.

Strong nodded weakly.

"But you made a mistake. You pocketed that little Yaqui Indian Antelope dancer."

Strong started. "Was that it?"

Montagne downplayed the sculpture. "It's like this. That's a burglary, a state felony, class two or three. Normally wouldn't involve us. So, why'd you do it?" Montagne had seen many a man fall to pieces in detention. But the look on Strong's face was the saddest he had ever seen.

"I just thought about the missus. If she was still alive—" Strong choked up.

Montagne waited for him to regain composure.

"If she hadn't died this past winter— I just thought how much she would have liked it. We were in the house for a completely different op, but when I saw that little statue, I thought of her and—" Strong stopped speaking. He took his fingers from the glass, wiped his eyes, and grasped the phone with both hands. "I ruined everything!"

Montagne chose his words carefully. "It was a major slip. But Paul, first, let me say I'm so sorry for your loss. And even though we haven't gotten to it, I know you're worried about your son Phil. We've notified him of your whereabouts. He's nineteen, we know, but still, it's scary to be without both parents at home so suddenly."

"Thank you."

"The thing is, Paul, that we have this mounting other evidence. Evidence that includes you and other people in the MCSO. I'm sure you're aware of the number of arrests of Hispanics, many of whom were law-abiding citizens. Just in the wrong place at the wrong time, right?"

Strong nodded.

"And you were part of the team that arrested many activists later acquitted by several Judges."

"Yeah." Strong shrugged.

"So, Paul, the situation is like this. I don't believe you intended to abuse your power. I don't believe you intended to do racial profiling. I honestly believe you thought you were enforcing the law and doing your job as you should."

"Yeah."

"But, Paul, an increasing number of people see it another way. Several judges and lawmakers think there was an abuse of power and racial profiling at the highest levels of the MSCO."

"Oh."

"The highest levels."

"Oh."

"And I don't think you carry the most responsibility for what has occurred."

"Oh."

"I know you worked with Len Snyder in almost every operation."

"Yeah."

"And, if you can think back, you can probably remember things Snyder said or did that were out of line."

"Yeah."

"Paul, I suspect that you even remember the number of times Chief Deputy Bullard or even Sheriff Bardo himself gave orders on how to execute an operation."

Deputy Strong began to understand. Finally, he could feel firm ground reappearing underneath his feet. "Yeah."

"But, Paul, burglary is a felony if it's in a residential structure, and criminal trespass is also a felony. Furthermore, if there is a search without a valid warrant, it's a violation of the Fourth Amendment. A Federal offense."

For Strong, the gravity of likely prison time began to sink in. "But my son. I can't leave him alone—"

"Paul, this is a grim situation. We've looked at the evidence on persons of interest. We believe you have intel about other individuals in the MCSO and the County Attorney's office that could help us evaluate the information more accurately. Cooperation with names, dates, and places could mitigate your charges and reduce sentencing. I'll give you some time to think about it. Do you understand?"

Holding the jail phone close, MCSO Deputy Paul Strong whispered, "Yes."

CHAPTER 46

AN INVITATION OR TWO

Friday, July 30th, 2010, Phoenix

Ivan and Emily drove to the Fourth Avenue Jail.

A dozen protesters had chained themselves across the entrance to the MCSO garage. Metal tubes sliding across the chains made disconnecting the chains almost impossible. Finally, several Deputies managed to separate the activists' chains with bolt cutters. Hours dragged before Bardo's cars emerged for the touted but much-delayed early morning "anti-illegal" sweep. Count one for the activists.

All the chained protesters were arrested for trespass and jailed. Count one for the MCSO.

Emily and Ivan returned to Steele Park on Indian School Road, where a large crowd was forming to march down Central Avenue and over to the Federal Court building. Thousands of noisy and dramatic protesters hailed from Los Angeles, Chicago, and New York, many carrying signs. As the demonstrators moved south along Central Avenue, Emily and Ivan looked to see if police were making improper arrests.

"Ivan, see that older man sitting on the curb? It looks like one of the Phoenix police is about to arrest him. Let me go see what's up." Emily asked the officer some questions.

The man looked ill and seemed to be having a great deal of difficulty breathing.

Suddenly Jonah arrived on a bicycle, a purple cross painted on his white armband. Jonah offered the man a bottle of water and took his blood pressure. Emily and the officer stood back as Jonah helped him walk to a bench on the sidewalk, in the shade, away from the crowd and the march.

Emily returned to Ivan's side. "It looks like Jonah helped avoid one unnecessary arrest today."

Meanwhile, sympathetic copycats on both sides of the immigration issue also demonstrated in Colorado and California.

It was a day of peaceful protests against SB 1070 with some pro-SB 1070 activists at the Federal Courthouse Plaza.

———————

As evening approached, Ivan invited Emily to Durant's for a quiet dinner, far from the madding crowd. Familiar legislators and City Council members chatted quietly in this well-known political haunt. The waitress seated them in a dimly lit leather booth in the far corner.

"Thanks, Emily. It was good to be on the street to see what the activists did and to watch you move around observing, taking notes in case something misfired."

"The Phoenix police generally handle the situation more professionally than the Sheriff's people."

"Better than getting arrested again, right?"

Emily grinned. "I wonder if we will have to go to trial, given the footage provided by your neighbor."

They ordered dinner. By now, both had become accustomed to a comfortable silence that sometimes sat like a welcome friend between them. This evening, though, the silence was awkward.

Ivan cut his steak. "Emily," he began, a piece of meat poised on his fork, "Someday soon, I want to show you something."

Emily sipped her ice water.

Ivan chewed slowly.

"What do you want to show me?"

"We've gotten to know each other somewhat, right?"

"Yes."

"And you're a crackerjack trial attorney, correct?"

"Yes."

"And I'm a competent mechanic, true?"

"Yes. And why do I feel like you're cross-examining me?"

"And we're now co-defendants in litigation, isn't that so?"

"Yes. You didn't answer my question."

"That's because you are my witness, and I'm cross-examining you. You can only answer yes or no. Cut me a little slack, Emily. I'm new at this."

She smiled. "So far, you're doing a pretty good job."

"Okay, let's move on, Ms. Hartwell. And have I been a danger to you?"

"No." *Very much a no.*

"In fact, wouldn't you say I helped you out of a pickle, and on July 4th of this year, I helped you enjoy one of the best nights of your life?"

"Where are you heading with this, Professor Wilder? Relevance?"

"Your honor," Ivan said toward the waiter across the room, who could not possibly hear a word, "I will demonstrate relevance shortly." Then, turning back to focus on Emily, he continued. "Ms. Hartwell, have you ever been to Hart Prairie?"

"Ahhhhhhhhh. So that's where you're going with this. No. Isn't that somewhere around Flagstaff? What's so special about—?"

"And so far, you have found me to be trustworthy?"

Sigh. "Yes. You win. What do you have in mind?"

"Ladies and Gentlemen of the jury, what you have heard just now from the witness is that she knows I am trustworthy," Ivan stated again to the out-of-earshot waiter. To Emily, he said, "On August 12th, I want to drive you out on the Hart Prairie Road for an overnight camping trip to spend an evening gazing at the sky."

"Mmmm. And what is so special about that particular night?"

"Ms. Hartwell, I have it on good authority that the evening will not be a waste of your time."

"You are such a man of mystery. Sure, if it broadens the horizons of a workaholic city girl, I'm game."

Ivan smiled. "Bring a sleeping bag and a sweatshirt. And like we say out of court, you can trust me."

He paid for their dinners and then dropped her at her apartment. As she stepped out and headed for her front door, he said, "Goodnight, Emily. See you next week."

Heading home alone, he stopped at his front door, the queasy feeling of confronting the MCSO not entirely gone. Grateful to his paranoid neighbor, he waved at a camera hidden among the oleanders and went inside.

CHAPTER 47

MORE EVIDENCE

Tuesday, August 3rd, 2010, Cronkite Campus

Ivan grabbed a burrito and a large coffee at El Portal, thought about one last smoke, and stopped. He had finally mustered the courage to call a specialist to help him kick the habit. It had been cold turkey, but Ivan already felt a difference in outlook—a feeling of solid resolve and hope. Then he strolled through the entrance and took the elevator upstairs. He placed the stack of papers in alphabetical order by last name on the table inside the door for the students to pick up.

After a while, a quiet knock presaged the onslaught of office hours. Students came in steadily, some offering thanks for the class and then leaving with their papers and grades. Some dropped off extra-credit reports from their weekend observations.

After a lull, another knock came, but the door didn't open.

"Come on in," Ivan called from his desk.

Phil entered and closed the door behind him—slumped shoulders, eyes red, brows furrowed.

"Want to sit down?" Ivan motioned to a chair on the other side of his desk.

"No thanks. Uh—"

"I'll lock the door. That way, no one can barge in."

"Thanks, yeah." Phil landed heavily in the seat as Ivan returned to his side of the desk.

"Phil, you can talk to me. You know I don't bite. What is it?"

"Professor Wilder, I didn't think the arrest would look like that! I mean, when the Deputies took the girls away. And the others. They were just like me, just students. And they took only the Hispanics. Harry gave me those names. I just handed them to my dad. I didn't realize how it would go down. I just—" Phil looked at his hands, picking a hangnail.

Ivan had known this much from Sullivan. He had not expected to see Phil again, thinking either the kid got what he wanted or might have been ashamed. But here the guy was, making an unsolicited apology. "That must have been pretty painful, knowing your people, the guys from the MSCO, could be pretty rough. And your dad is one of them. So, it must have been hard for you to watch all that, feel everything, and then still come to class."

"Yeah."

"Phil, this may sound odd, but I think it took courage for you to keep showing up, knowing that many students probably suspected you because of what you had said in class. I respect you for that."

"That's not all, Professor Wilder." Phil paused. Then he gulped. "You know the burglary of Ms. Milagro's house that she mentioned in class? I didn't believe her. I thought it was a crazy accusation. But it really was done by Sheriff Bardo's men. My father was one of them. Some U.S. Marshals arrested my dad for stealing a sculpture from her house on Thursday night. I'd seen it on his desk. He had said he thought my mom would have liked it if she was still alive. I never realized he stole it!"

"Your father?"

"Yeah. Dad's been in some Federal Jail all weekend. They let me see him on the weekend. I've been on my own at the house. They're thinking about letting him out on bail—" Phil looked up at Ivan with red, watery eyes.

They both sat still, absorbing the weight of Phil's disclosure.

Finally, Phil stood up and turned as if to go, standing awkwardly in front of the desk, hands limp at his side.

Ivan moved around the desk and hugged this hulk of a kid who, just weeks ago, had been so cocksure of himself. Phil leaned into him, head on Ivan's shoulder, shaking in hesitant sobs.

They stood there for a few minutes, Phil trying to pull it together, Ivan propping him up.

Another knock at the door broke the moment.

"Here's a tissue," Ivan whispered. "Just a minute," he called in a cheery voice that would carry to the hall. Quietly, he asked, "You okay now?"

Phil nodded.

"Take your papers, Phil. I want you to know that I did not expect much from you since I knew you were a repeat after the spring semester. But you surprised me. You did a good job and earned a B."

"Thanks, Professor Wilder—"

"The going will be rough for a while. But hang in there. You've learned some painful lessons. And if you ever want to talk, call me. I'll be here."

After the last students picked up their papers and left Ivan's office, he called Nick Montagne.

The U.S. District Attorney came on the line. "Calls are adding up, Professor Wilder. You too?"

"I guess you've heard this line recently, Mr. Montagne, but I think I have something you should see."

"Come on over. Now's a good time."

Half an hour later, they watched the paranoid neighbor's video.

"By now, you'd think I would be conditioned to abuse in its raw form," commented Montagne as he watched the two Deputies shove Ivan and Emily into the MCSO sedan. "But I'm not. I was raised on integrity, on the principles of carrying out our Constitutional duties. These arrests offend the hell out of me, violating people's civil rights with impunity."

"I have to hand it to my paranoid neighbor," said Ivan. "If it hadn't been for him, yet another abuse would have gone unrecorded."

"Maybe he's just realistic."

At a small conference room on the ground floor of the Arizona Supreme Court building, Elliot Forbes, Assistant Counsel for the Arizona Bar Association, watched Emily's DVDs from the 2008 arrests. "Ms. Hartwell, you certainly had good evidence as you went to trial."

"The prosecution's own videos, Mr. Forbes. Ironic, isn't it, that they would keep the footage that would be so damning to themselves. But from their behavior, I don't think they realized how bad they were."

"You know that you and your clients are small potatoes compared to some of the other cases involving the County Attorney. Mr. Shatigan was not shy about going after big fish—judges, developers, and county supervisors. If there is a bar complaint against the former County Attorney, it's possible that the authorities might not mention or even include your letter."

"I recognize that, Mr. Forbes. But at the same time, I felt professionally obligated to contact the ethics committee. I believe in practicing law according to our rules. His conduct, and Mr. Tanner's, ranged so far outside the pale that I was frankly stunned. I think the judges have all been horrified."

"Well, as you know, it's a process that takes a long time. Thank you for showing me the footage of the arrests. May I keep these DVDs as potential evidence?"

"By all means."

CHAPTER 48

A NEW VICTIM

Early August 2010, Phoenix

Unsettled by an inexplicable anxiety, Harry wandered into his father's office. Mom had abruptly taken off to visit relatives in Utah, saying she wasn't sure when she would return. Dad had left the house shortly afterward, extremely angry, and didn't say when he'd be back.

His father's computer screen listed over thirty dates and titles of documents and referenced specific DVDs. "Willow, 1992. Drape, 1997. Twin Sisters, 2001." The list went on. He looked at the DVD case next to the computer, a case that sat on the floor somewhat out of view. The labels on the spine of each disc case matched one of the titles on the screen. He picked one at random, dated 1993, and inserted it into the C drive.

At first, the shapes were gravelly. Gradually Harry perceived discreet figures. There was video footage of girls, not yet teenagers, in various positions of sexual activity. Riveted to the screen, Harry clicked the mouse to continue. Semi-clad or naked girls moved about on the screen as if following directions. The girls' eyes would sometimes face what must have been the person making the video. Some girls were gaunt, others expressionless, but the intent of their movements and positions was something any twenty-one-year-old man would understand. They were offering or performing sex— vaginal, oral, and anal—with adult men. Harry, fascinated and repulsed, became aroused. *But the girls are too young! They've got to be just kids. Is this what child porn is all about?*

Abruptly the scene changed. It was another under-lit room, but the images now showed naked boys. In groups of two, they were simulating oral or anal sex with each other. Some appeared to be posing for the camera. In like manner, the boys' childlike faces showed vacant emotions in contrast to the explicit nature of their bodily movements.

A lone boy appeared on the screen in his underpants. He seemed to be three or four years old. He had his back to the camera. A garish shag rug in front of the bathtub covered part of the stark white bathroom tile. It seemed that someone was directing the boy to remove his underpants. Harry watched with titillated apprehension as the lens zoomed in on the boy's buttocks. He turned around as if ordered to face the camera. The boy handled his penis, which became hard. He played with it for a few seconds as if under instruction. Then he peed into the toilet.

Something is wrong. The tile looks familiar. Harry broke into a cold sweat as the video panned briefly to the boy's face before fading out. *This isn't documentation for a prosecution. Dad was filming me!*

Suddenly the doorbell rang. Harry opened the door. Four Phoenix police officers crowded onto the porch.

"Are you Harold Tanner?" one asked.

"No, officer. I'm his son Harry. He's out tonight. I don't know where he has—"

"We have a warrant to search the house," said another. "Is anyone else home?"

"No, my mom went to Utah."

The four officers entered the house. Two moved quickly past Harry and found his father's office, where images were still on the screen. "Hey, guys, you need to see this." The two officers guarding Harry brought him into his father's office. The images on the DVD showed two young boys in explicit poses.

"No!" Fear chilled Harry's flesh. "Wait a second! This isn't what it looks like—"

"Harry Tanner, you are under arrest. You have the right to remain silent. And we are authorized to take you into custody."

CHAPTER 49

PERSEUS AND THE GORGON

August 12th, 2010, Flagstaff

After packing the Wrangler, Ivan drove to Emily's apartment, just as they had agreed. While waiting for her, he read the story downloaded from the Internet.

> "Perseus was the first of the mythic heroes of Greek mythology whose exploits in defeating various archaic monsters provided the founding myths of the Twelve Olympians. Perseus killed the Gorgon Medusa. Zeus came to Danae in the form of a shower of gold, and soon Perseus was born."[3]

> "With cloudless skies and in a dark viewing site, observers can expect to see between 60 and 100 shooting stars each hour of the night of the peak. The meteors appear to originate from a point in the constellation of Perseus. Unlike many other astronomical phenomena, watching meteors needs no special equipment and in fact they are best viewed with the unaided eye. August 12th will make the annual maximum of the Perseid meteor shower. At its peak and in a clear dark sky, up to eighty shooting stars or meteors may be visible."[4]

When Emily appeared, Ivan got out to help load her gear in the back seat. Driving in light traffic, they soon passed Black Canyon City. They wound their way uphill through the serpentine section of I-17 until it gradually flattened out on the high chaparral mesa approaching Cordes Junction.

"I'm guessing you haven't done much hiking, Emily?" Ivan said as they passed the turnoff to Prescott, continuing toward Flagstaff.

"No, I've been far too addicted to my work," Emily replied, taking in the view of the mountains in the distance.

They descended into Camp Verde and started the final climb past the Route 179 turnoff to Sedona.

Emily appeared relaxed, watching scrub oak disappear as juniper and the taller Ponderosa dominated under a sky dotted with puffy white clouds.

"Well, you know, every addiction can have its downside," Ivan said, smiling. "Are you breaking your workaholic habit by enjoying the outdoors side of Arizona?"

"Absolutely."

"Speaking of addictions, have you noticed anything different about me recently?"

"No, should I?"

"I went to see a doctor."

"Are you sick? You didn't tell me."

"You didn't ask."

"Smart aleck."

"Ms. Hartwell, did you see me smoke any cigarettes at the demonstration on July 29th?"

"Come to think of it, no."

"Did I take a cigarette break at Durant's during dinner?"

"No."

"For seven hours. Didn't that raise some suspicions?"

"I was busy thinking of other things—like people possibly getting busted."

"I guess you're right. But I didn't."

"What?"

"Smoke."

"Oh?"

"I've quit cold turkey, it's already been two weeks, and I've started going to a support group. We decided to call ourselves NA for Nicotine Anonymous."

"So?"

"I have to credit you with some of my motivation. I'd been hanging on to this crummy little habit since Marti was in hospice. It was ironic. It seemed to be a way to still be with her."

"Did it work?"

"For a while, yes. But after I named a star after Marti—that weekend you and I met up at Fossil Creek—it seemed that she started scolding me."

Emily remained silent.

"After spending time with you, it seemed less of a good idea."

"Ahh." Touched by Ivan's vulnerable admission, Emily kept her eyes on the mix of juniper and Ponderosa covering the roadside hills in the climb uphill past Mund's Park.

"The least you could say is congratulations or good effort."

Emily replied softly, "Good going, Ivan."

Arriving in Flagstaff, Ivan drove north on Milton and then under the railroad tracks as the road curved east and became Main Street, the nationally known Route 66. After they stopped to buy binoculars and insect repellent at the local Peace Surplus, Ivan said, "I seem to be the tour guide tonight, so let me suggest a nice little place to eat called Stage Left—a local spot just west of the Orpheum Theater. Let's get some sandwiches and a beer and sit outside."

"Sounds great. The weather is so pleasant."

A handsome local guitarist in jeans, boots, and a cowboy hat regaled fans with his country "I done her wrong" songs. Friends came by, bought supper, and listened. A few couples with small children occupied two tables close to the south end of the patio. Their kids, familiar with the venue, ran between tables without disrupting the musician or the fans.

"I wish we had more places like this in Phoenix," lamented Emily. "There's such a nice feel of people knowing each other, being part of a community."

"I love my work at ASU so much I'd have a hard time leaving town," agreed Ivan. "But it's so inviting here. I know a few professors at NAU. I'll aim to spend a few more weekends here."

After an hour of country music listening, they dropped a well-earned ten-spot in the musician's guitar case and headed out. Ivan turned north onto Route 180, the Fort Valley Road, toward the South Rim of the Grand Canyon. Twenty minutes later, they turned right off the highway, heading east and uphill on a dirt road. At approximately eight thousand feet, the mountain left the oaks behind. Soon the Ponderosa mingled thickly with Douglas fir. Gray-green aspen leaves trembled in the light evening wind. After about a mile, they parked the Wrangler. They took their sleeping gear and packs and, walking a few hundred feet, their flashlights soon helped them find a flat spot in the open meadow of Heart Prairie. An occasional stretch of the old broken-down fence of pine logs bordered the fields.

They spread out the tarp together and then set down their sleeping bags on the cushions on top of it. Emily donned her sweatshirt to be cozy in the dusky chill air.

"Before you slide into that bag, Emily, just look up." Ivan was already staring at the sky.

Gazing at the stars, Emily exclaimed, "Wow, what a night! The air is so fresh, and I love the scent of the Ponderosa and spruce." She did a 360-degree turn and admired the tops of the trees silhouetted against the darkening sky. "I'll keep my balance if I'm sitting down." She sat on the tarp and quickly tucked her legs into her mummy-style sleeping bag.

Ivan stood a few more minutes taking in the stars and then slid into his. "Keep watching, Emily, you are about to witness the Perseid meteor shower."

The southwestern sky showed only the shadow of a crescent as the new moon moved into its first quarter. Soon, it would slip below the horizon and stop competing with its astral cousins. Then the already cloudless night would provide a perfect stage for the show. They didn't have to wait long. Soon, a spattering of meteors illuminated the sky. Seeming to originate from a central cluster named the Perseid constellation, shooting stars zoomed across the sky every few seconds, their golden dust particles falling and fading into the darkness.

"So, this display is what you wanted to show me?"

"Yes. But not just because it's beautiful."

"Does there have to be any other reason? The sky is magnificent."

"Emily, the other reason is you. You exemplify the myth of Perseus. Taking on those three lawsuits, getting verdicts of not guilty, and then winning damages claims against the MCSO makes you a modern-day Perseus slaying the snake-haired Medusa. And Lord knows Bardo and his shop of horrors are about as ugly as Medusa and her head full of serpents. The Perseid Meteors remind me of your part in slaying the Gorgon—if our local Gorgon will ever be slain."

"Wow! Thanks." Emily was quiet for a moment. Then she said, "Ivan, I know I said it earlier, but congratulations on kicking the habit. You stepped out into new turf—beating an addiction."

"Thanks. I'm glad you like the evening sky. I like the company too, Em."

Silence took over. Meteor sprays burst across the sky every few minutes and burned into oblivion.

Finally, after a pronounced, very audible yawn, Emily said, "Now I'm going to sleep." She rolled toward Ivan and surprised him with a quick kiss on the cheek, rolled back on her other side, and curled up like a cocooned butterfly.

Ivan lay awake a while longer, gazing at the intermittent shower of golden sparkles evaporating into the midnight ether. Soon he spotted his special star. *Marti, if you don't mind, I'm breaking two habits. First, I finally quit smoking—for you. Second, I will stop living like a hermit and appreciate life while on this side of the firmament.*

CHAPTER 50

WALTER CRONKITE WOULD BE PROUD

Late August 2010, Cronkite Auditorium

Almost three years since John McCormick had called to tell him of the arrest of Bradley and Woodward at the hands of the Maricopa County Sheriff's Office, Ivan stood at the lectern in the auditorium at the ASU Cronkite School of Journalism.

Tripods, cameras, and reporters formed a phalanx in the first row. Elected officials, attorneys, members of the Board of Regents, and the curious public had filled the auditorium early. Hector and Lupe sat toward the back of the room.

A neatly dressed mid-sized man with salt and pepper hair approached Ivan. "Professor Wilder, we haven't met, but I wanted to say hello. I'm Asa Johnson from the Board of Supervisors. Your class this past summer and some of the footage from Ms. Hartwell's trials exposed the ugliness we had to contend with. I hear you handled it with professionalism and balance. Thank you." He returned to join other officials in one of the front rows.

Emily, fifth-row center, smiled at Ivan. Rafe manned one of the cameras. The photograph on the Internet of Rafe and Jester shimmying down their cables, unfurling the flag, had made national news. Bardo and his guys could never track them down.

The Attorney for the University provided an overview of the events that led up to the lawsuit. Cronkite had filed a Notice of Claim in Federal Court against the County, Sheriff Bardo, his Chief of Operations Sid Bullard, and Deputies Paul Strong and Len Snyder for violating Ivan's civil rights through the office burglary and the rights of the twelve arrested students with Spanish surnames. Dean Mitch Sullivan of Cronkite, Dean Allen McNeil of Public Policy, the Provost of the University, and the Chairman of the Board of Regents, stood alongside Ivan. Behind them, on the SmartScreen, ran the video of the Cronkite marquee with "Freedom of the Press" and the words of the First Amendment running in a continuous loop.

Ivan realized that in a few short months, the defendants had become plaintiffs. "Enforcers of the law" faced civil and criminal charges. It was the most significant Federal lawsuit against State officials since the 1960s. Starting with the arrests of Deputy Strong and the unfortunate young Harry Tanner, an odoriferous pile of information had landed in the office of the U.S. District Attorney. At the Federal level, a Grand Jury had taken testimony from Jonah, Beatrice, Eleanor, Alicia, Ivan, Emily, Judge Dunmire, Marcia Henderson, Asa Johnson and other staff. At the State level, based on the damning DVD from the paranoid neighbor, the Interim County Attorney who replaced Shatigan petitioned the Superior Court to dismiss charges against Ivan and Emily. Then, as a result of the young security guard's confession, he initiated felony charges against the perpetrators of the burglary of Ivan's office.

Suddenly reminded of his mortality, Paul Strong shared what he knew of the MCSO. Due to his cooperation, he avoided incarceration and stayed home—on house arrest—with his son, Phil. Len Snyder, arrested on the same illegal search and seizure charges from the Milagro burglary, sang his socks off about Bullard, Bardo, and Harold Tanner. Bullard denied he had done anything wrong and accused the defendants-turned-plaintiffs of terrorism. Bardo denied he knew anything. Since Harold Tanner was part of the Maricopa County Office, a prosecutor from Yavapai County petitioned to dismiss charges against young Harry and indicted his father on multiple charges of child pornography.

For a short while, it appeared that Shatigan, immune as County Attorney from prosecution, would sail safely toward election as Attorney General. But bar complaints from many sources, extending far beyond Emily's DVDs, resulted in a finding by the ethics committee that the former County Attorney's conduct merited disbarment.

Back in the Cronkite auditorium, lights flashed, and cameras rolled. The peripatetic Rafe, shouldering his omnipresent video cam, gave Ivan an informal head's up that the press conference would start soon.

Ivan tapped the mic and began. "Ladies and gentlemen, honored guests and dear friends, I would like to read a poem. It is a little rough, but it covers my thoughts. It is very much in the spirit of Pastor Martin Niemöller from Germany in the 1930s and 1940s.

"First, they arrested the day workers,

"But I wasn't a day worker.

"I was a professor, so I did not protest.

"When they finally came to arrest me,

and my attorney, and my students,

"There was no one left to protest."

CHAPTER 51

LYDIA

Late August 2010, Phoenix

Lydia's father handled the steering wheel as they navigated traffic into downtown Phoenix. *Señora* Flores smoothed down her dress and freshened her lipstick with a pocket mirror from her purse. *Señor* Flores turned into the parking lot of a building on East Washington Street. The bilingual receptionist greeted Lydia in English and her parents in Spanish and directed them toward the conference room.

The law offices of Bustamante and Jordan in central Phoenix displayed dedication and success. A large oil painting of *La Llorona*, hovering over an *arroyo* in the Sonoran Desert seeking her lost children, dominated the south wall of the conference room. Photographs of Bustamante or Jordan with Cesar Chavez, Congressman Valenzuela, past Presidents of the United States, and civil rights leaders covered the west wall.

Mr. Bustamante and Mr. Jordan shook hands with Lydia and her parents and gestured for them to sit in the plush leather chairs at the large conference table.

"Lydia, you realize this is not a slam dunk," said Mark Jordan. As the immigration expert, he let Elias Bustamante handle the defense work.

"Yes, sir."

"We now have your green card for temporary legal status. You'll have to request renewal every six months."

"Yes, sir." Having just turned nineteen, Lydia felt awed by these two senior attorneys. She recalled her time in the Fourth Avenue Jail with the other girls in a smelly cell. Mr. Bustamante had appeared to obtain her release, introduced himself, and said they were going home to her family.

Contacted by Mr. Jordan, a Congressman, and a Senator, ICE (Immigration and Customs Enforcement) found no reason to detain Lydia. She was granted temporary legal residence with an agreement to expedite the matter with the appropriate hearings. Meanwhile, ICE did not seem interested in Lydia's undocumented parents because they were law-abiding and had jobs.

Jordan continued. "Naturally, I need to know more about you and your family to present a successful case."

Señor Flores looked toward Bustamante.

"El habla español, es bilingüe," said Bustamante. Regardless of what their surnames might suggest, both attorneys spoke fluent English and Spanish.

Señor Flores spoke first, in Spanish. "After our Lydia was born, and with the NAFTA hurting our local businesses, we decided to come to *El Norte*, Arizona. I found a job with a landscape company. I am now a crew foreman. Sometimes I do repair and maintenance work on some of *Señor* Mendez's apartments when he needs me." He paused. "Lydia was about two or three when we came. It was not such a big deal then. A lot of people came across and found work. My wife sometimes cleans houses. We both work. We save to help our children get an education. Things are bad in Mexico. There is corruption. The drug cartels make it so dangerous." He looked at his hands. "We don't know what to do if she is deported."

Señora Flores added in halting English, "Lydia ees very good student. She has never be trouble. She help her brother Jesus. We so much hope for her she can go college. Maybe she be a teacher." She patted Lydia's hand under the table, her hand shaking.

Lydia patted her hand back. *It's okay, Mama, está bien. They want to help us.*

Señora Flores handed Mr. Jordan a copy of Lydia's school records.

Jordan skimmed the folder, smiling at the columns of A marks. He passed it to Bustamante. He then nodded to Mr. and Mrs. Flores and turned to Lydia. "Lydia, since you are my client in the immigration part of the case, I want to suggest something you can do to build your case," Jordan smiled at her reassuringly. "You'll be a student at ASU downtown, but there is a legal way to earn money on the side. If you form a limited liability company, an LLC, you can go into business for yourself. It will be entirely legal. You obtain a Federal Employee Identification Number (an EIN) and pay into the Social Security system like everyone else. You become both a student and a productive member of society. It will look good on your record."

"But what can I do?" A mere freshman at ASU, Lydia was not fully aware of her abilities.

"Your English is excellent. You could start classes for students coming to Arizona who want to learn English. Many will happily pay to study with someone of your background and ability. You are fluent in Spanish too. People wanting to learn Spanish could come to your school as well."

Lydia beamed. "I can teach English and Spanish! And I would like to help people in Arizona learn a new language."

Jordan and Bustamante smiled at each other, then looked at Lydia's parents for approval. *Señor* Flores smiled widely. "My Lydia, a teacher!"

Señora Flores looked at her husband. "If Lydia agrees, we agree."

The law partners made a date to meet with Lydia again in a week to finalize papers for filing an LLC.

And so, the Lydia Flores School for Language Learners was born.

AUTHOR'S AFTERWORD

Our democracy cannot normalize serious criminal conduct disguised as "enforcing" or obeying the law. Yet, in the United States, over several decades, we have witnessed unethical and even felonious behavior, especially from individuals in high-ranking positions of power.

In Arizona, for twenty-four years, Joseph Michael Arpaio abused the power entrusted to him as Sheriff of Maricopa County. He mistreated individuals detained in his jails. Several inmates died wrongfully under his watch. He targeted Hispanics and those who openly disagreed with him. With Maricopa County Attorney Andrew Thomas, he initiated numerous unsubstantiated investigations and invalid arrests. He fraudulently mishandled funds, moving them from legally required responsibilities to operations of his choice. His misconduct resulted in charges against him and his office, which, as of January 2023, reached a running total of over three hundred million dollars.

In the decade since we first published *A DRY HATE*, five patterns have become more noticeable that constitute abuse of power by the Sheriff's Office—all of which are dangerous to our democracy.

When we talk about abuse of power, we mean "the misuse of a position of power to take unjust advantage of individuals, organizations, or governments."[5]

Five forms of abuse are:

1. Physical—where the harm is not accidental
2. Emotional—sometimes called psychological abuse
3. Neglect—the persistent failure to meet someone's basic physical or psychological needs

4. Sexual—abusing another human sexually without their [informed] consent

5. Bullying—deliberate hurtful behavior. It can be physical, verbal, or emotional.[6]

In the operations of the MCSO under Sheriff Arpaio, all five of these kinds of abuses were present or occurred. Most could have been avoided. The Sheriff committed these abuses in the following ways:

1. **Violation of his oath of office and the Constitution, including the misuse of Federal and State funds**

   Sheriff Arpaio's refusal to investigate and prosecute sex crime complaints violated his oath of office since investigating crimes was an MCSO requirement. He repeatedly targeted Hispanics at traffic stops, worksites, and neighborhood sweeps, which violated each individual's right to equal protection of the laws under the Fourteenth Amendment to the U.S. Constitution. Additionally, he failed to allocate staff to transfer inmates from the jails to the courts for scheduled appearances, thus violating both the requirements of his office and the rights of individual detainees to Due Process under the Fifth Amendment.

2. **Retaliation against political enemies**

   The arrest of the *New Times* Editors, the trumped-up investigations of Judges and other Court personnel and County Supervisors, and the arrests of activists were all done in retaliation when others questioned his authority.

3. **Disrespect for laws and refusal to obey lawful Court Orders**

   Sheriff Arpaio violated one of our essential tenets of democratic governance—respect for the separation of powers. The Founding Fathers intended for the judiciary to function more independently, not beholden to or heavily influenced by politicians or ideology. While we as a people are not always happy, or even in agreement with, the decisions of our courts, we have historically honored them and the system of changing these decisions through the appeal process and electing legislators who pass different laws. This process avoids violence, autocracy, revolution, or insurrection.

When taken to Court and ordered by the Court to abstain from or adhere to specific procedures, Sheriff Arpaio both flagrantly ignored the court orders and bragged to his "base" that he could do what he wanted "to uphold the law," which amounted to breaking existing laws.

From 2010 to 2017, the Sheriff repeatedly— intentionally—ignored specific Federal District Court Orders, such as the order to stop targeting people of Latino appearance, in violation of the Fifth and Fourteenth Amendments in traffic stops and arrests. Therefore, in 2017, after lengthy deliberation, a Federal Judge convicted Arpaio of criminal contempt of Court based on the overwhelming evidence of Arpaio's misconduct. Yet, sadly for our justice system, he was pardoned by then-President Trump, a pardon which allowed a criminal to suffer no consequences for his illegal activity.

Meanwhile, Arpaio's ally, duly-elected County Attorney Andrew Thomas, violated his oath of office and code of ethics as an attorney. Under our legal framework, he could not be sued, but the State Bar Association disbarred him from the practice of law for multiple violations of legal ethics.

4. **Lies—the creation of distorted truth through the use of propaganda or misinformation to justify his abusive behavior and that of his deputies**

Sheriff Arpaio and County Attorney Andrew Thomas abused their power by gratuitously, strategically, and repeatedly articulating lies and making false claims against innocent persons.

The Sheriff and County Attorney fabricated allegations about corruption, criminal conduct, racketeering, and criminal conspiracies. Fabricated means that the allegations were completely unsubstantiated by evidence. They made up fake documents to pretend that there had been a Grand Jury hearing or that an independent judge had duly signed a warrant for a search or arrest. The Sheriff lied in court, claiming on the stand not to remember court orders, despite bragging to followers that he could continue to enforce the law.

5. **Cruelty is being callously indifferent to or taking pleasure in causing pain and suffering to others.**

Arpaio publicly marched undocumented detainees before the press. He marched activists in handcuffs or chains in front of the public and arrested Supervisor Don Stapley in a staged event in front of the press. The Sheriff then bragged about serving inmates green bologna and making them wear pink underwear. He deliberately reduced their meals from three to two per day. He failed to supervise the staff who caused the deaths of inmates in custody.

Frequently two types of abuse of power go together. Choosing not to prosecute sex crime complaints violated Sheriff Arpaio's Oath of Office—a legal responsibility of the MCSO—and was cruel to the victims who saw no safety or justice. Parading Don Stapley in front of the press was retaliation and malicious cruelty. Telling his supporters that he would continue to go after "illegals" was disrespectful to the judiciary and a lie to the Court about whether he knew about sweeps conducted by his Office.

Sheriff Arpaio's abuse of power resulted in four different kinds of costs:

1. **Cost of settlements for inmates who died while in MCSO custody**

Inmates are not always easy to handle, but it is the legal and professional responsibility of the Office of the Sheriff to ensure the safety of all the accused and all detainees in the County jails while awaiting trial or serving short sentences. (Those convicted of more serious offenses go to prison.) Part of the Sheriff's responsibility is to feed the detainees enough food to keep them in fair health and safe—from guards, each other, and even themselves.

Under Sheriff Joe Arpaio, from 1992 to 2016, at least four men died wrongfully while in the custody of MCSO—Ernest Atencio, Scott Norberg, Charles Agster, and Clint Yarberg. These unnecessary deaths resulted in lawsuits by aggrieved families, who then reached settlement agreements of $24.85 million.[7]

Professional conduct and oversight—not to mention humane treatment—could have prevented the loss of these men's lives, the heartbreak of their loved ones, and the financial cost to the taxpayers.

2. **Cost of cases brought by innocent victims whose civil rights MCSO violated**

Dozens of Judges, Court officials, County Supervisors, newspaper editors, activists, documented and undocumented workers, and other civilians experienced the violation of their civil rights under the abusive conduct of the Sheriff from 2006 to 2012. They filed claims in Federal Court against the MCSO for violating their civil rights. Most of them successfully achieved financial settlements paid by the County without going to trial because the Sheriff's attorneys advised him that he would lose at trial. Based on facts and evidence, the financial penalties would have been even more significant.

Ultimately, there was no penalty to the Sheriff or MCSO—it was all borne by taxpayers and aggrieved parties.

Federal and State Judges weighed immense amounts of evidence, concluding that there had been an abuse of power, violation of Constitutional rights, and illegal retaliation against political opponents by the MSCO.

Financial settlements against the MCSO included:

- Michael Lacey and Jim Larkin, editors of the *New Times* newspaper **($3.75 million)**
- Maricopa County Supervisor Mary Rose Wilcox **($1,086,397.82** paid out in damages, interest for delays in payment, and attorney fees)
- Maricopa County Supervisor Don Stapley **($3.5 million)**
- Maricopa County Supervisor Andy Kunasek **($123,000)**
- Superior Court Judge Gary Donahoe **($1.2 million)**
- Superior Court Judge Barbara Rodriguez Mundell **($500,000)**
- Superior Court Judge Ken Fields **($100,000)**
- Superior Court Judge Anna Baca **($100,000)**
- The "clappers" cited in the novel—Joel Nelson, Jason Odhner, Monica Sandschafer, Raquel Terán, and Kristy Theilen **($500,000)**
- **$25 million** in other legal fees

This list, while extensive, is not all-inclusive.[8]

In addition, the racial profiling case brought by Manuel de Jesus Ortega Melendres, also unjustly arrested, is ongoing.

The Sheriff should never have arrested, accused, or jailed these human beings who were innocent of all allegations charged. Yet, the MCSO investigated or detained them without probable cause. Our democratic system is robust enough that the Courts will entertain cases in which those who believe someone wronged them can sue. However, the legal process takes time, requires collecting massive amounts of evidence, and is a time, resources, psychological, and financial burden to all involved—all as a result of the Sheriff abusing the power of his Office.

3. **Cost of Compliance with Court Orders**

    The cost of compliance in the *Melendrez* racial profiling case, in which the current MCSO must train staff and follow new protocols to avoid constitutional violations, is ongoing. Still, according to some sources, the cost in January 2023 was over **$215 million.**[9] As late as November of 2022, the Federal Judge again cited MCSO for continued racial profiling from within the Office. Among other issues, candidates for the many MCSO vacancies know its legal problems. In a tight labor market, potential employees with no discipline history can easily find other employment. The mess made by Sheriff Arpaio continues to cause the MCSO problems today.

4. **Cost incurred for improper expenditures and legal fees**

    It has been more difficult to document these costs. However, Sheriff Arpaio purchased vehicles without permission and paid staff to conduct raids, sweeps, and unlawful arrests that were not part of the job description of the Sheriff or MCSO. Instead, the Sheriff should have spent the funds on approved items in his budget, such as transporting jail detainees to hearings in Court.

Summary and Parting Thoughts

The U.S. Constitution is the general source of all the specific laws we must support. In addition, every elective office has job specifications and an oath or affirmation of office. Officials swear or affirm they will uphold the Constitution and the requirements of their Office. They will treat everyone equally under the law—their allies and political opponents.

It is the nature of abuse of power that we never know when the abuser will turn on us, which is true in family and politics. Life with a power abuser is uncertain and unstable. Furthermore, abuse of power by politicians in high office threatens our Constitution, laws, and regulations—the foundational base upon which we build our democracy. With an abuser, no one is safe. Sadly, abusers often fool their victims for a lifetime. Women stay with abusive partners. Children still love dangerous parents. Those attached to autocrats deny their faults and lies.

A political leader who repeats a lie attempts to manipulate his audience so that the people hearing the lie will perceive it as the truth. In addition, using hatred or abusive language in propaganda— basically, brainwashing techniques—can change brain chemistry, stimulate anger, and incite violence. Once we buy into the propaganda perpetrated by the one in power, we sometimes discard our willingness to be open to other evidence or another person's perspective or experience.

It's important to be more perceptive and less susceptible to propaganda as we, the American people, face our uncertain future. Let's consider the validity of our sources, use critical thinking, and be willing to change our minds in the face of factual evidence that may contradict our biases.

Together, let us seek what's best for everyone living in the United States of America.

QUESTIONS FOR DISCUSSION

1. What purpose does the Prologue serve? Are there any conflicts inherent in Arizona's history or geography?
2. What is "it" for Ivan? For Lydia? For Phil? For Sheriff Bardo? For Asa Johnson?
3. How does Sheriff's Deputy Paul Strong see his job? Does he see any conflicts with coworkers or events as they unfold? Should he?
4. How are Lydia and Alicia similar? How are they different?
5. What drives Phil Strong? What works for him? What problems or conflicts arise? How does he deal with them? How does he change?
6. Who is Eleanor Jones? How does she fit into the attitude held by the Sheriff's Deputies about women? How does she not fit?
7. What issues does Tony Mendez have to wrestle with? How does he change?
8. When does Ivan begin to realize there are problems with his class? What does he do or not do about it? Could he have done things differently?
9. What appears to drive Harry Tanner? How does he change?
10. What role does Asa Johnson play throughout the novel? How is he different than Lydia? How is he similar?
11. How is the setting, in the Cronkite School of Journalism, associated with the storyline?
12. Did anything in *A DRY HATE* influence you to consider acting in a different manner?
13. Is there anything in the Afterword that surprised you or that you did not know?
14. Do you believe that the things listed as actions by Sheriff Arpaio are actual? Why or why not?

15. Do you think Sheriff Arpaio abused his power as elected Sheriff? Why or why not?
16. Do you think the abuse of power, as described in the Afterword, threatens democracy in the United States? Why or why not?
17. Can you describe other examples of power abuse by other leaders in the United States? Who and what?
18. Are there any policies in the U.S. that you would like to see changed? Is there something you can do to influence that course of events?

A LIST OF TYPICAL PROPAGANDA TECHNIQUES[10]

This list can be used as a guide to allow students, teachers, and others to analyze the speeches and comments in the story for propaganda.

1. **STEREOTYPING OR LABELING.** Stereotyping and labeling attempt to paint all people of similar backgrounds with a negative name or image.
2. **SLOGANS.** Anti-immigrant groups use the slogans "Secure the border" and "We enforce the law." Pro-immigrant groups say, "Stop hate," and "They just want to work."
3. **SCAPEGOATING.** When a speaker blames an individual or a group for something, as if they alone were the cause of a complex problem, they do so to arouse prejudice.
4. **ISOLATE, SEGREGATE, MARGINALIZE.** The dominant groups have regularly used propaganda and political power to marginalize and segregate minorities, making them appear of less value as human beings.
5. **CONFUSION AND DIVERSION.** Talking about something other than the real issue is a diversionary tactic.
6. **DISINFORMATION, SMEARS, AND LIES ABOUT ONE'S OPPONENTS.** The claim that the winning political candidates stole the 2020 election by fraud was a lie, smear, and disinformation because there was—after numerous investigations—no evidence of fraud.
7. **APPEAL TO FEAR.** Claiming that all Mexicans crossing the border into the United States bring disease, increase crime rates, and are rapists and murderers, is fearmongering.

8. **APPEAL TO AUTHORITY.** Claiming the righteousness of one's religion, political position, or "upholding The Law" are examples of appealing to authority.
9. **BANDWAGON.** Appealing to anyone to join your side without logical reasoning is trying to get them on the bandwagon.
10. **GLITTERING GENERALITIES.** "We're against terror," "The other side is weak," and "Immigrants bring disease" are examples of glittering generalities that appear to apply to all.
11. **RATIONALIZATION.** Saying a wrong action is justified because it accompanies a (theoretically) good action means that it constitutes rationalization.
12. **OVERSIMPLIFICATION.** Making one issue seem like it will solve a complex problem or blaming one person when many factors are at play are examples of oversimplification.
13. **GENERATE INTENTIONAL VAGUENESS.** Referring to "they" or "people are saying" intentionally casts doubt on the proven evidence and facts.
14. **TRANSFERS.** Projecting praise or blaming a group that makes them all seem good or bad, for example, praising all "Christians" as good or all Muslims as "terrorists," are transfers.
15. **APPEAL TO THE COMMON SENSE OF THE PEOPLE.** Use ordinary language to make people feel you are one of them.
16. **TESTIMONIALS.** When people speak about the good qualities of a political candidate or someone receiving an honor at a ceremony—whether accurate or earned—they offer testimonials.
17. **USE VIRTUOUS WORDS FOR YOUR SIDE.** "We believe in peace" or "I just enforce the law" are phrases that sound good, although they may not indicate what the people are doing.

ENDNOTES: CITATIONS AND SOURCES

1. https://en.wikipedia.org/wiki/Walter_Cronkite, p. 3 of 25.
2. https://blogs.uoregon.edu/frengsj387/vietnam-war/
3. https://en.wikipedia.org/wiki/Perseids
4. https://www.sciencedaily.com/releases/2008/08/080808123912.htm
5. https://safeguardingassociation.com/5-main-types-of-abuse
6. *Ibid.*
7. https://www.azcentral.com/story/opinion/op-ed/laurieroberts/2019/08/27/joe-arpaio-maricopa-county-sheriff-election-campaign/2131407001/
8. *Ibid.* ["clapping" costs provided by author]
9. "A racial profiling case has cost Maricopa County $215 million," Sasha Hupka, *Arizona Republic/USA TODAY NETWORK* (1/26/2023 & 1/28/2023).
10. https://www.baschools.org/pages/uploaded/file
    https://www.en.wikipedia.org/wiki/Propaganda
    https://www.yourarticlelibrary.como/sociology/propaganda

Book

Sterling, Terry Greene, and Joffe-Block, Jude, *Driving While BROWN: Sheriff Joe Arpaio versus the Latino Resistance* (Oakland, University of California Press, 2021).

Articles

https://en.wikipedia.org/wiki/Andrew_Thomas_(American_politician)

"Arpaio's immigration patrols to cost public $202 M," Jacques Billeaud, ASSOCIATED PRESS, *Arizona Republic,* May 19, 2021.

"Racial Profiling Plagues MCSO: Lawsuit costs projected to reach $200 million," Rafael Carranza and Jimmy Jenkins, *Arizona Republic, USA TODAY NETWORK,* March 4, 2022.

https://www.aclu.org/sb-1070-supreme-court-whats-stake

"The Collected Crimes of Sheriff Joe Arpaio," by Danielle Tcholakian, August 28, 2017, as per and with added comments by Elizabeth Graham, February 2023.

https://nymag.com/intelligencer/2020/02/dumb-as-a-rock-9-times-trump-insulted-people-he-appointed.html

https://www.cnn.com/2020/06/04/politics/officials-who-criticized-donald-trump/index.html

Statutes

https://www.azleg.gov/ars/11/00441.htm [ARS S. 11-441. Powers and duties, A. Sheriff]

https://www.azleg.gov/ars/38/00231.htm [ARS S.38-231. Officers and employees required to take loyalty oath]

ACKNOWLEDGMENTS

Numerous people contributed to this book, knowingly or not, in conversations, through their articles, or by working together on several legal matters. I want to express my deep appreciation to the following individuals for their varied contributions to the original 2012 publication of *A DRY HATE:* Joy Bertrand, Kevin Bumstead, Thomas Cesta, Angie Delgadillo, Charlie Dell, Wyatt and Terry Earp, Dennis Gilman, Tom Haines, John Hay, Shana Higa, Lynn Hoffman, Jameson Johnson, Wallace Kleindienst, Sean Larkin, Steven Lemmons, David Lujan, Rob McElwain, Nick Moceri, Joel Nelson, Jason Odhner, Daniel Ortega, Dan Pachoda, Randy Parraz, Joel Robbins, Andrew Sanchez, Monica Sandschafer, Alan Scheidt, Bettie Smiley, Raquel Terán, John Templeton, Kristy Theilen, Dave Wells, and Candace Wilkinson.

The extensive research and high quality of coverage of local events by numerous journalists from the *Arizona Republic, AP*, and the *Phoenix New Times* and online news outlets, deserve high praise. Nevertheless, I have not named any journalist, reporter, author, or video contributor unless personally credited for a specific article or other contribution. Extrapolation and use of information are the responsibility of the author.

I particularly appreciated the early encouragement from my *novelista* critique group: Trish Dolasinski, Rudri Patel, and Linda Stryker. You helped me improve the characters in my novel. In addition, Mary Holden provided highly professional editorial guidance on both form and substance.

More recently, conversations with individuals who were acutely aware of some of the events portrayed herein were constructive. Thanks to Maricopa County Superior Court Judges Gary Donahoe (retired) and William P. Sergeant III (retired), civic leader Lydia Guzmán, former Maricopa County Supervisor Don Stapley, author Terry Greene Sterling, and U.S. District Court Judge Neil Wake (retired), for their insights and information about this era. Author Elizabeth Graham and attorney Dianne Post significantly improved the Author Afterword. My husband, Vance, supported the project and gave me the room and time—including Wi-Fi in my woman cave—to pursue my passion for justice.

Finally, thanks to my publishing and production team. Collaborative editing with Lynn Thompson gave me a new appreciation for both the use of our language and how she gave time, attention, and skill to help create a much better product. Thanks also to Becky Norwood of Spotlight Publishing House for her skillful coordination of all phases of the work, including the designer's cover concept, to bring the second edition of *A DRY HATE* to the light of day.

Nancy Hicks Marshall

ABOUT THE AUTHOR

Author Nancy Marshall was born in New York, graduated with honors from Smith College (BA), obtained a Masters in Teaching from Wesleyan (MAT), and received her law degree from Rutgers University (JD). She spent several years teaching high school history and political science and also served as a field officer with the New York State Division of Civil Rights.

In 1975, Nancy moved to Arizona, where she served almost five years as Executive Director of the Arizona Civil Liberties Union. She married, raised a family, created a newsletter for the Arizona Family Planning Council, and wrote two editions of *SEX AND THE LAW, Arizona Legal Guide on Reproduction, Sexual Conduct and Families*, in the 1990s. At the same time, she wrote a series of vignettes, *DEAR GRANDMA*, told by a toddler to his scribe of a mother for Grandma, who was far from home.

Growing up on the south shore of Long Island, Nancy appreciated the beauty of the marshes and the wildlife visible from her backyard—pheasants, cardinals, rabbits, blue herons, and white egrets. During one college summer, she worked on the South Rim of the Grand Canyon and hiked to Phantom Ranch, mesmerized by the raw beauty of this natural wonder. When living in New York, Nancy frequently hiked with the Appalachian Mountain Club, again appreciating nature, especially our wild animal brothers and sisters. In Arizona, she and her family visited their cabin in the woods of the Prescott National Forest. In 2020, she wrote *A RATTLER'S TALE: When Wild Animals Encounter Humans*, a beautifully illustrated children's book narrated by an Arizona Black Rattlesnake.

Having attended schools with an active sports program and expectations of high academic achievement for girls and women,

Nancy always understood that women are equal. But she has found that some people, and the law, have frequently treated women as less than equal. The denial of equal pay and full reproductive rights are two persistent examples of inequality in the law.

Nancy found a disturbing pattern in Juvenile Court, where she participated in hundreds of cases. Of all girls and women in Juvenile court cases—whether removed from a dangerous home, teen delinquents, or mothers whose children had been removed— over 80% were sexually abused as children. On occasion, this abuse spanned two or three generations! She saw time after time, the negative impact of such abuse. This realization prompted her to write the novel *ROSIE'S GOLD* in 2010.

For a few years during the 1990s, Nancy worked as a substitute teacher in the Phoenix and Scottsdale public schools. Then, taking and passing the Arizona Bar Exam in her late 50s, she worked for ten years in the Juvenile Court. Her professional career in the courts reached an apex when, in 2008-09, Nancy defended a young man, one of four people arrested by Sheriff Arpaio's Deputies for clapping in a public meeting. The arrest was a pure and callous violation of her client's right to freedom of expression. She and other attorneys won verdicts of innocent for their clients and damages of $500,000 against the Sheriff for civil rights violations. This case and the events of that time inspired Nancy to write *A DRY HATE* in 2012. The ongoing relevance of the themes of this novel prompted the publication of a second edition in 2023.

Dismayed by the results of the Presidential election in 2016 and the vehement reaction to the election, Nancy set out to write a book to offer common ground. In 2018 she published *THE BOOK OF PRO-S: An Alphabetical Chat About Things We Can Like,* including (from A to Z) Accuracy, Bubble Bath, Journalism, National Parks, and Zumba. Everyone will find a few things on which we can agree!

Marshall lives in Phoenix and Flagstaff with her husband and their dog, Chelly. She loves hiking, nature, music, growing a vegetable garden, and learning Spanish.

Made in the USA
Monee, IL
07 July 2023

38091683R00164